*"Well, then, may[be there'll be another]
time."*

"No, there won't be another time," Reilly said flatly. "You might as well know that now. If you've set your sights on me, you're wasting your time. I'm not interested."

Stunned, Janey couldn't believe she'd heard him correctly. He actually thought that she…that she was the kind of woman who would…

Unable to finish the thoughts whirling in her head, Janey almost laughed at the ridiculousness of his accusations. He couldn't be serious! She'd never come on to a man in her life—she wouldn't even know where to begin! But she drew herself up proudly. So he wasn't interested, was he?

Well, neither was she!

Dear Reader,

It's the beginning of a new year, and Intimate Moments is ready to kick things off with six more fabulously exciting novels. Readers have been clamoring for Linda Turner to create each new installment of her wonderful miniseries THOSE MARRYING McBRIDES! In *Never Been Kissed* she honors those wishes with the deeply satisfying tale of virginal nurse Janey McBride and Dr. Reilly Jones, who's just the man to teach her how wonderful love can be when you share it with the right man.

A YEAR OF LOVING DANGEROUSLY continues to keep readers on the edge of their seats with *The Spy Who Loved Him,* bestselling author Merline Lovelace's foray into the dangerous jungles of Central America, where the loving is as steamy as the air. And you won't want to miss *My Secret Valentine,* the enthralling conclusion to our in-line 36 HOURS spin-off. As always, Marilyn Pappano delivers a page-turner you won't be able to resist. Ruth Langan begins a new trilogy, THE SULLIVAN SISTERS, with *Awakening Alex,* sure to be another bestseller. Lyn Stone's second book for the line, *Live-In Lover,* is sure to make you her fan. Finally, welcome brand-new New Zealand sensation Frances Housden. In *The Man for Maggie* she makes a memorable debut, one that will have you crossing your fingers that her next book will be out soon.

Enjoy! And come back next month, when the excitement continues here in Silhouette Intimate Moments.

Yours,

Leslie J. Wainger
Executive Senior Editor

Please address questions and book requests to:
Silhouette Reader Service
U.S.: 3010 Walden Ave., P.O. Box 1325, Buffalo, NY 14269
Canadian: P.O. Box 609, Fort Erie, Ont. L2A 5X3

Never Been Kissed
LINDA TURNER

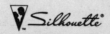

INTIMATE MOMENTS™
Published by Silhouette Books
America's Publisher of Contemporary Romance

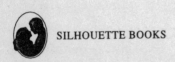 SILHOUETTE BOOKS

ISBN 0-373-27121-2

NEVER BEEN KISSED

Copyright © 2001 by Linda Turner

Visit Silhouette at www.eHarlequin.com

Printed in U.S.A.

Books by Linda Turner

LINDA TURNER

began reading romances in high school and began writing them one night when she had nothing else to read. She's been writing ever since. Single and living in Texas, she travels every chance she gets, scouting locales for her books.

Prologue

Every Labor Day the Jones family gathered for their annual picnic, and this year's get-together was wilder than ever. By 10:30 a.m., the beer and sodas were flowing, the barbecue was sizzling on the grill and a spirited game of volleyball was in progress on the beach. The object was to win, at all cost, and cheating was not only allowed, but heartily encouraged. Laughter echoed up and down the beach, along with the ribald comments from the cheering section on the sidelines.

In the past Reilly Jones would have been right in the big middle of the game, leading his team to victory and enjoying every second of it. But not this year. He didn't feel like playing—or mingling with the family. He wouldn't, in fact, have even showed up if it hadn't been for his older brother, Tony, who'd nagged and bitched and hounded him to put in an appearance until he'd finally given in just to shut him up.

Standing alone, well apart from the rest of the family,

Reilly stared broodingly out to sea and knew he shouldn't have come. He didn't belong here. The trouble was he didn't belong anywhere and he hadn't for a long time now. Ever since Victoria had died.

Pain lanced his heart just at the thought of her. God, he missed her! Every second of every day. He'd been told that with time, the hurt would lessen and eventually fade, but it had been eight months since a teenager in a stolen car had slammed into her and killed her, and the pain was as fierce today as it had been that fateful day. He couldn't eat, couldn't sleep, couldn't work. There was a gaping hole in his heart, in his life, where she had once been, and all he wanted to do was die so he could be with her again.

Behind him he heard a footstep and didn't have to turn around to know his brother had joined him. Tony had appointed himself his personal guardian angel, and lately he seemed to always know when his thoughts were at their lowest. Not taking his eyes from the shadowy blurred images of Catalina in the distance, Reilly said gruffly, "You don't have to worry. I'm not going to do anything stupid like drown myself or anything. I was just thinking."

Tony, to his credit, knew better than to ask him about what. The answer, as usual, was written in the sad, grim lines of his somber expression. Victoria. There'd been a time when Tony had envied his brother the rare love he shared with Victoria, but not anymore. Her death had nearly destroyed Reilly, and Tony didn't know if he would ever recover from it. He hadn't laughed since the day she died, and eight months later the grief that tore at him was stronger than ever. He'd turned his medical practice over to his partners and had lost all interest in life. When he wasn't sitting at home in his study staring at her picture, he was either at the cemetery or in his car, driving the endless freeways of L.A., looking in vain for a peace that was nowhere to be found.

And Tony didn't mind admitting he was worried about him. He was slowly destroying himself, and if something wasn't done soon to pull him out of the depression he had slipped into, he was going to be in serious trouble.

"I've been thinking, too," he replied, "and I think you should get out of here."

Surprised, Reilly dragged his eyes away from the ocean to arch a dark brow at him. "What's gotten into you? For the last two weeks, you've done nothing but preach about how important it was for me to come to this thing, and now you're telling me to leave?"

"Not the picnic," Tony corrected him quietly. "L.A."

That was the last thing Reilly expected him to say. "Are you serious?"

"You're slowly killing yourself here, grieving yourself to death," he said bluntly. "With Victoria gone there's nothing here for you anymore. So sell everything—the house, your practice—and get the hell out of here while you still can."

It was a logical suggestion—and everything inside Reilly rebelled at the thought. He couldn't leave L.A. His last memories of Victoria were here. Everywhere he turned he could see her, hear her, smell her. How could he turn his back on their home and the life they had built together and start over as if she had never existed? He couldn't. He wouldn't!

But even as he opened his mouth to tell Tony he would never even consider such a suggestion, he knew deep down in his soul that his brother was right. The grief that already consumed his every waking and sleeping moment was on the verge of swallowing him whole. If he didn't do something soon to save himself, he was going to be lost.

"Where would I go?"

Encouraged, Tony said, "Do you remember Steven Michaels? He was my chemistry lab partner in college."

The name conjured up images of a tall, gangly kid who had been all arms and legs and six foot five if he was an inch. Frowning, Reilly nodded. "Yeah. He should have played basketball. What about him?"

"I ran into him last month at a convention and he was telling me about an uncle of his who's looking for someone to join his family medical practice and eventually take it over so he can retire. His name's Dan Michaels. I think you should consider calling him."

"I'm a heart surgeon, Tony."

"You're a doctor," he reminded him. "You take care of sick people. Just because you normally spend your days operating on people's hearts doesn't mean you can't treat colds and allergies and high blood pressure instead. Think about it. It might be a really nice change for you."

Reilly had to admit he had a point. There'd been a time when he'd thrived on the stress and challenge of surgery. But that was before he'd lost Victoria. Now the operating room—like everything else—held little appeal. But a family practitioner? Could he be content with that?

"So where is this uncle's practice?"

"Colorado," he replied. "A little town called Liberty Hill. From what I understand, it's southwest of Colorado Springs. It's right in the middle of ranching country, but Aspen's not that far away."

It sounded like a wide spot in the road, as different from L.A. as day was from night, and Reilly knew that if he had any sense, he'd laugh in his brother's face and tell him to think again. If he was going to start his life over, it was going to be someplace where he could at least get Brie without people asking him what it was.

But even as he tried to convince himself that he needed to live someplace more sophisticated, he knew it didn't matter. L.A., New York, Liberty Hill, Colorado. What difference did it make where he lived? Without Victoria, he wouldn't care if he was in the middle of the Sahara.

"All right, I'll give this Dr. Michaels a call if it'll make you happy," he said with a grimace. "Give me the number."

Chapter 1

The rain was a cold mist that stretched as far as the horizon in every direction. Surrounded by rolling ranchland on all sides, Reilly noted the highway sign that informed him he was ten miles from Liberty Hill and knew just how Dorothy must have felt when she found herself in Oz. He wasn't in Kansas—or L.A.—anymore, and he couldn't help wondering if he'd made a mistake by accepting Dr. Michaels's offer to join his practice. It was, however, too late to back out now. He'd already sold his practice and everything else in L.A. Even if he decided he wanted to go back to California, there was nothing to go back to.

Which meant that, like it or not, he was stuck with a new life in Colorado. A life without Victoria. If it looked less than appealing at the moment, he couldn't find the strength to care. His blue eyes bleak with despair, he continued toward Liberty Hill with little enthusiasm, the steady beat of the windshield wipers echoing the lonely beat of his heart.

Lost in his misery, he didn't notice there was a problem

with his car until the motor suddenly began to make an odd sound. Surprised, he glanced down at the dash and swore at the sight of the Check Engine light flashing at him angrily. Immediately lifting his foot from the accelerator, he slowed down and carefully eased over to the shoulder.

It wasn't until he reached for his cell phone and came up empty-handed that he remembered he'd thrown the damn thing away the day before he left L.A. He hadn't been able to do anything but grieve for Victoria, and he'd taken a long, solitary drive around L.A. He'd been gone for hours. Later he couldn't have said where he'd gone— he hadn't cared. He'd just wanted to be left alone. No one, however, had respected that. First his partners had called him one by one to check on him, then his brother. They'd all just wanted to make sure he was okay, which he'd assured each of them he was, then he'd hung up and tossed the phone out the window. In the never-ending stream of cars that raced the city freeways, the phone had been instantly smashed. Relieved, he hadn't bought another because he hadn't thought he would need one where he was going.

Which meant he was now stuck in the middle of nowhere, with no way to call for a tow truck. Glancing ahead, then in his rearview mirror, he swore roundly. The road curved among the rolling hills before it disappeared over the hill in the distance, and there wasn't another car in sight in either direction. Liberty Hill was ten miles away. It was going to be a long, cold walk.

Another man might have lifted the hood and at least given the motor a quick look before facing a ten-mile hike under such miserable conditions, but Reilly knew his strengths and weaknesses. He could perform the most intricate heart surgery with his eyes practically closed, but a mechanic he was not. Muttering curses, he turned on his emergency flashers, grabbed his jacket and keys and pushed open his door.

His thoughts already focused on the long walk ahead of him, he didn't see the red Jeep that came around the curve behind him until it pulled up beside him. The electric window on the passenger's side silently lowered, and from across the width of the vehicle, the woman driver shot him a sympathetic smile. "I saw your flashers. Anything I can do to help?"

If Reilly needed further proof that he was a long way from home, she just gave it to him. No one in L.A., especially a woman alone, stopped to help someone who appeared to be in trouble—not if she valued her life. For all she knew, he could be an ax murderer.

But if she was the least bit leery, she certainly didn't show it. The passenger window was all the way down, and he wouldn't have doubted that the doors were unlocked. With one quick move, he could have been inside and had her in his clutches before she even knew what he was about. Granted, she could have driven off at the least sign of danger from him, but danger wasn't always recognizable at first.

Marveling at her bravery—and stupidity—he frowned at her in puzzlement. "I appreciate the offer, but you don't know me from Adam and this is a lonely stretch of road. Didn't your mother ever tell you to be wary of strangers?"

Her lips curling into a half smile, she said, "Actually, it was my father who drilled that particular lesson into my head—which is why he bought me a shotgun when I was twelve and taught me how to use it. If you'd like, I can demonstrate."

"You mean you have it with you?"

"Of course. It wouldn't do me any good if it was locked away in a gun cabinet at home, would it?"

She appeared to be dead serious, but Reilly would have sworn he caught a glimpse of mischief in her brown eyes before that was quickly blinked away. Intrigued, he arched a brow at her. "Does the sheriff know you drive around with a loaded gun in your car? That's illegal, you know, if you don't have a permit."

Far from worried, Janey McBride only grinned. Nick Kincaid, the local sheriff, was not only a friend, but her brother-in-law. As protective as her brothers, he'd chew her out for *not* carrying a gun if she even suggested driving the road to town and back without any means of protecting herself.

"I'm not worried about the sheriff," she said dryly. She had, in fact, called Nick the second she spied the unfamiliar BMW with its California license, sitting on the side of the road with its flashers on. It didn't hurt to be too careful. "In fact, I think that's him coming our way now," she added, and nodded down the road to the patrol car that just came around the curve half a mile away. "If you don't mind, I'm going to leave you in his hands and be on my way. I hope nothing's seriously wrong with your car."

With a wave and a smile she drove off, leaving Reilly staring after her with a frown. She hadn't even given him time to thank her for stopping—or given him a chance to ask her her name.

The sheriff arrived then, circling around to park on the shoulder behind his car, the whirling lights on his lightbar warning anyone who approached from either direction to do so cautiously. A tall, lean man with an angular face that could have been carved from stone, he didn't look nearly as friendly as the shotgun-toting, unidentified Good Samaritan who'd just driven off, but Reilly supposed the hard look he gave him was one of the requirements of the job.

"Having trouble?" he asked coolly as he approached and asked for his driver's license.

Reilly nodded and handed over his identification. "The Check Engine light came on and I didn't want to chance driving all the way into town."

Noting his name and address on the license, some of the sheriff's stiffness melted. "That's probably a wise move on your part, Doctor. You're a long ways from Los Angeles. Where're you headed?"

"Liberty Hill."

Surprised, Nick lifted a dark brow at him. "No kidding? Would you mind telling me why? Don't get me wrong—I grew up here, and I can't imagine living anywhere else, but it's not the kind of place that normally draws tourists from California. We're too far from the ski slopes to draw that bunch. And we wouldn't know a convention if we tripped over it, so I doubt you drove all the way from L.A. for that. I could understand if you took a wrong turn and got lost, but you didn't. You're here on purpose. Why?"

There'd been a time when it wouldn't have taken much more than the other man's totally bewildered expression to make Reilly smile. But that was before—before Victoria died, before all the joy went out of his life. Appreciation glinted in his eyes, but his lips didn't so much as twitch with humor. "Trust me, you're not asking anything I haven't asked myself," he said dryly. "Actually, I'm moving here. I'm joining Dan Michaels's practice."

Nick couldn't have been more shocked if he'd told him he planned to grow marijuana once he was settled into his new home. "Dr. Michaels? You're going to work with Dan?"

He nodded. "Yeah. You know him?"

"He delivered just about every baby in town for the past forty years," Nick said with a smile. "He's a good man."

And if Dan was taking on a partner, it went without saying that he wouldn't trust his practice to just anyone. He would have made sure Reilly Jones was a good man himself. Relaxing, he held out his hand with a grin. "It looks like I'm the welcoming committee. Welcome to town, Doctor. I'm Nick Kincaid. If I can do anything to help you get settled in, just let me know."

Just that easily the introductions were made and Reilly was accepted. "Thanks," he said, returning his handshake. "And the name's Reilly. I don't stand much on ceremony."

"Then you should fit in just fine around here," Nick replied, his brown eyes twinkling. "We're a pretty casual group. C'mon, let's take a look at your car and see what's wrong with it."

Standing in the cold mist, Reilly watched the tow truck driver hook up his BMW for the tow into town and wondered what the hell he was going to do now. When Nick had lifted the hood, he'd spotted the problem immediately—a broken fan belt—which Reilly had assumed could be easily fixed. All he had to do was get a new fan belt.

In L.A. that wouldn't have been a problem. But he wasn't in L.A., and the tow truck driver—and owner of the only garage in town—had quickly informed him that he didn't keep spare parts for BMWs in stock since no one in town owned one. The fan belt would have to come from Colorado Springs—on the bus. If he was lucky, Reilly would have his car back in a couple of days!

"Damn!"

Sympathizing with him, Nick made no attempt to hold back a grin. "Don't look so glum. Things aren't as bad as they seem. This isn't L.A.—you don't really need a car. The town's so small, you can walk just about anywhere you want to go in ten minutes. C'mon, I'll show you. Where are you staying?''

Reilly grimaced. "Good question. I don't know yet.''

"What do you mean, *you don't know?*''

"Just what I said. I didn't want to make arrangements long-distance without getting the lay of the land first. That'll be hard to do without a car, so if you wouldn't mind taking me to the nearest hotel, I'll stay there until I get the car back.''

This time it was Nick's turn to grimace. "I'll take you if you want, but you might want to reconsider.''

"Why? Is it a dump or what?''

"No, actually it's a very nice place," he replied. "In Gunnison—thirty miles away.''

Reilly swore. "There's no hotel in Liberty Hill? What the hell kind of town is it?''

"A small one,'' Nick said wryly. "Myrtle Henderson rents out spare rooms, but she's booked the rest of the week with a writers' group, so you're out of luck there.'' Studying him through narrowed eyes, he said, "What kind of place were you looking for?''

With no conscious effort on his part, Reilly found himself thinking of the Tudor house he'd shared with Victoria in West Hollywood and still thought of as home. Built in the twenties, he and Victoria had fallen in love with it the second they stepped through the front door for the first time. They'd never even considered looking at anything else.

He'd thought he would live the rest of his life there, but he'd sold it and everything else when he'd left L.A. His heart flinching at the thought, he reminded himself the whole purpose of moving to Colorado was to let go of the past and get on with his life. He just hadn't expected it to be so painful.

"I don't want anything fancy," he said gruffly. "There's just me to consider, and I don't plan on doing any entertaining, so something small would be nice. And secluded, if I can find it. After living in the city for so long, I really just want to be left alone."

A man was entitled to his privacy, Nick thought. And his pain. And Reilly Jones's went soul deep. Oh, his tone was casual enough, and his expression gave away little of what he was feeling. But his eyes spoke volumes. Dark with misery, they were the windows of a tortured soul. Whatever his story was, it was eating him alive.

Feeling for him, Nick knew he should talk to Merry before he offered him his cabin, but the poor guy was obviously hurting and needed a place to hole up and lick his wounds. And it wasn't as if he and Merry were using the cabin. Since they'd gotten married last year, he'd moved into her place on the ranch, and the cabin had been sitting empty. He'd actually been thinking about renting it, and here was the ideal renter, complete with excellent references. If Dr. Dan was willing to trust him with his patients, Nick thought he could certainly trust him with the cabin.

Making a snap decision, he said, "I've got a log cabin north of town you might be interested in renting. You said you didn't want fancy. Trust me—it's not. Some friends helped me build it seven years ago, so I'll warn you up front that it's not perfect. Some of the doors stick on humid days, and the upstairs floor has a tendency to creak. But it's airtight, warm in the winter and surrounded by trees. If you want privacy, you ought to take a look at it. The nearest neighbor's a half a mile away."

"How far out of town is it?"

Nick winced. That was the kicker. "A mile and a half. But your car's only going to be out of commission for three days,'' he reminded him. ''When do you start working with Dr. Dan?''

''Tomorrow,'' he replied, ''but the distance isn't a problem. I can walk if I have to. When can I see it?''

''Right now,'' Nick said, grinning, and led the way to his patrol car.

There was a time in his life when Reilly wouldn't have looked twice at a log cabin. He wasn't an outdoorsman, and the rustic look had never appealed to him. But when Nick drove down the winding drive that led to the cabin, Reilly had to admit there was something about the place that immediately caught his eye.

Just as Nick had promised, the cabin offered all the privacy anyone could possibly want. Nestled among a thick stand of pines and set well back on a two-acre lot, it blended in with the trees and was virtually impossible to see from the road. The nearest neighbor may have been a half mile away, but it might as well have been a hundred. You couldn't see another living soul for what looked like miles in any direction.

He liked the idea of not being bothered by neighbors as he had been in L.A. He'd known they were concerned about him, and he appreciated that, but all he'd wanted was the silence of his own company. Living out here, so far from anyone, he wouldn't have to worry about someone dropping by to borrow a cup of sugar, thank God. And for no other reason than that, he was prepared to love the place even if it turned out to be an architectural nightmare.

The cabin that Nick had built with the help of some friends, however, was far from the leaning shack that Reilly had expected. It may have been rough-hewn and a quarter of the size of his old house in L.A., but it had a porch across the front and back, a fieldstone fireplace, and paned windows that gave it an old-fashioned charm that would be nice to come home to after a long day at work. As Nick braked to a stop in the circular drive and cut the engine, Reilly took one long look and didn't need to see anything else.

"I'll take it."

Already in the process of stepping from the car, Nick leaned down to swivel a sharp look at him. "Don't you want to look inside?"

"Sure, but it's just a formality," he retorted. "This is just what I was looking for. Is it furnished?"

Amazed that he could make a decision so easily, Nick nodded. "I didn't take much when I married Merry and moved into her place—just a chest and a couple of end tables. When do you expect your things from California? You can go ahead and move in today if you like, but it's going to take me a couple of days to find a place to store everything—"

"Don't bother. I'll take it the way it is, if that's okay with you. I sold all my things in California with the house."

Surprised, Nick wanted to ask him what could bring a man to sell everything he owned and cut all ties with his past, but Reilly's expression had turned distant, his eyes shuttered. Wondering what his story was, Nick didn't push. In his business, he'd learned that people talked when they were ready. And judging from the wall he had built around himself, Reilly was a long way from ready.

Respecting his privacy, Nick said easily, "Sure. No problem." Naming a fair market price for the rent, he arched a brow at him. "How does that sound to you?"

"More than fair," Reilly replied, and stuck out his hand. "So we have a deal?"

Pleased, Nick grinned and shook his hand. "Deal!"

* * *

"Sorry, Wanda, darling, but a full house beats three of a kind. If my calculations are right you now owe me six million big ones and a handful of M&M candies. I'll take the candy now, thank you very much."

"Not so fast, Robin Hood," Janey drawled before Scott Bradford could grab the colorful candy piled high in the middle of the table. "You may have a full house, but if I remember correctly, that can't hold a candle to a royal flush." Smiling hugely, she laid down her cards on the table to the cheers of Scott's wife, Wanda, who was down to her last piece of candy. Her brown eyes dancing, Janey smiled smugly at Scott. "Now what was that you were saying about candy, pretty boy?"

For an answer he shot her a less-than-polite hand gesture.

Far from offended, Janey only laughed. She'd known Scott all her life—his uncle's ranch boarded her family's, and they'd gone through school together. And for the last few years he and Wanda invariably spent two evenings a week with Janey at the local volunteer fire department volunteering as emergency medical technicians. And tonight, as most Thursday nights, they passed the time playing poker while they waited for the radio to crackle to life with the report of an accident or the phone to ring with an emergency call.

They rarely got either.

Oh, they got their fair share of calls, but the calls were usually for something minor—like a twisted ankle or heart pains that turned out to be heartburn, and then there was the time Margaret Hopper got stuck in the bathtub and it took not only the entire EMT team but two firefighters, as well, to get her out. Tonight the phone was thankfully silent. Janey hoped it stayed that way.

A grin twitching at his lips, Scott watched her rake in her winnings and groaned in pretended pain. When Janey arched an inquiring brow at him, he pressed a hand to his stomach and moaned again. "I think I must be going through withdrawals. Help me, Janey. You wouldn't deny your old friend a few M&Ms, would you? I'm dying here."

"Then we've got to do something!" Jumping to her feet, she grabbed her stethoscope. "Quick, Wanda, help me get him into the ambulance. We've got to get him to the hospital."

"Do you want me to call your mama, honey?" his wife crooned, laughing when he scowled at her. "I'm sure she would want to know about this—"

Enjoying themselves, she and Janey would have continued to tease him unmercifully, but before they got the chance, the radio suddenly started to crackle and Nick's voice, rough with static, filled the room. "This is County One calling County 911. Janey? Are you there?"

Her smile fading, Janey stepped quickly over to the radio and grabbed the mike. "Yes, go ahead, Nick. What's the problem?"

"We've got a one-vehicle accident out on Eagle Ridge Highway ten miles north of town. The driver took a curve too fast and rolled his SUV. He and his girlfriend weren't wearing their seat belts, and were both thrown from the vehicle. You'd better get out here as quick as you can."

He didn't have to tell her twice. Already reaching for her bag, Janey said, "We're on our way."

They may have been volunteers, but they, like the rest of the local residents who worked the station on a regular basis, prided themselves on always being ready for whatever emergency cropped up. And this time was no exception. The ambulance was stocked with everything they needed, and by the time Janey ended the call a few seconds later, the rest of the team was already in the cab of the vehicle and waiting for her. She quickly jumped in next to

Wanda, who sat in the middle, and was still reaching for her seat belt when Scott pulled out of the garage of the volunteer fire department with sirens blazing. Seconds later they turned north on the Eagle Ridge Highway and left town far behind.

If it hadn't been for the flares Nick had set out marking the spot of the accident, they might have driven right past without even noticing it. In the dark it was impossible to see the wrecked car at the bottom of the ravine that ran parallel with the highway.

Nick had, however, managed to get his patrol car down there, and Scott carefully followed his path in the ambulance. "Ouch," he said when the vehicle's headlights landed on the smashed SUV. A foreign make that obviously didn't stand up well to crash tests, it was banged in on all sides and nearly as flat as a pancake.

"It looks like a tin can that's been run over by a semi," Wanda said.

Janey had to agree. "I don't know how anyone made it out alive."

As it was, the two survivors weren't in the best of shape. The driver was bleeding and unconscious, while his girlfriend was suffering from a broken leg and arm and going into shock. Janey and her team took one look at them and went right to work. They knew the routine, and although Janey was the only one who actually worked in the medical field, both Scott and Wanda had had extensive training in emergency medical care. They didn't need instructions to know what to do.

Within minutes the girlfriend's broken bones were immobilized, and she was given fluids to help counteract the shock. Her boyfriend wasn't so lucky. He'd regained consciousness, but his pulse was thready, his blood pressure falling, and Janey was sure he was bleeding internally. They didn't have a lot of time to waste. Hurriedly easing both victims onto stretchers, they quickly loaded them into the ambulance, then raced back to town.

Scott radioed the hospital with a report of the victims' condition and their estimated time of arrival, but Janey hardly noticed. With all her attention focused on her patient and his rapidly falling blood pressure, she never even noticed that they made it back to the hospital in record time. Suddenly the back doors of the ambulance flew open, and there were hands to unload both patients and rush them inside.

In the organized chaos that was the emergency room, the driver and his girlfriend were taken to separate cubicles and quickly examined. Vital signs were hurriedly taken and called out, and in the madness, Janey heard a nurse working on the girlfriend tell someone to call for X rays and Dr. Easton, the only orthopedic surgeon in town. But it was the driver that Janey was worried about. He'd slipped back into unconsciousness again. If he didn't get into surgery soon, they were going to lose him.

Hurriedly she helped cut away his clothes and hook him up to a heart monitor. During the entire procedure she never took her eyes off his still figure. "Where's Dr. Michaels? Has anybody paged him? Somebody send an orderly for him—"

"There's no need to send an orderly," a cool, husky voice cut in smoothly. "I'm taking over for Dr. Michaels tonight."

Startled, Janey looked up from the patient, directly into the deep-blue eyes of the stranded California motorist she'd stopped to help the day before yesterday when his BMW broke down on the side of the road. She'd only seen him that once, and then only for a few minutes, but she would have known those eyes of his in the far reaches of Mongolia. As dark as the sky before a winter storm, they were tinged with a sadness that touched her heart.

She'd never been able to stand to see anyone in pain and wanted to ask who or what had put that look in his eyes, but he had a reserve about him that didn't encourage questions. Then, with a blink, recognition flared and his only expression was surprise.

It was her—the woman who'd stopped to help him his first day in town. He'd thought she was some rancher's wife—she'd had the look of one, driving a Jeep and wearing jeans and cowboy boots that were scarred from use— but here she was in an EMT's uniform and right at home in the emergency. Who the hell was she?

If a patient hadn't lay there bleeding to death right in front of him, he would have asked. As it was, all he could do was growl, "Let's get this man to surgery," and quickly help push the stretcher down the hall to the surgical wing of the small two-story hospital.

She didn't accompany him and the other nurses, but stayed behind in the E.R. Watching him disappear behind the double doors that led to surgery, she frowned, questions swirling like a swarm of bees in her head. Who was he? There was no question that he was a doctor—she only had to see him in action in the E.R. to know that—but what was a doctor from California doing in Liberty Hill, for heaven's sake? She'd just thought he was a traveler passing through town who'd made a wrong turn.

"Isn't he the best-looking man you've ever seen in your life?" a dreamy voice sighed beside her. "It's the eyes, you know. So sad and lonely. I'll bet he needs a good woman."

Turning to face the head nurse of the E.R., Janey tried not to flinch. Tanya had never been one of her favorite people—she was too bold and wild, and since her recent divorce, she'd become even more so. She'd already come on to every eligible man in town, not to mention a few married ones, since she'd walked out on her husband. Considering that, Janey wouldn't have been the least bit surprised if she'd set her sights on the new doctor without bothering to ask—or care—if he was married or not.

"I wouldn't know," Janey said quietly. "Who is he?"

"Dr. Reilly Jones," Tanya replied, savoring the name as if it was some new tasty treat. "He just joined Dr. Michaels's practice today."

Shocked, Janey couldn't believe she'd heard correctly. "Dan never said anything about taking on a partner. What's going on?"

"I wish I knew," Tanya said with one last longing look at the doors Reilly disappeared behind. "The word going around the hospital is Dr. Michaels is retiring and Reilly Jones is taking over his practice for him. Nobody knows who he is, though, or what his story is. I almost asked, but then I thought it'd be better not to push my luck. He seems to be a very private man, so I figured I'd give him some time to get comfortable here, then make my move."

Janey didn't care about Reilly Jones—if he was stupid enough to be taken in by Tanya, than he was dumber than she thought he was. No, it was Dan she was concerned about. He and his wife, Peggy, had been her parents' best friends, then when Peggy and Janey's father had both died, Dan and her mother had continued their friendship over the years. He was like a member of the family, and if he was retiring without telling anyone, something had to be horribly wrong.

Afraid he might be sick or something, Janey almost woke her mother to find out what was going on, later that evening when her shift was over and she went home, but she didn't want to scare her. So she spent what was left of the night worrying about Dan and barely slept. Up by five-thirty and scheduled to report to work at her regular job at the nursing home by seven, she hurried downstairs just as soon as she was dressed.

As usual her mother, Sara, was already up and in the kitchen making breakfast. Seeing her at the old O'Keefe and Merrit stove that her mother wouldn't have traded for anything, Janey had to smile. For as long as she could remember, her mother had been right there every morning of her life when she came down to breakfast. And today, as always, it amazed Janey how time had hardly touched her at all.

Sara Dawson McBride was sixty-four and didn't look a day past fifty. She'd always claimed she was lucky to have good bone structure, but Janey knew better. Her mother had a good heart, the kind that would keep her forever young. Janey only hoped she was as lucky.

Glancing up from the stove, Sara sent her a smile that was as bright as the copper teakettle whistling happily on the stove. "Good morning, sweetie. Did you sleep well?"

She'd meant to wait until after breakfast to ask about Dan and Reilly Jones, but she found that she couldn't. "Not really. I met a new doctor at the hospital last night. His name's Reilly Jones. Apparently, he's Dan's new partner. I was shocked. Is Dan sick or something? The word going around the hospital is he's going to retire."

"But not because he's sick," her mother assured her quickly. "He's been thinking about retiring for some time now, but he didn't want me to say anything until he had someone lined up he felt comfortable turning his practice over to."

"And Reilly Jones is that man?"

Unable to speculate on that, Sara poured them both a cup

of tea. "It's too early to tell. Right now they just have a temporary partnership—after three months they'll decide if they want to make it permanent. Dan's keeping his fingers crossed that it'll work out. A doctor of Reilly's caliber doesn't come along every day. He's an excellent heart surgeon."

In the process of setting the table for breakfast, Janey frowned. "But Dan has a family practice. I wouldn't think a cardiologist would be interested in that at all, especially in a small town like Liberty Hill. Most of the local surgeries are pretty routine."

"He apparently wanted a break from L.A.," Sara said simply. "His wife died recently, and he decided he needed a complete change of scene."

That explained the sadness in his eyes. "That must have been very difficult for him. What happened?"

Sara shrugged. "He didn't want to talk about it to Dan, so all I know is that he showed up in town the day before yesterday with only a fancy foreign car and two suitcases to his name. He didn't even have a place to stay until Nick rented him the cabin."

That stunned Janey almost as much as the news that Dan had taken on a partner. "Why am I just now finding out about this?"

But even as she asked, she knew. She'd worked double shifts at the nursing home all week because they were shorthanded due to an early flu bug that was going around. Then last night she'd spent half the night working with the volunteer fire department. She hadn't seen any of the family except in passing all week.

"I guess I haven't been around much," she admitted with a grimace. "Obviously the good doctor impressed Nick—that cabin's his baby. He wouldn't rent to just anybody."

"Dan says he's a good man," her mother replied. "Nick thinks so, too."

And that said a lot. Besides her brothers, Janey couldn't think of two men she respected more. If Reilly Jones made a good impression on them, that should have been enough to silence any questions she had about the man. It didn't. As far as she could see, it just didn't make sense. A man didn't leave a million-dollar practice in L.A. for a significantly smaller one in the wilds of Colorado without a darn good reason. So what was Reilly Jones's story? It would be interesting to find out.

Chapter 2

Reilly wasn't surprised that he was the latest topic of conversation everywhere he went. Gossip was the grease that made most small towns run, and he was the new man in town. He'd expected questions, and there were plenty of them. But he had no intention of answering any of them. Not now, not ever. He'd come to Colorado to start fresh and put his past behind him, and he couldn't do that if he was continually talking about it. So when people asked everything from how much money he'd made in L.A. to why he wasn't married, he coolly replied that that was private information and he preferred not to talk about it.

It didn't win him many friends.

Another man might have been bothered by that, but Reilly told himself he didn't care. He wasn't there to make friends. Friends took an emotional toll, and that was more than he could give at the moment. Which was one of the reasons he'd moved to Liberty Hill in the first place. He didn't know anyone there and didn't *want* to know anyone.

He just wanted to work, then escape to the cabin in the woods he'd rented from the sheriff and just be left alone. After everything he'd been through, he didn't think that was too much to ask.

Dan Michaels, his new partner, had other ideas.

Inviting him to lunch at the local diner to discuss the matter after he'd observed Reilly with the patients that morning, Dan took a chair across the table from him and ordered a grilled chicken sandwich without bothering to look at the menu. A tall, trim man with snow-white hair and the kindest eyes Reilly had ever seen, he waited until Reilly had given his order and the waitress had moved on before he met his gaze with a frown.

"We've got a problem," he said quietly. "And if this partnership between us is going to work, I feel it's important that we start it off right by discussing problems that crop up as soon as possible. Agreed?"

"Of course," Reilly replied, surprised. Frowning, he thought back to some of the patients he'd seen that morning. He'd treated colds, allergies, a sprained wrist, even a minor burn, nothing that a first-year medical student couldn't have handled with one hand tied behind his back. So what was the problem? "I thought everything went fairly smoothly. Did I miss something?"

"The patients," the older man retorted, not unkindly. "Don't get me wrong. I was watching you, and you were right on the money when it came to your diagnoses. There isn't a doubt in my mind that when it comes to medicine, you're a gifted doctor."

"But you just said I missed something with the patients," he said, confused. "I don't understand."

Careful to keep his voice down so it wouldn't carry to the other diners, Dan said quietly, "I don't have to tell you that there's more to practicing medicine than handing out prescriptions and doing everything right procedurally. In L.A., your patients might accept—and even expect—a cool business relationship with their doctors, but that won't work here. This is a small town, Reilly. Your patients will expect you to not only be their doctor, but a friend, confidant, priest and therapist. They'll treat you like family and ask you private questions they've got no business asking. And they won't understand if you don't tell them anything about yourself."

Not liking the sound of that, Reilly scowled. "I have a right to my privacy."

"Yes, you do," he agreed. "And I know you're still grieving. After my wife died, I just wanted to crawl in a hole and be left alone. But I couldn't, and neither can you. Because you have patients who need you. And to them you're a stranger. They want to accept you, to like you, but they don't know anything about you. If you don't open up a little and let them know who you are, there won't be much trust between you. And without trust, you won't be much good to them as a doctor."

He wasn't saying anything Reilly didn't already know. A good doctor did a lot more than just treat physical ailments. But wasn't he allowed to keep his private life separate from work? Couldn't he earn patients' trust without telling them about the house he'd owned in Beverly Hills and if he'd ever dated a movie star? Wasn't he at least entitled to that?

"What's important here is that the patients trust my judgment as a doctor," he replied. "They don't need to know anything about my private life to do that."

Not a pushy man, Dan had said his piece. There was no point in beating the subject like a dead horse. "You know what's best for you," he said simply. "So how were things at the hospital last night? After the fancy operating rooms you practiced in in L.A., our little hospital must have been quite a shock to you. You probably felt like you'd stepped back in time.''

Reilly had to grin at that. "Well, maybe just a little, but I didn't encounter anything I couldn't handle. By the end of the evening, I felt right at home.''

"Good." Pleased, Dan sat back as the waitress delivered their food. "I can't remember the last time I had a night off. It was great, thanks to you.''

"That's what I'm here for," Reilly said with a wry shrug. And Dan was no more grateful than he was. After sitting at home and brooding for months in L.A., he hadn't realized how much he'd missed work. Last night he'd been so busy that he hadn't had much time to think about Victoria.

His brother had been right—he had needed a change of scene and he hadn't even realized it. He'd needed to work again, to find himself in medicine, and Liberty Hill, at least so far, seemed like a good place to do that. Dan was an excellent doctor—intelligent, thorough, kind—and Reilly hoped that their temporary three-month partnership worked out for both of them. He liked Dan and felt sure he was someone he could work with.

As for the patients Reilly was confident they would come around. He'd never lived in a small town before, but people were pretty much the same everywhere. All he had to do was give them time. If they were nosy, they'd learn soon enough that he had no intention of discussing his personal life with them. Once they accepted that, they'd all get along fine.

Satisfied that he had everything well in hand, he and Dan finished their lunch, then walked back to the office, which was conveniently located two blocks from the town square in an old craftsman cottage Dan had converted into office space ten years ago. Not surprisingly, the waiting room was full. Dan had warned him that once word got out that he'd joined the practice, they'd be flooded with patients wanting to get a look at him, and he'd been exactly right. Patients had come in and out of the office in a steady stream all morning, and only a handful of them had really been sick enough to require the attention of a doctor. The rest had used everything from a hangnail to a fake cough as an excuse to see Reilly, and they'd made no apologies for it.

Amused, he took the chart from the door of the first examining room and read the name on it. Myrtle Henderson. Stepping inside, he found an older woman pacing the small confines of the examining room impatiently. Tall and spare, with a lively step, she appeared to be in her early seventies and in excellent shape for her age. Reilly didn't doubt for a second that she, like so many of the others, had come to check him out. According to her chart, she'd come in complaining of dizziness, but the second she heard him step through the door, she whirled to face him without the slightest sign of unsteadiness. If she was dizzy, she hid it well.

"You must be Dr. Jones," she said with a delighted smile, holding out her hand for a firm shake. "Welcome to our neck of the woods, Doctor. It's good to have you here."

Amused, Reilly couldn't help but like her. She looked as if she could be as tough as nails when the occasion called for it, but there was a twinkle in her direct blue eyes that was hard to resist. "Thank you, ma'am. It's nice to be here. I understand you're having a problem with dizziness. Why don't you sit down and I'll take your blood pressure?"

Reluctantly she took the chair he motioned to, all the while assuring him that she was sure it was nothing. "I didn't eat breakfast, and that always makes me a little light-headed. And it was just for a second, anyway. In fact, now that I think about it, I'm sure I just imagined it.''

Biting back a smile, Reilly didn't doubt that, but he took her blood pressure, anyway. Just as he'd suspected, it checked out fine. Removing his stethoscope from his ears, he sat back and arched a dark brow at her. ''Well, it's not your blood pressure. Have you had this problem before? Maybe I should schedule some tests—''

''Oh, no,'' she laughed, dismissing the suggestion with a wave of her hand. ''We don't need to do that. I'm healthy as a horse—always have been. You look like you are, too,'' she added, neatly changing the subject. ''I bet you spent a lot of time playing golf and tennis at a fancy country club in L.A., didn't you? You've got that healthy, outdoor California look to you.''

''Thank you,'' he said dryly, and neatly sidetracked her question by not answering it at all.

Undaunted, Myrtle examined him with bright, curious eyes. ''So what brought you to Liberty Hill? I'd think a good-looking young man like yourself would go stir crazy here by the end of the week. It's pretty quiet. There's not much nightlife. Though I could introduce you around, if you like. I know a couple of nice girls you might like to meet.''

Reilly cringed at the idea, but all he said was, ''I appreciate the offer, Mrs. Henderson—''

''Myrtle,'' she corrected him with a broad grin and a motherly pat on the hand. ''Everyone calls me Myrtle.''

''But right now I don't have time for a social life. Maybe some other time.''

She surprised him by accepting that with a rueful shrug. ''It never hurts to try. If you change your mind, you let me know. I was born and raised here and know everybody in town.''

Her mission accomplished and curiosity satisfied, she sailed out without mentioning her dizziness at all, and Reilly could only smile and shake his head. Unfortunately, the patients he saw after her weren't nearly as polite. By the time the office closed early at three so he and Dan could go on rounds at the local nursing home, he'd been grilled about everything from his credit history to the number of children he one day hoped to have. And then, there were the women who'd come on to him. He didn't even want to think about that.

Dan took one look at him as they headed for the nursing home and arched a brow. "Rough afternoon?"

"No, thanks," he said dryly. "I've already had one. Are the women around here always so aggressive?"

To his credit, Dan didn't laugh. But his lips twitched with wry humor. "So the feeding frenzy's starting already, has it? I was afraid of that. I went through the same thing after Peggy died."

"There were some women in L.A. who made it clear they'd be happy to help me through my *grief*," Reilly said with a grimace of distaste, "but they were friends. These women don't even know me!"

"Unfortunately, they know everything important they think they need to know about you," the older man said as they walked the three blocks to the nursing home. Normally not a cynical man, he ticked off Reilly's attributes. "You're single, young, reasonably attractive. And you've got M.D. after your name. Every mama wants her daughter to marry a doctor—you know that. It's not any different here than in L.A. Except that in a town the size of Liberty Hill, doctors are harder to come by. As long as you're walking around free, you'll be considered fair game."

He spoke nothing less than the truth, and they both knew it. Reilly had married Victoria the summer before he started medical school, so he hadn't been chased by marriage-minded women looking to land a rich doctor who could support them in the manner to which they wanted to become accustomed. But he'd been to more than his share of weddings where thrilled mamas of the bride paraded the groom around the reception hall as if he was a prize, introducing him to everyone as "my new son-in-law, *the doctor.*" Just thinking about it made him cringe.

That was *not* going to happen to him!

"They're wasting their time," he told Dan grimly as they reached the nursing home and the older man held the door open for him. "Victoria might be gone, but I still love her. I'll always love her. If I can't have her, I don't want anyone."

Sympathizing with him, Dan knew exactly how he felt. When Peggy had died, he'd thought his world had ended and he could never look at another woman as anything but a friend. He'd been wrong. Reilly would love again, too, but that was something he wasn't ready to hear yet.

"You're still new here," he said diplomatically. "Once the women get to know you and realize you're really not interested, they'll back off. Just give them time."

That sounded good, but Reilly wasn't holding his breath. Women were the same all over, and as long as they thought he was free, they'd think they had a chance with him. He would have no peace. Resigned, he stepped inside the nursing home, where he would be making rounds twice a week, and braced for more questions as Dr. Michaels began to introduce him to the staff and patients.

He didn't have to wait long.

"Oh, Dr. Reilly, it's so good to finally meet you. I heard you were living out at Sheriff Kincaid's cabin all by yourself. Don't you have a wife and family?"

"We've heard so much about you, Dr. Reilly. Is it true

that you had a house on the beach in Malibu and used to date Meg Ryan? Is she as sweet as she looks?''

"Are you married, Doctor? I was just telling my granddaughter she needed to meet you. Why don't I give you her phone number and you can call her?''

Gritting his teeth as one patient after another quizzed him about his personal life, Reilly admitted that he wasn't married and had never had the good fortune to meet Meg Ryan. The staff, thankfully, was more restrained, but he didn't fool himself into thinking that the nurses weren't listening to every word. More than a few of them had a gleam in their eye that he found all too familiar.

And he wasn't the only one who noticed. Disapproval glinting in his eyes, Dan sent several of the younger girls back to work with just a frown. "C'mon,'' he told Reilly. "There's someone else I want you to meet. This time of day, she's usually in the solarium with the Lester sisters.''

Leading the way through the east wing, Dan stepped into the solarium and grinned at the sight of the nurse overseeing a lively game of Parcheesi between two old women in wheelchairs who sat at a wrought-iron table that overlooked an outdoor patio. "Janey! I thought I'd find you here. Come and meet my new partner.''

In the process of rolling the dice for Margaret, who had lost partial use of her right hand due to a stroke four months ago, Janey turned at Dan's call, a smile already starting to spread across her face. Then she spied the man at his side. He was scowling at her, just as he had when she'd stopped to help him the other day when his BMW broke down on the side of the road.

"Actually, we've already met,'' she told Dan as she excused herself from the Lester sisters and stepped forward with a smile. "Well, sort of,'' she amended wryly, offering Reilly her hand. "We ran into each other at the E.R. last night, but there wasn't time for an introduction. It's nice to finally meet you, Doctor. I'm Janey McBride.''

"Reilly Jones," he said, giving her hand a matter-of-fact shake. "You're Nick Kincaid's sister-in-law."

"Guilty as charged," she replied, amusement glinting in her brown eyes. "Just for the record, he knows all about my shotgun."

Chuckling, Dan grinned. "Everybody knows about that shotgun. As far as I know," he told Reilly, "she's never had to use it, but that doesn't mean she can't. She's a crackerjack shot. And one of the most caring nurses you'll ever have the good fortune to work with. You can always depend on her to see that your patients get the finest care."

It was a glowing recommendation, one that brought a blush to Janey's cheeks. "I just do what anyone else would do," she said modestly, and immediately changed the subject. "Liberty Hill's quite a change from L.A.," she told Reilly with a smile. "But I guess you know that already. What do you miss the most so far?"

Privacy, Reilly wanted to answer, and just barely held his tongue. Dammit, what was wrong with everyone around here? Every time he turned around, someone was asking him a damn personal question. He wanted to give people the benefit of the doubt—they were just being friendly and trying to find something to talk about—but he felt as if he'd been prodded and poked all day for information that was none of their business, and he was heartily sick of it. Didn't they understand? He just wanted to be left alone!

"Nothing," he said coolly. "That's why I left. Now if you'll excuse me, Dr. Michaels introduced me to some patients who need my attention. It was nice meeting you."

With a curt nod he turned and strode out of the solarium, leaving behind a stunned silence. Taken aback, Janey turned to Dan in confusion. "What was that all about? What did I say? I didn't mean to offend him."

"Of course you didn't," he assured her with a comforting pat on the shoulder. "It wasn't you, dear. Reilly's just had a difficult afternoon." Making a snap decision, he motioned to her to take a seat at one of the nearby tables. "Sit down, Janey. I need to tell you a few things about Dr. Jones."

The Lester sisters had turned their attention from their game to Oprah, who'd just come on the television in the corner, so Janey had time to talk. "If this is about his wife dying, I already know," she said as she settled into a chair across the table from him. "Mom told me. Obviously he's going through a rough time."

Dan nodded grimly. "That isn't something a man gets over in a hurry. Trust me—I know. Peggy's been dead eighteen years, and there are still times when I go home at the end of the day and expect to find her in the kitchen. It's the loneliest feeling in the world when you realize she's not there."

"Is that why he left L.A.?" she asked quietly. "He couldn't stand to live there without her?"

"I don't know," he admitted. "He's a private person and never really said. And I didn't push. I do know, though, that he was looking for a change. But change isn't always easy, especially when you're in a strange town where you don't know anyone. That's why I wanted to talk to you. He could use a friend, Janey. I know the two of you didn't get off to a good start, but I was hoping you would do what you can to make him feel welcome. I imagine he's pretty lonely."

An astute woman, Janey knew when she was being manipulated. But she was also a soft touch, and she could not only forgive Dan for tugging on her emotions, but Reilly, too, for his hostile attitude. If their situations had been reversed, and she'd not only lost a husband she'd loved with all her heart, but moved to L.A., where she knew no one, she would have been miserable, too.

Smiling fondly at Dan, she gave in gracefully. "Okay, you can stop twisting my arm. I'll be nice to the guy. If he hands my head to me on a platter, I guess you can stitch it back on for me."

Pleased, he rose to his feet with her and hugged her. "I knew I could count on you. You're just like your mother."

Janey couldn't think of anyone she'd rather be like, but Dan had it wrong. Her mother was strikingly beautiful, and Merry was her spitting image. She, on the other hand, was more like her father and Joe. Quiet and plain as apple pie, she'd accepted long ago that she would never have her mother's or Merry's striking beauty or outgoing personality. That just wasn't who she was. And that was okay. She would have never been comfortable being beautiful. Happily married to Nick and eight months pregnant, Merry still drew constant male looks wherever she went. Janey couldn't imagine that. She would have hated it.

Convincing Dan of that, however, would have been impossible. An old family friend, he'd known her all her life and made no secret of the fact that he thought she was every bit as beautiful as the rest of the family. Returning his hug fondly, she promised, "I'll do what I can."

She told herself it would be easy. She would make a point of seeking him out when he came by the nursing home for rounds, and she was bound to run into him at the hospital when she was working rescue with the volunteer fire department. There wouldn't, however, be much time to talk during work, so she had to find another way to make him feel welcome.

"I'll make him a cake and take it over to the cabin," she decided as she drove home after her shift. It was the neighborly thing to do, and her mother had an excellent chocolate cake recipe. She'd never made it before, personally, but how hard could it be? All she had to do was follow directions.

Wednesday night was the regular meeting of her mother's bridge club at Myrtle's, so Janey wasn't surprised to find the house deserted when she got home. Her mother loved bridge and seldom missed a night out with the girls. Thankfully, Janey knew where she kept her recipes. Taking time only to change out of her nurse's uniform into jeans and a T-shirt, she hurried back downstairs and tied on an apron.

She should have known she was in trouble when she finally found the recipe in her mother's recipe box and discovered that it was nothing more than a list of ingredients written down in Sara's neat hand. There were no directions, no indication of what order the ingredients were mixed or even what temperature the cake should be baked at. Frowning, Janey considered calling Sara at Myrtle's, but she really hated to disturb the game, especially for something so minor. She'd watched her mother make the cake dozens of times over the years. Surely she could figure it out by herself. Quickly gathering all the ingredients and setting them out on the counter, she began.

Her memory wasn't the best, but if she remembered correctly, the sugar, chocolate, butter and vanilla were in the icing, so by process of elimination, she deduced the contents of the cake. Pleased with herself, she tossed everything into the mixing bowl and turned the mixture on high. Now all she had to do was grease and flour the sheet cake pan and she could start baking. Grinning, she could just see

her mother's face when she came in and discovered she'd
actually baked a cake. She'd be shocked!

The scent of burning chocolate hit Sara in the face the
second she stepped through the front door. Surprised, she
frowned. What was going on? She was sure she hadn't left
anything in the oven, and Janey didn't usually venture into
the kitchen on her own unless it was to heat up something
in the microwave. Scrambled eggs was about the extent of
her culinary repertoire, and with good reason. The last time
she'd tried to bake something, she'd been twelve, and she'd
nearly set the house on fire.

Alarmed by the memory, Sara rushed into the kitchen to
find Janey peering doubtfully into the oven. "Janey!" she
sighed in relief when she saw there was no smoke filling
the room as she'd half feared. "What's going on? I smelled
something burning and thought the house was on fire!"

"I was making a cake," she replied in disgust as she
looked around in vain for the pot holders, "but I think I
burned it. Don't you put the oven on five hundred when
you bake a cake?"

"Good Lord, no, honey! Not if you want it to be edible."
Quickly grabbing the pot holders she kept on a hook next
to the stove, Sara jerked open the oven door and rescued
what was left of the cake. Not surprisingly, it was a pitiful
sight. Shrunk to half the size of the sheet pan, it was nothing but a hard, charred glob.

When Janey groaned at the sight of it, it was all Sara
could do not to laugh. Pressing her lips tightly together, it
was several long moments before she could manage to turn
to her with a straight face. Even then her voice had a tendency to wobble with laughter. "Is that my chocolate cake
recipe?"

Janey nodded glumly. "Somehow it didn't turn out like yours does. What'd I do wrong besides cook it to death?"

From the looks of it, *everything,* but Sara couldn't bring herself to say that. Not when Janey had gone to so much trouble. Pulling out a chair at the kitchen table that had been in the family longer than anyone could remember, she patted the spot next to her. "We'll get to that. First, sit down and tell me what brought this all about. The last time you wanted to cook, you still had braces on your teeth."

Wincing, Janey remembered that occasion all too well. Her brothers still teased her about it. "Please," she begged, "let's don't even go there. I was just trying to be nice to Reilly, like Dan asked me to, and I blew it."

"Reilly?" her mother repeated, surprised. "All this was for *Reilly Jones?*"

Janey nodded and told her about her first meeting with Reilly several days ago, then her encounter with him earlier in the day at the nursing home. "He's a very unhappy man. Dan thinks he needs a friend, so I thought I would make him a cake and take it over to the cabin. You know, sort of a welcome-to-the-neighborhood type thing." Wrinkling her nose at the miserable excuse for a cake, she had to laugh. "So much for good intentions. I guess I should have just stopped at Ed's on the way home from work and bought a pie. At least that would have been edible."

So why hadn't she? Sara wondered. What was it about Reilly Jones that had inspired her to make a cake for him? Janey had never done such a thing before for any man, let alone one she'd only just met. What in the world was going on?

Questions buzzing around in her head, Sara told herself not to be nosy. Janey was a grown woman and certainly didn't have to answer to her mother. And Sara didn't want to say anything that might make her feel self-conscious.

Not when she appeared to be showing an interest in a man for the first time in her life. "Don't give up hope," she said, dumping the burned cake in the trash. "He'll be able to eat yours, too. We'll just make another one."

Sara could have whipped up her famous hot fudge cake in record time, but this was Janey's cake, not hers. So after helping her assemble fresh ingredients, she patiently gave her step by step instructions, then watched her every move to make sure she didn't make any mistakes.

Pleased with herself when she finally pulled the finished product from the oven, Janey had to admit that the cake didn't look anything like the one her mother usually made, but she couldn't complain. It might not look pretty, but compared to her first effort, it was a virtual masterpiece.

"Thanks, Mom," she said, hugging her. "I don't know what I would have done without you. Do you think it's too late to take it over to the cabin tonight?"

"No, it's early yet, and I'm sure Reilly will appreciate the gesture," she assured her. "While you're there, why don't you invite him to join the decorating committee for the Christmas festival? The festival's just two weeks away, and the first committee meeting is Monday."

It was a great idea, one Janey knew she should have thought of herself. Every year the town celebrated Christmas by turning the town square into a winter wonderland the second weekend in December. There were food and crafts booths, not to mention a complete village for Santa and his elves, and they were all constructed by the decorating committee, which was comprised of volunteers from all over the county. Because the committee meetings were as much fun as the festival itself, there was never any shortage of volunteers, but no one was ever turned away. The more, the merrier.

"It'll give him a chance to meet people," she said, pleased. "Thanks, Mom! I'll do that."

Made of logs that had been cut from the property itself, Nick's cabin sat in the middle of a thick stand of pines and looked as though it had been there forever. With a deep front porch and paned windows that were designed to let in the light and bring the forest inside, it had a charm to it that Janey had always loved. Tonight, only a single lamp burned in the living room, but that was enough to cast an inviting glow across the porch.

Parking in the circular drive, she wasn't surprised when the porch light came on as she started up the stairs to the porch. The cabin sat at the end of a long private drive, and in the dark of the night, Reilly would have seen her headlights the second she turned down the drive.

Janey didn't consider herself a shy person. She liked people and enjoyed talking to them, but something happened to her on the way up the steps to his front door. Suddenly her heart was pounding, her knees weren't quite steady, and the little welcoming speech she had all prepared flew right out of her head the second he opened the door to her. And for the life of her, she didn't know why. Flustered, she forced a weak smile and couldn't think of a thing to say except, "Hi."

His face expressionless, he arched a brow at the sight of the cake pan in her hand. "What's that?"

"What? Oh!" Suddenly remembering why she was there, she blushed to the roots of her hair and abruptly thrust the pan into his hands like it was a hot rock. "It's a cake," she said unnecessarily. "To welcome you to the neighborhood."

"I see."

Janey wasn't too sure of that. From his expression, he'd

never seen a cake before, and Janey couldn't say she blamed him. It was awful looking. Suddenly appreciating the humor of the situation, she grinned. "I know it looks terrible—I'm not much of a cook—but trust me, this is a real prize compared to the first one I made. That one ended up in the trash can."

"You made two?"

"I didn't want to poison you," she said simply. "The whole point of this was to make you feel welcome."

He should have laughed. She expected him to. When he didn't, she reminded herself that he was going through a difficult time and probably didn't mean to be rude. If she was going to be a friend to him, she had to remember that.

Shrugging off her hurt feelings, she forced a smile that didn't come as easily as she would have liked. "Well, it's getting late. I just stopped by to give you the cake. Oh, and to invite you to a meeting of the decorating committee for the Christmas festival," she added. Quickly telling him about the festival and how much fun the committee meetings were, she said, "Our first meeting's next Monday, and I thought you might like to come. It'll give you a chance to meet people and have some fun at the same time. If you're not busy, of course."

There was nothing the least bit offensive about her little speech, but Reilly knew better than to be taken in by the apparent innocence of it. Did she really think he was so gullible? Ever since Victoria's death, he had been hit on by just about every woman who crossed his path, and he was heartily sick of it. There were three casseroles in his refrigerator from three other women who'd had the same idea as Janey. And despite their claims to the contrary, he knew they weren't just being neighborly. He'd played the game too many times with the women in L.A. after Victoria had died. By bringing him a covered dish, they were each ensuring that they could return in a few days with the excuse that they were there to pick up their cookware.

Just thinking about it irritated the hell out of him. From the little he'd seen of Janey McBride, he'd thought she was different. Obviously, he'd been wrong.

"I'm busy Monday night," he said coldly.

"Oh. Well, then, maybe some other time."

When she started to turn, her smile now gone, he should have let her go. If she wanted to go on thinking there was a chance they'd get together at a later time, that was her problem, he told himself. He wasn't responsible for what she thought. But even as he tried to convince himself of that, he knew he had to set the record straight. He wasn't a man who led women on—he never had been. Honesty wasn't always appreciated, but it prevented a lot of problems in the long run.

"No, there won't be another time," he said flatly. "You might as well know that now. If you've set your sights on me, you're wasting your time. I'm not interested."

Stunned, Janey couldn't believe she'd heard him correctly. He actually thought that she...that she was the kind of woman who would...

Unable to finish the thoughts whirling in her head, she almost laughed at the ridiculousness of his accusations. He couldn't be serious! She'd never come on to a man in her life—she wouldn't even know where to begin. This had to be some kind of a joke.

But there was nothing the least bit amusing about the hard glint in his blue eyes. He actually thought she was making a play for him, and he wanted nothing to do with her.

Later—years from now—she told herself, she might be able to look back and laugh about this. But for now she'd never been so insulted in her life. Pride coming to her rescue, she drew herself up proudly and stared down her nose at him with all the regalness of a queen. So he wasn't interested, was he? Well, neither was she!

"Someone here has an overinflated ego," she said coolly, "and it's not me. For your information, Doctor, the only reason I brought the cake over was because Dr. Michaels asked me to be nice to you. Since I've obviously failed at that, I won't bother you anymore. Good night."

Chapter 3

She didn't slam the door, but she didn't need to. She'd made her point, not that Reilly cared. Watching her storm out, he told himself he was lucky to be rid of her. If he was any judge of character, Janey McBride, unlike the other women who had tried to sweet talk their way into his home, wouldn't be back. He'd hurt her pride, and as she drove away and her taillights disappeared into the darkness, he knew she was probably consigning him to the devil. And that was all right by him. He wasn't interested in her or any other woman.

The problem was, she seemed to be the only one who'd gotten the message, he thought irritably as he shut the front door and headed for the kitchen. The others who'd come bearing gifts and a come-hither smile hadn't been nearly as easy to discourage. Refusing to take offense at his rudeness, they'd just shrugged off his bad manners with an irritatingly forgiving laugh and promised to lighten his mood. All he had to do was give them a chance.

Sex. He hadn't pretended to misunderstand what they were offering. That was what they wanted, how they thought they could catch him. They could pretend to themselves and everyone else that their motives were pure—they were just being friendly by welcoming the new widower to the neighborhood—but he knew a woman on the prowl when he saw one. And everyone who'd knocked on his door that evening had had that gleam in her eye that had sent alarm bells clanging in his head.

Everyone, that is, except Janey McBride.

He tried to deny that, but he couldn't forget the look on her face when he'd told her she was wasting her time if she'd set her sights on him. She'd been shocked—there was no other way to describe it—as if the thought had never entered her head. And now that he thought of it, she hadn't been dressed like a woman bent on seduction. Far from it, in fact. Unlike the others, who'd delivered their culinary gifts decked out in full makeup and body-hugging sweaters that were designed to make a man drop his teeth, Janey had worn faded jeans and an old college sweatshirt that still bore traces of cocoa and flour from her baking. As for makeup, her face had been bare and natural but for mascara and lip gloss.

Yeah, the lady's really after you, Jones, a voice in his head sneered. *She was decked out like a real Jezebel. It's a wonder you were able to control yourself.*

The truth hit him then like a slap in the face. Janey McBride was, in all likelihood, everything she'd appeared to be—considerate, caring, generous. The only reason she'd brought him a cake was because Dan really had asked her to be nice to him. It was something his partner would have done. And how had he responded to her kindness? By mocking her efforts and accusing her of coming on to him.

"Son of a bitch!" he groaned. How could he have been

so stupid? He would have liked to use the excuse that he'd just met her and didn't know what kind of woman she was, but anyone with eyes could see that she just wasn't the type to blatantly chase a man. With her prim-and-proper manner, she was too old-fashioned for that. She'd wait for a man to approach *her,* not the other way around.

Cursing softly, he wanted to kick himself. He was an intelligent man who knew women—he should have seen the kind of woman she was from her appearance alone. Instead, he'd jumped to all the wrong conclusions and acted like a general all-round jerk—after she'd spent hours slaving over a hot stove, baking not one cake, but *two* for him! No wonder she'd stormed off like an insulted queen. He didn't blame her. Just thinking about the way he'd spoken to her disgusted him. He'd been raised better than that.

There was no question that he would apologize the next time he saw her, he promised himself. He'd been wrong, and he owed her that, at the very least. He didn't, however, regret making it clear to her that he wasn't interested in having a relationship with anyone. The only woman he wanted was dead, and he didn't expect to ever love anyone else again. The sooner the women of Liberty Hill knew and accepted that, the happier he'd be.

Sinking down onto the couch, he picked up the medical journal he'd been trying to read all evening, but with a will of their own his eyes kept drifting to the picture of Victoria that sat right next to him on the end table. Young and beautiful, her blond hair flowing loose around her shoulders and her green eyes impish with laughter, she smiled at him with a love that lit up her whole face.

It had been eight months since he'd seen that smile, eight months since the warmth of her love had made him feel whole. Everyone had told him that the hurt would fade with time, that the wound to his heart would scar over and eventually heal, but it hadn't. Every time he saw her picture, every time he thought of her, he ached so badly, his very soul hurt.

Tears glinting in his eyes, he reached for her picture, just as he did every night. Because he couldn't reach for her. He wanted to touch her, to feel her, to love her, but this was all he had left. Pictures. *Things,* dammit! And memories. And that wasn't nearly enough.

Fuming all the way home, Janey wasn't surprised to see Dan's Suburban parked in the circular drive in front of the house. He usually dropped in several nights a week to visit with her mother, especially when Janey was out. He claimed he didn't like the idea of Sara being alone at night, but Janey suspected he really wanted a chance to have her mother all to himself. And her mother didn't seem to have a clue.

Another time Janey might have smiled at that. Everyone seemed to know that Dan was crazy about Sara—everyone except Sara, herself. But Janey could find no humor in the situation tonight. Not when all she could think of was Reilly Jones and how she'd like to string him up by his thumbs. Damn the man, what kind of woman did he think she was?

"Don't answer that," she snapped to herself as she stormed inside and slammed the door behind her. "You already know the answer to that one."

And that was what hurt the most. She wasn't some loose floozy who made a play for every good-looking cowboy who came along with a fat wallet. The very idea was ludicrous! Didn't he look at her? Couldn't he see that she was just an ordinary—

"Janey? Is that you?"

Wincing, Janey wanted to kick herself for not slipping

quietly inside and making her way upstairs without anyone being the wiser. Her mother would want to know how Reilly had reacted to the cake, of course, and she didn't want to talk about it. Not now. She wouldn't be able to hide her anger, and that would just lead to more questions, and she really didn't want to repeat Reilly's outrageous accusations.

But her mother wasn't going to let her escape upstairs without some kind of explanation, so there was no hope for it but to go in and try to put the best spin on the situation as possible. Forcing a grimace of a smile, she called back, "Yeah, Mom. I'll be right there."

She wasn't much of an actress, but she thought she hid her anger well. She should have known, however, that she couldn't fool Sara. The second she stepped into the great room and greeted her mother and Dan, who were watching their favorite detective show on TV, Sara took one look at her and immediately frowned. "What is it? What's wrong?"

"Nothing," she said easily, hanging on to her smile for all she was worth. "I'd like to stay and talk, but it's been a long day and I'm worn out. I think I'll go to bed."

She would have rushed up the stairs, but Sara stopped her before she could take a single step. "How was Reilly? Did he like the cake? What did he say?"

Another time Janey would have found a diplomatic way to answer. After all, Reilly was Dan's partner, and she didn't want to put Dan in the position of having to defend him. But she was still so steamed, the words just popped out. "Trust me, you don't want to know. He was horrible."

"What?"

"Oh, Janey!"

"I know you wanted me to be nice to him, Dan," she told the older man, "but I just can't. He's rude and conceited and I wish you'd never taken him into your practice. God knows how I'm going to work with him. As far as I'm concerned, I never want to lay eyes on him again!''

''But what happened?'' her mother asked, stunned by her daughter's vehemence since she rarely lost her temper. ''From what Dan said about him, he was nice but reserved. What did he do? You just took him a cake. Why would he be rude about something like that? Most men would have been thrilled to have someone cook for them.''

Janey would have preferred not to discuss it—now or ever. Just thinking about the things Reilly had said to her brought the painful sting of a blush to her cheeks. But she knew her mother and Dan. They were both as protective as mother hens, and they wouldn't let the subject die until they had some answers.

Left with no choice, she blurted out, ''He thinks I had an ulterior motive.''

''Good Lord, how? You just baked him a cake.''

''He accused me of setting my sights on him and told me I was wasting my time. He wasn't interested.''

For a long moment there was nothing but stunned silence. Embarrassed to death, Janey couldn't bring herself to look either her mother or Dan in the eye, so she didn't see the surprise that flared in their eyes—or the sudden smiles they quickly bit back.

''He didn't want to help with the decorating committee for the Christmas festival, either,'' she added stiffly. ''When I offered to introduce him around some other time, he made it clear that wasn't going to happen. He was busy.''

Dan winced at that, feeling responsible. He'd only been trying to help, and instead, he'd messed up everything. ''I'm so sorry, Janey,'' he said gruffly. ''I never meant for you to get your feelings hurt. I know he's still grieving for his wife, but he can't take his anger out on other people. I'll talk to him.''

She should have let him. Every instinct she had urged her to jump at the offer. Then she wouldn't have to deal with the oh-so-conceited Dr. Jones anymore except on a professional level. She wouldn't have to speak to him, be nice to him, even acknowledge his existence on a personal level, and that sounded just fine with her. After the way he'd treated her, she wanted nothing to do with him ever again.

But even as she considered letting Dan fight her battles for her, she knew she couldn't. She wasn't the helpless female type—she never had been. Her parents had raised her and her sister, Merry, to stand on their own two feet and handle what life threw at them with confidence. She didn't go running to her brothers or Dan or any other man when something difficult cropped up. She took care of it herself. She'd do the same with Reilly Jones.

The glint of battle lighting her brown eyes, she raised her chin a notch. ''I appreciate the offer, Dan,'' she replied quietly, ''but I can handle Dr. Jones just fine all by myself. Now if you'll excuse me, I think I'll go up to bed. I run rescue tomorrow night, so it's going to be a long day. Good night.''

She turned and sailed proudly out of the room and never saw the speculative looks her mother and Dan exchanged. In the quiet left by her leavetaking, Sara arched a brow at Dan. ''Are you thinking what I'm thinking?''

He nodded, his lips twitching with wry humor. ''I've never seen her this way before. Reilly's definitely stirred her up.''

''And she seems to have done the same to him. But do you think that's possible, Dan? Maybe we're reading too much into this. After all, Reilly's still mourning his wife. And Janey..."

She hesitated, searching for words to describe her oldest daughter. "I've prayed that she would meet someone someday and find happiness with a good man she could share her life with. But she never seemed to want that for herself. She's always been so dedicated to her work. And if she ever took an interest in any of the boys she went to school with, I never knew about it. She just always seemed so content to be alone."

"Maybe that's because the right man hadn't come along yet," Dan replied.

"And you think Reilly might be that man?"

He shrugged. "It's too soon to say. But they definitely seem to have struck sparks off each other."

"But he's still in love with his dead wife!"

There was, unfortunately, no denying that. "And a part of him will always love her. They obviously had a wonderful relationship, and you and I both know how hard it is to let go of something that was so perfect. But a man can only take so much loneliness before he's forced to admit that the woman he loved is gone forever. If he doesn't want to be miserable the rest of his life, he has to let go of the past and find someone else."

He spoke from experience. After months of heartache and long, empty nights he'd thought would never end, he'd come to accept the fact that Peggy was never coming back. Admitting that had been the hardest thing he'd ever done. It was like losing her all over again. He'd cried for days. But then, when his tears had dried, a peace unlike anything he'd ever known before had settled over him, and he'd gradually begun to heal. He'd found himself looking forward to each new day rather than dreading it. And that's when he'd looked up and found Sara.

Just thinking about that day he'd noticed her as a woman for the first time still brought a smile to his lips. She'd smiled at him just as she always did, and every nerve ending in his body had sat up and taken notice. It had shocked the hell out of him. Up until then she'd always just been Sara, the widow of his old friend Gus, and one of Peggy's best friends. For years the four of them had been like family, spending holidays and special occasions together, and that hadn't stopped with Gus's death. Sara and the kids had still been a huge part of his and Peggy's life, and never once had he looked at her as anything other than a friend.

Then she'd smiled at him one day, and everything changed.

He loved her. It still amazed him how much. And she didn't have a clue. Oh, she knew he loved her as a friend, but that apparently was as far as she thought it went. She didn't begin to suspect the depth of his feelings for her, and he didn't know how to tell her. He loved her and needed her in his life, but he wasn't sure if she would want anything more from him than friendship. So rather than risk losing her completely, he kept his feelings to himself and they went on as they always had.

"There is another possibility," she said. "I've never known Janey not to get along with anyone before, but this could just be a case of a personality clash between the two of them. They might not be attracted to each other at all."

"That's true," he agreed. "Whatever it is, I'm sure they'll work it out. After all, it's not like they can avoid each other. Not when they'll be working together at the nursing home and the hospital."

Watching Janey and Reilly come to terms with the sparks they rubbed off each other would, in fact, be damned interesting. For now, though, it was his own romance he was concerned about. "But enough about the youngsters," he said, abruptly changing the subject. "What I want to know is when are you going to go out with me?"

It was an old joke between them, one that went back to that day when he'd first looked at her in a new light and realized that his feelings for her went much deeper than friendship. Caught up in the headiness of his newfound emotions, he'd asked her out, and she'd mistakenly thought he was joking. At the time he couldn't blame her. She'd been spending a lot of time with him, helping him through Peggy's death, and the town gossips had begun to wonder if they were dating. He'd suggested they go out to give the busybodies something to talk about, and she'd been joking about it ever since.

And this time was no different. Her blue eyes sparkling with merriment, she laughed gaily. "Why? Are the gossips having a slow day? Shall we give them something to talk about?"

They could give them more to talk about than she suspected, but that wasn't something she was ready to hear. Grinning, he said easily, "I'm game if you are. There's nothing I like better than setting the phone lines buzzing."

He wouldn't have given a damn about the phone lines if she'd said yes, but she didn't. Still thinking he was teasing, she chuckled. "Maybe next time."

It was that thought that got him through the long, lonely nights. The only problem was next time never seemed to come.

When the alarm went off the next morning, Janey felt as if she hadn't slept a wink. Every time she'd closed her eyes during the night, she'd seen nothing but Reilly Jones and the coldness in his eyes when he'd told her he wasn't interested in her. When she'd finally fallen asleep from sheer exhaustion, the infuriating man had followed her into her dreams.

Cursing him, she rolled out of bed with a groan and hoped she wouldn't have the misfortune to run into the irritating Dr. Jones today. Because if she did, she promised herself as she changed into her nurse's uniform and left for work, she just might tell him what she thought of him. It was no more than he deserved.

Her chin set at a determined angle, she marched into the nursing home a few minutes before seven with a look in her eye that had her co-workers lifting their brows in surprise. She never came to work with an attitude, and more than a few of her fellow nurses didn't know what to make of it.

"Are you okay, Janey?"

"Has something happened to your mom?"

"It's not Merry and the baby, is it? When is she due?"

Realizing she must look awful, Janey shook her head, her smile more than a little forced. "Merry's due Christmas Day. And no, nothing's wrong. I just didn't get much sleep last night. I couldn't seem to turn my brain off."

That wasn't the complete truth, but she had no intention of sharing her experience with Dr. Jones with the entire nursing home staff. And that's what would happen if she made the mistake of telling so much as a single soul. The story would spread like wildfire through every room in the nursing home within an hour.

There was, fortunately, no time for anyone to ask her what she'd been thinking about that had kept her up all night. It was time for her shift to start, and she had work to do. Sending up a silent prayer of thanks, she headed for the east wing nurses' station and began the day just as she always did—by reading her patients' charts to see if there'd been any change in their conditions since yesterday.

She was well into the first chart and wondering if Mr. Drisco needed his medication changed when Cybil Greer, one of the night shift nurses, stopped to talk to her. "I guess you heard about Hannah."

There was only one woman there by the name of Hannah, and she was not only Janey's patient, but one of her favorite people. And she hadn't been doing well lately. Alarmed, she said, "What's wrong?"

"She's developed pneumonia," Cybil said grimly. "It doesn't look good."

Already rising to her feet, Janey said, "Thanks for telling me. I'll check on her right now."

Hannah Starks wasn't the oldest patient on Janey's floor, but she'd been there the longest, and there was just something about her that touched Janey's heart. Small and frail, with eyes that still sparkled like a girl's, she, like so many of the other women in the nursing home, had lost her husband years ago and now had to depend on the mercy of strangers to get her through the day. And she did it all without complaint.

If she'd been in her shoes, Janey wasn't sure she could have been as gracious. It wasn't as if Hannah had no one to care for her. She had a son—William—who lived in Seattle, and Hannah adored him. If William's love was as strong as his mother's, he gave no sign of it. Over the course of the last year, he hadn't been to see his mother a single time. Both Dan and Janey had both talked to him on several occasions, telling him how desperately his mother wanted to see him, but he still hadn't come. And poor Hannah kept making excuses for him.

Her heart breaking for her, Janey wasn't surprised to find her frailer than yesterday. At eighty-two, she was as thin as a rail and had little strength to fall back on when she became ill. Still, she smiled at the sight of Janey and struggled to sit up.

"No, you don't need to get up!" she said quickly, hurrying across the room to help ease her back against her pillow. "You lie there and take it easy. I heard you weren't feeling up to snuff this morning. Can I get you anything? Breakfast, maybe? Scrambled eggs? Or how about some pancakes? You name it, and I'll get it for you."

If she'd said eggs Benedict, Janey would have called Ed's diner and asked Ed to make the special dish for her, but Hannah had simple tastes and there was only one thing in life that she really wanted. Pale as the bedsheets, she smiled and shook her head. "No, thank you, dear. I'm not really hungry this morning. But I would like to see William. Once he hears that I need him, I'm sure he'll come."

Her faith was unshakable, the love in her eyes heartbreaking to see as she lifted her gaze to the wall across from her bed. There, family photos covered nearly every available space. Some of the pictures were of Hannah's parents and husband, all of whom had died years ago, but the majority were of her only child, William. Taken at all stages of life, there were pictures of him at two and eight and forty-two, with his first dog, his first girlfriend, his first wife.

"He's such a handsome boy," Hannah murmured fondly. "And just like his father. Don't you think so?"

Her heart breaking for her, Janey wondered how the son could be anything like the husband who had adored her. Granted, William favored his father in looks, but from what Janey could see, the resemblance ended there. The only feeling he'd shown for his mother so far was cold, hard indifference.

And she deserved better than that, Janey thought resentfully. Unlike some patients who complained about every little ache and pain, Hannah never did. She always had a kind word and a smile for everyone and seldom thought about herself, even when the arthritis that plagued her was at its most painful. And whenever she called William and asked him to come see her, she always made excuses for him when he promised to come and never did.

And it tore Janey apart. She wanted to tell her not to torture herself this way—he wasn't going to come. But it was thoughts of William that kept her going day in and day out, so Janey told her what she wanted to hear. "I know you're very proud of him," she said diplomatically. "Why don't we get you ready for company just in case he's able to come today?"

Not surprisingly, Hannah beamed at the suggestion in spite of the fact that she wasn't feeling well at all. "That's an excellent idea! Can you help me into the pink bed jacket? It's my favorite."

Janey had worked with the elderly ever since she'd graduated from college, and she'd learned a long time ago that patients felt much better when they were able to get out of bed whenever possible and dress in regular street clothes. Hannah was obviously too weak for that, but just combing her hair and brushing a little rouge on her cheeks invariably gave her a lift. And she did love her pink bed jacket.

So Janey helped her spruce herself up a little and couldn't help but notice how weak she had become over the course of the last week. She was eighty-two, for heaven's sake, and could die at any time without ever seeing her son again. Didn't he realize that? Or was he really such a bastard that he didn't care?

Knowing she was overstepping her bounds but not caring, Janey was determined she wasn't going to let him get away with such neglect. So as soon as she had Hannah settled and as comfortable as she could make her, she promised to be back later to check on her, then hurried to the nurses' station to look up William's phone number in Hannah's file.

"You're calling her son."

Glancing up from the file to see Erin, one of her co-workers, watching her with knowing eyes, she didn't deny it. "I'm just doing what's right. If Hawkins doesn't like it, she can take it out of my hide later. This has gone on long enough."

Gloria Hawkins was their immediate supervisor and a stickler about procedure. According to the nursing home's policy, a patient could call their loved ones as often as they liked, but a nurse only called at the instructions of a doctor. And no doctor had requested that William Starks be called…yet. Janey knew Dan would do it if she asked him, but the mornings were his busiest time. By the time she tracked him down and he found a moment to call William, it might be too late for him to get there before she died.

And Janey's heart broke at the thought of Hannah dying without seeing her son one last time. So she took matters into her own hands and did what she had to do.

Taking advantage of the fact that Gloria was on vacation, Janey slipped into her office and quickly dialed William's home number. It was an hour earlier in Seattle, and luck was with her. He hadn't left for work yet.

"Mr. Starks?" she said as soon as he came on the line. "This is Janey McBride calling from Liberty Hill Nursing Home."

If receiving a call from the nursing home alarmed him at all, he gave no sign of it. He didn't even ask about his mother. "Yes? What can I do for you?"

It was his tone, more than his words, that rubbed Janey the wrong way. Cold and impatient, he sounded as if he couldn't be bothered with her or his mother and just wanted her to state her business so he could be on about his. How, she wondered indignantly, could he possibly be the son of someone as sweet and loving as Hannah?

"You can come and see your mother," she said bluntly. Normally, she would have found a way to be more diplomatic, but with a man like William Starks, she didn't think that was possible. He didn't take hints, so she gave him the truth, plain and simple, and hoped that would get his attention. "Your mother has pneumonia, and I don't think she has the strength left to fight it. So if you want to see her before she dies, I suggest you find a way to get to Liberty Hill as soon as possible, Mr. Starks. She doesn't have a lot of time left."

For a moment she thought she'd finally gotten through to him. There was a long silence, as if he was collecting his emotions, and she almost sighed in relief. He did care! Then he said, "I can't possibly come this week. I'm going to a convention in Hawaii. It'll have to be sometime after that."

Stunned, Janey couldn't believe she'd heard him correctly. His mother was dying, and he didn't have time to see her because he'd already planned to lie on the beach and drink martinis? The nerve of the jackass! Was he really that inhuman?

Out of patience, she snapped, "I didn't call so we could pencil your mother's death into your schedule when it was convenient, Mr. Starks. Personally, I don't care what you've got planned. All I'm concerned with is Hannah. She wants to see you before she dies, and I don't think that's too much for a mother to ask of her son. Especially after all she's done for you."

That was a low blow, reminding him that he owed his mother, but at this point Janey didn't care. Not only had Hannah and her husband raised their son with every luxury, they'd paid for an Ivy League education and given him thousands of dollars to start his own business after he graduated from college. Today he owned one of the most successful computer chip firms in the country, and he owed that all to the generosity of his parents.

And although she didn't expect him to admit it, Janey knew she'd struck a nerve. For a long moment there was nothing but silence. Then, just when she was beginning to wonder if she was wasting her time trying to get through to him, he said grimly, "I'll see what I can do."

He hung up without making any promises, but Janey had to believe he would be there soon. Only a monster would ignore his mother's dying request.

On his way to the nurses' station to read the charts of two patients he'd been called about, Reilly heard Janey McBride's voice coming from a nearby office and stopped in his tracks. "...pencil your mother's death in when it was convenient, Mr. Starks. Personally, I don't care what you've got planned...." He didn't intend to eavesdrop, but the office door was open, and he could clearly hear every word. It didn't take much intelligence to figure out that she was chewing out a patient's son and doing a darn good job of it.

Impressed, Reilly shouldn't have been surprised. After last night, when she'd put him in his place in no uncertain terms, he'd realized that when push came to shove the lady had no difficulty speaking her mind. Especially when she felt an injustice was being done. And even though he'd felt the sting of her tongue last night, he couldn't help but feel she was the kind of person you would want in your corner in a fight. She stood up for herself and others, and her patients were lucky to have her. With her to watch over them, they didn't have to worry about getting screwed by the system or neglected by family. Janey would never let that happen.

Unabashedly listening to the one-sided conversation, Reilly would have given his eyeteeth to hear the negligent son's response to Janey's scolding, but before he could even imagine that, she hung up. A split second later she stepped through the office doorway.

Reilly was caught red-handed and there was nothing he could do but swear under his breath and try to make the best of the situation. "Good morning," he said gruffly.

He hadn't forgotten that he owed her an apology, and he fully intended to give her one. But before he could explain why he was lingering in the hall listening to a private conversation, she gave him a look that could have blistered paint. "Don't mess with me, Jones," she growled. "I'm not in the mood." And brushing past him as if he were of no more importance than a gnat, she strode off down the hall.

He should have been not only insulted but furious. He was a surgeon, for God's sake, and a damn good one at that. For no other reason than that, he was entitled to her respect as a doctor. He couldn't think of a single nurse in L.A. who would have dared dismiss him the way she just had. Especially at work.

But even as he tried to work up a good case of indignation, he couldn't. His ego wasn't so fragile that he couldn't stand to be put in his place once in a while. Especially by a woman like Janey McBride. She might appear to be quiet and reserved, but that, he was discovering, was only a front. There was a heck of a lot more to her than met the eye.

Staring after her as she strode down the hall without bothering to acknowledge the fact that she knew he was watching her, he had to admit that life wasn't going to be boring with her around. And for the first time since Victoria had died, he found himself actually looking forward to what the day would hold. Humor glinting in his eyes, he smiled, and he wasn't even aware of it.

Chapter 4

"Mrs. Boothe is in examining room three, Judge Perkins had to reschedule for noon, and Mary Lou Foster is on line two and needs to talk to you again. She thinks she's having a heart attack."

Rattling off his schedule, Ruby Jean, his nurse, rolled her eyes as she relayed that latest message from Mary Lou Foster, and Reilly couldn't blame her. In the short time he'd been working with Dan, he already had three conversations with Mary Lou about her heart. The first time she'd called, Reilly had mistakenly assumed that she was in serious trouble and had rushed over to her house, which was just three blocks away—only to discover that the only thing the woman was suffering from was indigestion. Later that same afternoon she'd claimed she was short of breath and needed to see him. He had, however, had time to take a look at her records by then, and it hadn't taken him long to realize that Mary Lou was a hypochondriac. For years she'd been calling Dan's office every time she had gas.

Already reaching for Mrs. Boothe's chart, Reilly said, "Squeeze the judge in where you can. If I have to miss lunch, I'll grab a sandwich in between patients later."

"What about Mary Lou?" Ruby asked wryly. "She'll just call back if you don't talk to her, you know."

Muttering a curse under his breath, Reilly knew she was right. Mary Lou was nothing if not persistent. "All right," he sighed with a grimace, rubbing at the headache that throbbed between his eyes. "Have her come in to have her blood pressure checked. If it's okay—"

Ruby snorted. "What do you mean…*if?* Do you honestly think there's something wrong with that woman? Something," she amended with a quick grin, "that can't be fixed by a psychiatrist?"

Reilly shouldn't have let her talk that way about a patient, but damned if she wasn't right. His lips twitching, he tried and failed to frown disapprovingly. "Be that as it may, we have to check her, anyway. If she's okay, send her home. If not, I'll have to see her."

And God only knew where he'd find the time. He was already running behind because of his unexpected call to the nursing home earlier that morning, and he was booked solid with patients the rest of the day. What little time he'd saved for a break would now be used to see Judge Perkins, so there went lunch. Yesterday the same thing had happened when Cara Robinson had to be seen at noon for a bad case of strep throat. The day before that it had been Roger Fischer with a spider bite. He hadn't had lunch since he'd started working there!

Stepping into examining room three, where Mrs. Boothe and her sprained wrist waited patiently for him, he wondered how Dan had handled the practice by himself all these years. The workload was incredible—and that was with *two* doctors now on staff! How had he managed to see all his patients, do rounds at the nursing home, be on call at the hospital and still have any kind of a life? No wonder he wanted to retire. He had to be exhausted!

You wanted to lose yourself in work, he reminded himself. Now's your chance. Enjoy.

In a crazy kind of way he was. The rest of the day was as busy as the morning, and he hardly had time to turn around before the next patient was being shown in, and he loved it. He hadn't worked this hard since he was in medical school, and when he arrived home at nine o'clock that evening, he was dead on his feet. And he thanked God for that. Because last night, for the first time since Victoria had died, he'd actually fallen asleep almost as soon as his head touched the pillow.

And tonight she wasn't the one he thought of when he walked in the door at the end of a very long day. Instead his gaze landed on the cake that Janey had made for him and the piece that he'd cut from it last night and eaten before going to bed. Rueful amusement glinted in his eyes. As far as cakes went, it really was a pitiful looking little thing, but he had to admit, it tasted a hell of a lot better than it looked. He'd have to remember to tell her how good it was…if she ever let him speak to her again.

"You really screwed up, Jones," he said aloud, shattering the quiet of his lonely existence. "So what are you going to do about it?"

That was a good question, one he didn't have an answer for. How could you apologize and make peace with someone if they wouldn't even listen to you? He could write her a letter, but he doubted she'd even read it. Which left him back at square one. They had to work together, dammit! he thought in growing frustration. Didn't she realize how much easier that would be—and better for their patients— if they could speak without growling at each other?

Stymied, he was still searching for a way to reach her without antagonizing her more than he already had when the phone rang. Groaning, he seriously considered not answering it. The only calls he'd gotten at that time of night since he'd moved to Liberty Hill were emergencies, and he wasn't on call tonight. Someone else could take it.

But even as he considered that, he knew he couldn't just ignore a call for help. Not in a town the size of Liberty Hill, where doctors were in short supply. If he was dead on his feet, that was just something he'd have to ignore.

Resigned, he snatched up the phone. "Hello?"

"Reilly? You okay?"

At the sound of his brother Tony's voice, a slow smile transformed his face. "Hey, big brother, how's it going? I haven't heard from you in a few days."

"I thought I'd give you time to settle in. The locals treating you okay?"

He shrugged, thinking of Janey. "That depends on what you call okay. Not that I can complain. I'm getting exactly what I deserve."

"Uh-oh," Tony said, a sudden frown in his voice. "What does that mean? What's wrong?"

There'd been a time in his life when he would have shrugged off his brother's concern and distracted him by asking how things were going in L.A. He'd never liked to talk about his problems. Instead he preferred to handle them in his own way and act as if he had everything under control. But he wasn't that man anymore and never would be again. If he'd had things under control, he would have never had to leave L.A.

"Oh, I just acted like a jerk when one of the nurses at the nursing home baked me a cake to welcome me to town," he said with a grimace. "I accused her of coming on to me."

"And was she?"

If he hadn't felt so rotten about his own behavior, he would have laughed. "Are you kidding? She's just about the only woman in town who *hasn't* come on to me! She's not that kind."

There was something in his tone that had Tony lifting a brow in surprise. The last time he'd seen his little brother, he would have sworn it would be years—if ever—before he showed an interest in another woman. But here he was, worrying about what one thought of him. It looked like there was a God, after all!

Encouraged, he said, "So what kind is she?"

In the few rare moments when he'd had time for reflection over the course of the day, Reilly had asked himself the same question and come up with few answers. "She's different," he said simply. "I can't think of any other way to describe her. At times she seems quiet and reserved, but then she'll turn around and chew out the son of a patient for not visiting his mother enough. She does volunteer EMT work with the local fire department and carries a shotgun in her car. The first time I met her was the day I arrived and the car broke down on the way into town. She stopped to help me. Then this morning she cut me dead at the nursing home because I offended her."

He'd expected Tony to sympathize with him. He laughed instead. "I like this girl. What's her name?"

"Janey McBride. Her family owns one of the largest ranches in the state."

"It sounds like she has her feet on the ground. If you've got any sense, you'll apologize for acting like a heel."

"I've tried, but she won't talk to me, dammit! And don't go getting any ideas about her," he warned, suddenly realizing that his brother was reading more into the situation than was there. "I'm not interested in her as a woman. But

I did hurt her feelings and we have to work together. It's awkward. This is a small town, and we can't turn around without running into each other.''

"So send her some flowers!"

"And give her the wrong idea? I don't think so.''

Personally Tony didn't think that would be so bad— whoever this mystery woman was, she sounded as if she was just what Reilly needed to jump-start his heart again, but that was obviously something he wasn't ready to hear. "Okay, so flowers are out. Then maybe you need to spend some time with her so she'll see you're not such a bad guy, after all.''

"Well, she did ask me to join some committee for a Christmas festival the city has every year," he replied, only just then remembering it. "There's a meeting Monday night, but I told her I was busy.''

"Why?"

"You know why. Let it go.''

If he'd loved his brother less, Tony might have done that. Reilly didn't take kindly to interference in his personal life, and a wise man would have done just as he suggested and changed the subject. But Tony had been taking care of his baby brother all of his life, and he wasn't going to stop now. Not when he obviously needed someone to talk some sense into him.

"Victoria wouldn't want you to martyr yourself for her," he said quietly. "You have to start living again, and that means having a life other than work. Go to this meeting. It'll be good for you. You can meet people, get involved in a civic project and make some friends. It'll also give you a chance to show Janey McBride you're not such a bad guy. She might even let you apologize.''

Reilly knew he was right—Victoria would want him to go on with his life. But he wasn't sure if he was ready to step into a social setting without her at his side. After all, it had only been eight months. He needed more time.

"I'll think about it," he promised.

And he did. Over the weekend he gave serious consideration to taking Tony's suggestion and going to the meeting of the decorating committee. If Victoria had been there, she would have told him it was the right thing to do. It would take his mind off her and give him an opportunity to meet the local residents he hadn't yet met. It would be good for him.

He knew that, accepted the wisdom of that and actually thought he'd made up his mind to go. But then Monday rolled around, and his mood changed. It was a cold, wet day, dark and dreary, the kind that reminded him too much of the day of Victoria's funeral. He couldn't stop thinking of her, and as the time for the meeting grew closer, he knew he couldn't go. The committee would be working on Christmas decorations for the festival, and everything inside him froze at the thought of the coming holidays. This would be his first Christmas without Victoria, and the last thing he wanted to do was celebrate it.

And there was no question that the meeting would be festive. He'd been to this kind of thing before—he knew how they operated. There would be food and music and lots of kidding and laughter, and there'd been a time when he would have loved that. But not tonight. He would stay home and watch Monday Night Football on TV, he decided as he saw his last patient for the day. Better that than to go to the meeting and dampen everyone's spirits.

The decision made, he spent the next twenty minutes catching up on paperwork in his office, then cleared off his desk and grabbed his jacket. Just as he stepped out into the hallway, Dan did the same.

"Hey," the older man said with a broad grin, "you going to the meeting tonight? You did hear about it, didn't you? The meeting of the decorating committee for the Christmas festival? Sara said Janey invited you.''

Wishing he'd slipped out five minutes earlier, Reilly was forced to admit that she had. ''But I'm not going to be able to go,'' he added. ''I'd already made other plans.''

He spoke nothing less than the truth—he hadn't watched a game all season and didn't want to miss this one—but he still couldn't bring himself to look Dan in the eye. If he had, he would have seen the quick grin that he hurriedly suppressed.

''I see,'' Dan said solemnly, his blue eyes twinkling knowingly. ''That's too bad. I was hoping that you were going so I could catch a ride with you.''

Surprised, Reilly arched a brow at him. ''Is something wrong with your car?''

It had only just that moment developed carburetor problems, but that was something Dan kept to himself. He knew what Reilly was doing—he'd done the same thing the first Christmas after Peggy had died. He'd come up with any excuse he could to avoid facing the holidays without her. Consequently he'd spent most of that time holed up in his house, brooding. He'd never been more miserable in his life.

He was determined not to let Reilly make the same mistake. He needed to be around people. He needed friends. And with time, he would let go of the hurt from the past and find himself a good woman. Someone like Janey, Dan decided. But it was too soon for that now. At the moment Dan just wanted to get him back into the mainstream of life. And if he had to pretend to be afoot to accomplish that, then that's what he'd do.

''It's been hard to start lately, and this morning it gave up the ghost,'' he fibbed without so much as blinking an eye. "I had to have it towed to that new garage that just opened over by the library, but it won't be ready until sometime tomorrow. I can call Sara, though, if you don't have time to give me a ride," he added quickly. "I'm sure she wouldn't mind stopping by to pick me up."

When Reilly hesitated, Dan thought he was going to take him up on his suggestion and wanted to curse himself for bringing up Sara's name. But then, Reilly only shrugged and said, "Sure, no problem."

Relieved, Dan swallowed a sigh of relief. "Good," he said, pleased. "I wasn't looking forward to walking in the rain, and sometimes Sara runs late. I hate walking in on something after it's already started."

"Then we'd better get going," Reilly replied. "It's almost seven now."

The night was cold and rainy and miserable, and anyone with any brains in their head would have been at home in front of a warm fire. The parking lot of the VFW hall was nearly full, however, as Reilly pulled up before the hall's front door a few minutes later. Surprised—he'd thought the turnout would be poor because of the rain—he said, "It looks like you've got a full house. I didn't think that many people would want to brave the weather."

Far from surprised himself, Dan smiled. "This isn't one of your regular civic-type committee meetings. The same people have been working on the decorating committee for years, and they take great pride in what they do. They wouldn't let a little rain scare them away."

Reaching for his door handle, Dan added casually, "They're a good group, you know. I think you'd like them. Why don't you come in for a few seconds and let me introduce you around? It'll just take a few minutes."

Not a slow-witted man, Reilly saw the glint in his eye

and suddenly knew exactly what he was doing. Why, that conniving old goat! he thought in growing amusement. So his car was acting up, was it? Yeah, right! And he was Tom Selleck. He'd obviously conned him into giving him a ride so he could finagle him into coming inside, and Reilly hadn't even seen it coming.

He was good, he acknowledged, fighting a smile. Damn good. And the only reason Reilly wasn't mad was because he knew Dan's heart was in the right place. He was a good man, and he understood what he was going through because he'd been there himself. Still, it would have served him right if he'd turned him down flat.

If he'd been a different kind of man, Reilly might have considered it. But he couldn't do that to Dan, not when he was just trying to help him. "All right. But only for a few minutes," he warned. "I'm not staying, Dan."

All innocence, the older man said, wide-eyed, "Oh, no, of course not. I know you have other plans. I'm just going to introduce you to a few friends. It won't take five minutes. I promise."

Later Reilly knew he should have known better. Dan was one of the most popular doctors in town and knew just about everyone in the area. The second they walked inside the hall, he found one person after another to introduce him to. Five minutes stretched into ten, then twenty, and to his surprise Reilly didn't even think about leaving as he shook hands with the movers and shakers of Liberty Hill.

He was still trying to get all the names and faces straight when Dan suddenly smiled widely. "Oh, there's Sara! C'mon, I want you to meet her."

Reilly had heard him talk about Sara enough to know that she was Janey's mother, so as Dan wound his way through the crowd toward Sara McBride, he wasn't surprised to find Janey there, too. And from the look on her face as her eyes locked with his, she was none too happy to see him. As Dan introduced him to her mother and her two brothers, Joe and Zeke, Janey greeted him with nothing more than a stiff nod.

So she hadn't forgiven him, Reilly thought, frustrated. Damn, she was stubborn!

Caught up in his thoughts, he didn't realize that the others had noticed Janey's cool reception until her brothers arched a brow in surprise. And just that quickly, he knew he had to apologize again, in front of the whole town, if necessary. Maybe then she would believe him when he said he was sorry.

Shaking hands with her brothers and mother, he said gruffly, "I deserved that. In fact, I wouldn't blame her if she never spoke to me again. I was rude to her the other night when she brought me a cake to welcome me to town, and there was no excuse for that.

"I'm sorry, Janey," he told her quietly. "I realized I'd made a mistake almost immediately, but it was too late. I'd already hurt your feelings. If you'll accept my apology, I promise it won't happen again."

All but going down on his knee in abject apology, there was no doubting his sincerity. Hesitating when he held out his hand to her, Janey tried to harden her heart against him—she wouldn't make it this easy for him, dammit!— but she was fighting a losing battle. She'd never been one to carry a grudge, especially when an apology was offered so contritely, and just that easily her anger melted. Damn the man, she thought when her lips twitched. How was she supposed to stay mad at him when he humbled himself in front of her entire family?

"That sounds fair enough," she replied, and slipped her hand into his to shake on the deal.

Accepting his apology should have been just that simple, but the second his fingers closed around hers, she felt it again, that same spark that had set her pulse skipping when Dan had introduced them for the first time at the nursing home. She'd thought she imagined it.

Confused, her eyes searched his, but then Zeke distracted her when he grinned and told Reilly, "Janey doesn't get mad very often, but when she does, watch out. The fur's going to fly."

"If I remember correctly, she came close to scalping you a time or two," Joe said dryly, "and it was no more than you deserved."

"Hey," he said, pretending to be wounded. "So I put a frog in her bed once. I was only a kid. It was a joke."

"Which I didn't find particularly funny," Janey retorted, her brown eyes twinkling. "Until I got revenge."

"She painted his fingernails while he was sleeping," her mother confided to Reilly with a grin. "He wasn't amused when he woke up."

"He screamed bloody murder," Joe said, chuckling at the memory. "Talk about learning a lesson! He never so much as touched a frog again, let alone came near one of the girls with one."

"That's because I threatened to perm his hair if he ever tried anything like that again," Janey said. "I wouldn't have, but he didn't know that."

"Now you tell me!"

They all laughed at that, and Reilly couldn't help but like the McBrides. Their affection for each other was obvious, and he liked that. They reminded him of his own family and the innocent jokes he and Tony had played on each other.

"Do you have brothers and sisters, Reilly?" Sara McBride asked.

"A brother," he said with a smile. "My mother used to say she'd be gray by the time she was forty because we were so wild."

"And was she?"

His smile faded. "She died of breast cancer when she was thirty-eight. I was nine."

"Oh, I'm sorry! That must have been very difficult for you and your brother, growing up without a mother."

"It was," he said simply, "but we had each other and our father, and that helped."

With the ice broken and Janey's acceptance of his apology, he should have found an excuse to leave then, but he'd waited too long. Some of the single women in the crowd spied him and started toward him, cutting off all exits. From the gleam in their eyes, it was obvious that they saw this as their opportunity to get to know him better. He had other ideas.

Turning his attention back to the McBrides, he cast an eye over the painting supplies and building materials that they'd been working with when he and Dan arrived. "What's this?"

Joe grinned broadly. "What? You don't recognize Santa's workshop when you see it?"

"That's a crack at me," Zeke told Reilly, his blue eyes twinkling with devilment. "He's just jealous because I came up with a better design than he did."

Joe snorted humorously. "Yeah, it's such a good design that the man had to ask what it was."

"Now, boys," Sara said, just as she must have when they were kids. "Let's be nice."

"Try to remember you weren't raised in a barn," Janey added, her own lips twitching. "In case you've forgotten, we're here to do a little work."

Dan, who'd silently been watching the exchange between

Reilly and the McBrides said, "Reilly just came in for a few moments—"

"Oh, I can stay for a while," he said after a quick look over his shoulder at the women who were hovering nearby, waiting for a chance to talk to him. "What do you want me to do?"

Surprised, Janey almost reminded him about the plans he'd claimed the other night that he had for this evening—then she saw the women hovering nearby and understood. "Looks like the sharks are circling," she murmured. "Maybe you should help me with the painting."

She didn't have to make the suggestion twice. "Good idea," he said, picking up the can of paint she was reaching for. "Where do you want this?"

The man had never held a paintbrush in his life. That much was immediately obvious as they started to paint the plywood pieces of the workshop bright red. He didn't have a clue where to begin, which wasn't surprising. After all, high-priced L.A. surgeons didn't have to know how to paint—they paid someone to do it for them. In spite of that, Janey had to give him credit. He didn't let his lack of experience stop him from participating. Following her lead, he threw himself into the work and was soon slapping paint onto the workshop pieces as if he'd been doing it all his life. And when he got paint on his hands and clothes, he didn't complain as she expected him to, but simply went on with what he was doing.

"Not bad, Doctor. I'm impressed," she told him as they changed from red paint to white and started on the trim. "So is the peanut gallery. They haven't missed a stroke."

She nodded toward the three who had joined Martha Hoffsteader and her sons to work on one of the food booths they were constructing nearby. Lana Stevens, Beverly Green and Jennifer Pruitt were notorious flirts and had a reputation for chasing Martha's good-looking sons every chance they got. But not tonight. They may have been working with "the boys"—as they were called around town—but their attention was definitely elsewhere. With sharp, hungry eyes, they watched Reilly's every move. And he didn't spare them so much as a glance. Janey had to admire him for that. There weren't many men who could ignore those three when they set their minds to being noticed.

"Ignore them," he said with a shrug. "I am."

"So I see." Amused, she arched a brow at him. "Have you always had this ability to close out the rest of the world? Medical school must have been a snap for you."

"Well, it wasn't a walk in the park, but I never had a problem studying," he retorted, flashing her a grin. "I bet you didn't, either."

Caught flat-footed by the unexpected smile, Janey felt as though a Mac truck had come out of nowhere to flatten her. Dazed, she just stood there while the blood roared in her ears and her heart threatened to pound out of her chest. Good Lord, she thought, no wonder he had half the women in town drooling over him. When he smiled like that, he could make a woman forget her own name.

Observing them from a discreet distance, Dan made no attempt to hold back a smile. "Look, Sara," he said, nodding to where Janey stood staring at a grinning Reilly like she'd never seen a man before. "I'd say they've made peace, wouldn't you?"

Glancing over at her daughter, Sara had to admit that it certainly looked that way. And that worried her as much as it pleased her. For the last few days Janey had walked around the house like a bear with a sore tooth, and it was all because of Reilly. And now she was looking at him in a way she'd never seen her look at a man before. "I just don't want her to get hurt, Dan. I don't think it's even entered her head that she's attracted to him. What if she falls in love with him and he still doesn't want to get involved? She'd be devastated.''

"That's not going to happen."

"How can you be sure of that? He was obviously very hurt by his wife's death. There are people who lose a spouse and never get married again—look at us. It would break my heart if Janey waited all these years to find someone and he couldn't love her back."

Dan patted her hand and almost told her that didn't happen as often as she thought—*he* did love her, and with time she would realize that she felt the same way about him—but that wasn't something he planned to discuss when they were surrounded by a crowd of people. "That's not going to happen," he assured her again. "She has a wonderful, caring heart, and that's what Reilly needs—someone to care for *him*. Not Reilly Jones, the doctor, but Reilly Jones, the man with a broken heart. They already seem to like each other. Just give them time. Everything will work out fine."

She wanted to believe him—he could see it in her eyes—but in many ways, Sara was just like Janey. She was a natural caretaker and worried about the people she loved. And although she didn't have favorites among her children, Janey was very close to her heart. It would be very difficult for her to stand by and do nothing if Janey got hurt, even though she knew there was nothing she could do to stop it.

"Hey," he teased when her frown didn't lighten. "We're here to have fun, remember? And Janey's not the only one who's got a good-looking man working with her. Or hadn't you noticed, Mrs. McBride? For your information, I have it on good authority that I'm still a fine figure of a man."

That got her attention, just as he'd known it would. Turning her attention back to him, she lifted a delicately arched brow at him. "Oh, really? And who's been flirting with you now, Doctor? That conniving little gray-haired floozy from Mountain Springs? I warned you to watch out for her. All she's interested in is how fat your bank statement is."

Laughing, he just loved it when her blue eyes sparked with jealousy. "Now, Sara, you don't know that for sure. I think she really likes me. And her hair's not gray. It's white. Snow-white."

"Oh, *pleaaase,*" she sniffed. "Spare me the fairy tales. We're both too old for them. And so is that little—"

"Don't say it," he warned with twinkling eyes.

"Tart," she substituted. "She's older than the two of us together. And don't tell me she doesn't look it. She's had three face-lifts, for heaven's sake! Talk about vain."

Delighted, he started to laugh, and that's when the pain hit him hard and fast, right in the heart. Shocked, he gasped and couldn't seem to catch his breath. He clutched at his chest, but the pain was excruciating. Instinctively he reached for Sara as the blood roared in his ears. "Sara! Help me!"

Horrified, she sprang to catch him as his legs buckled. "Dan! Oh, my God! What is it? Somebody help us!"

At her first cry, everyone in the hall seemed to freeze. Then, suddenly Janey and Reilly were at her side, and she never even saw them move. "His heart," she gasped as they moved to quickly lower Dan to the floor. "I think it's his heart."

"Somebody get my medical bag out of Dan's car," Reilly ordered, never looking up from the older man's face as he quickly loosened his tie and jerked it off, then started on the buttons of his shirt. "And call an ambulance. Now!"

He didn't have to repeat himself. Joe ran outside and retrieved the medical bag while one of the Hoffsteaders called 911. Literally within seconds Reilly had his stethoscope in his ears and was bending over Dan to listen to his heart while Janey took the older man's pulse. From down the street they heard the scream of the ambulance's siren as it pulled out of the garage at the fire department.

It arrived in less than a minute, but that wasn't soon enough for Reilly. Dan was in serious trouble, and the quicker they got him to the hospital, the better. His eyes grim, he glanced up at Janey and saw that he didn't have to tell her they didn't have any time to waste. Everything he was feeling and more was reflected in her pale face.

Still conscious, his face gray with pain as the EMTs lifted him onto the stretcher, Dan grasped at his hand. "I'm going to be okay," he said weakly. "It's indigestion."

If Reilly hadn't already cared about the man, he would have then. There he lay in pain and possibly dying, and he was cracking jokes and trying to reassure his friends. Grinning affectionately at him, Reilly squeezed his hand. "Indigestion, my ass. You're having a heart attack and you know it. But you're right about one thing. You are going to be okay. I'm going to make sure of it. C'mon, let's get you to the hospital."

"I'm going, too," Sara McBride said quickly, stepping forward.

"We all are," Zeke said as he and Joe flanked their mother and Janey. "C'mon, let's go."

The hospital waiting room and nearby corridor were packed with Dan's friends and neighbors, but Sara hardly noticed. Numb with worry, all she could think of was that fateful day twenty years ago when she'd sat in this same waiting room, waiting for some kind of news about her husband, Gus. He, too, had suffered a heart attack. Unlike Dan, however, there hadn't been a doctor at his side when he had the attack. By the time she'd gotten him to the hospital, it had been too late. The doctors and nurses had done everything they could for him, but in the end they couldn't save him.

What if that happened again? How would she bear it?

Reading her mind—and the stark worry deepening the lines of her face—Janey hugged her close. "Hey, don't start thinking the worst," she chided softly. "Dan's a tough old coot. And I've heard him say more than once that Reilly is one of the best heart surgeons in the country. He couldn't be in finer hands."

She wanted desperately to believe that, but suddenly the faith that had kept her strong all these years without Gus by her side wasn't nearly as unshakable as she'd thought it was. "Sometimes it doesn't matter how good the doctor is. Things go wrong. If it's his time—"

"It's not."

"I lost your father. I can't lose Dan, too."

"Medicine's changed a lot since Dad died," Joe reminded her gruffly. "And Dan's a fighter. He'll beat this. You'll see."

The words were hardly out of his mouth when Reilly walked into the room. Already dressed in scrubs, he immediately strode over to Sara. "He's all right," he assured her immediately. "His condition has stabilized and he's conscious, but after further tests, we decided he needs a quadruple bypass. We're prepping him for surgery now."

She paled. "So soon?"

"It's for the best," he said simply. "Next time he might not be so lucky."

"Will the operation take long?"

He nodded. "If you'd be more comfortable waiting at home, I'll call you as soon as it's over with, or you can wait here."

Sara didn't even have to consider it. She wasn't going

anywhere until she saw with her own two eyes that Dan was going to be all right. Lifting her chin, she said, "I'll stay. If I'm not here when you're finished, I'll be in the cafeteria."

A half smile threatening to curl the corners of his mouth, Reilly knew she'd still be there if the operation lasted all night. Dan was lucky to have her in his corner. "I'll find you," he promised, and with a brief nod to the rest of the family, turned and walked out.

When he strode into the operating room a few minutes later, Dan was still conscious and refusing to let the anesthetist anywhere near him. Surprised, Reilly hurried forward with a frown. "What's the problem, Dan? I thought we'd agreed you need the surgery."

Pale and drawn, he said weakly, "I haven't changed my mind. I just wanted to talk to you first before I went under. There are some things I need to say—"

"You're not going to die, Dan," he cut in gently. "I'm not going to let anything happen to you."

He'd only meant to reassure him, but Dan's eyes filled with tears instead. Alarmed, he reached for his hand. "Hey, it's okay. You're going to be okay."

"I know," he choked. "I just wanted you to know that I'm glad you're here. Not just to operate on me. You're a good man. I can't think of anyone I'd rather have take over my practice."

Touched, Reilly didn't know what to say. They'd agreed that they would both take three months before they decided whether to make their partnership permanent or not. So far, Reilly had enjoyed working with Dan, but it was too soon to think about staying in Liberty Hill the rest of his life.

That wasn't, however, something Dan needed to hear right before going into surgery. Especially since Reilly knew he wasn't going anywhere until Dan was back on his feet. For now, at least, he was staying.

"I'll be here for you as long as you need me," he assured him. "Okay?"

That was all Dan needed to hear. Satisfied, he closed his eyes and sighed. "Okay."

Chapter 5

As far as waiting rooms went, the one down the hall from the operating rooms was as well or better equipped than most. Magazine and book shelves lined one wall, providing plenty of reading material to distract anxious family members, and the TV mounted from the ceiling in the corner had a zillion and one cable channels that played twenty-four hours a day. For those who were hungry, there were snacks in the vending machines and free coffee that was strong enough to choke a horse. One dose of the strong brew would jump-start anyone who even thought of nodding off.

Though how anyone could even think of sleeping in such an environment, Sara would never know. Her nerves wound tight, she found it impossible to sit still, let alone read or watch TV. With worry eating at her, she paced the confines of the waiting room like a tiger in a cage, but it didn't help. Every time someone walked down the hallway and passed the open door to the waiting room, her heart froze in her breast. Afraid it was Reilly coming to tell her that Dan had died on the table, she stopped in her tracks each time and went pale as a ghost, her eyes wide with fear as she watched the doorway. Then a nurse or orderly would walk by, and she'd press her hand to her heart and send up a silent prayer of thanks.

Minutes ticked by, then hours, and there was still no sign of Reilly. Sara knew she should have taken comfort from that. No news was good news. But she couldn't forget the look on Dan's face when the first pain hit him. He'd realized immediately that he was having a heart attack, and he'd been so scared. She couldn't blame him. She'd been terrified. She'd never considered the possibility that she could lose him. Not Dan. He was always so strong. Without him by her side, she didn't know how she would have gotten through Gus's death. He and Peggy had both been there for her and the children. Then, later, when he'd lost Peggy to cancer, she and the kids had helped him through the grief. He was a part of the family, and such a good friend to her. She couldn't imagine life without him.

Panicking just at the thought, she glanced at the clock on the wall and scowled. She knew they'd been there hours, waiting for news, but the hands on the clock didn't appear to have moved at all. "What's taking so long?" she cried suddenly, shattering the quiet that hung like a dark cloud over the waiting room. "We should have heard something by now."

"You can't rush a bypass, Mom," Janey said quietly, setting aside the magazine she'd been reading. "These things take time."

Rising to his feet, Joe slipped an arm around his mother's shoulders. "Why don't we all go to the cafeteria and get something to eat? It'll take your mind off things for a while."

Her stomach turned over just at the thought of food. "I'm not hungry."

"Then come and watch us eat," Zeke said. "I'm starving. It's been hours since I had supper."

Sara had to smile at that. "You sound like Merry."

Eight months pregnant and counting the days, it seemed her youngest daughter ate every hour on the hour. When Janey had called to tell Merry about Dan, she'd wanted to come to the hospital immediately, but she'd been on complete bed rest for the last two weeks because of high blood pressure, and Janey had, thankfully, convinced her she had to stay home for the sake of the baby.

"Sorry, Mom, no babies here," Zeke said with a grin, patting his hard belly. "And don't give Lizzie any ideas. Cassie's already been asking us both if Santa's going to bring us a baby for Christmas like he is Aunt Merry."

"She does need somebody to play with," Janey pointed out, her brown eyes twinkling at the thought of two little McBrides running around in Zeke's house. Three going on fourteen, Cassie was a delight—and wild as a March hare. With a little brother or sister as an accomplice, the two of them would turn Zeke's hair white before he was forty.

"So I'll get her a puppy," he retorted. "One big enough to hold its own with her."

"Oh, c'mon, Zeke," Joe teased, "you can't mean to keep her an only child her whole life. She can't climb a tree or go riding with a puppy."

"Or tell it ghost stories and scare it half to death like somebody I know," he said pointedly. "If I remember correctly, it was a dog who tied me to my bed one night while I was sleeping, but it was the two legged kind. I believe his initials were J.M."

Glad to see his mother was smiling at their banter, Joe

only grinned and played innocent. "I don't know what you're talking about. I don't remember tying you up."

"Aha! A likely story. If you're so innocent, why did you assume I was talking about you? Janey's initials are the same as yours."

Caught red-handed, there was nothing he could do but laugh. "Okay, so I gave myself away. But it could have been Janey."

Guilty of her share of mischief as a child, Janey sniffed in a superior way that was almost ruined by her grin. "It could have, but it wasn't. I was much more imaginative than that."

"You certainly were," her mother agreed, chuckling. "You and Joe together were a handful. I used to lie awake nights wondering what kind of mischief you were going to get into next."

"Then Zeke and Merry came along, and you realized you'd had it easy up until then," Joe retorted, chuckling. "Talk about holy terrors. Those two are the ones who gave you all that gray hair, not me and Janey."

Laughing, Sara started to deny it, but then Reilly stepped into the waiting room, still wearing his scrubs, and her smile abruptly faded. Suddenly pale, her heart pounding in alarm at the sight of his somber face, she took a step toward him. "You're finished already? Isn't it too soon? Is he—"

"He's fine," Reilly said gruffly, smiling as he took her hand and patted it reassuringly. "He came through the surgery with flying colors."

He'd only meant to reassure her. But instead of throwing herself into his arms in relief, as he half expected, she burst into tears.

"Mom? My God, what is it?"

"Didn't you hear Dr. Jones? Dan made it through the surgery."

"He's going to be okay."

As shocked as her children by her sudden meltdown, Sara nodded, wiping ineffectually at her damp cheeks. "I'm sorry," she sniffed. "I didn't mean to fall apart on you. I was just so afraid. If something had happened—"

Swallowing the sudden lump in her throat, her throat squeezed tight just at the thought of losing Dan, and she found it impossible to finish her sentence. Reilly, however, seemed to understand. Giving her hand a gentle squeeze, he smiled into her swimming eyes and said gruffly, "It's okay. I was worried, too. If he'd been anywhere else but right here in town when the attack hit him, he might not have made it."

"But he's going to be fine?" she asked worriedly. "You're sure?"

"I'd stake my career on it," he said simply.

Her eyes searching his, Sara couldn't doubt his sincerity. He meant every word. Relieved, she sighed, releasing the fear that had held her in its tight-fisted grip for the past five hours. "Thank you," she said thickly, and had to laugh when tears once again flooded her eyes. "I'm sorry. I don't mean to be such a crybaby. I'm just so glad he's okay. Can I see him?"

"Tomorrow," he promised. "He's still in recovery."

"Oh, but I wanted to stay the night!"

She had, in fact, planned to be right there by Dan's side every time he opened his eyes, but his doctor had other ideas. "He made it through the surgery, Sara, but he's got a long way to go before he's back on his feet again. He's going to need you in the days and weeks to come, so you need your rest, too."

Put that way, there was little she could say in the way of an argument. He was right and they both knew it. Still, she asked, "Can I at least let him know I'll be back in the morning? It won't take a second. I don't want to leave without telling him good-night.''

For a minute she thought he was going to tell her no, and she had to respect him for that. His number-one priority was Dan, and he was looking out for his welfare above all others—which was, no doubt, why he was such a good doctor. He put his patients first.

She wasn't asking for much, however, just a chance to see him and reassure herself that he really was all right.

And Reilly, thankfully, realized that. "Thirty seconds," he said. "Then you need to go home and go to bed."

Grinning, she impulsively hugged him. "I'm glad he has you on his side," she whispered. "Thank you."

"Me, too," he whispered back, touched. "Now get out of here before I change my mind."

He didn't have to tell her twice. With her sons at her side, she hurried out of the waiting room. Janey, staying behind for a moment, said quietly, "Thank you for that. This has really thrown her. If anything happened to Dan, I don't think she'd be able to stand it."

"She loves him."

Not sure if he was asking her or telling her, Janey smiled. "She's always thought of him as just a friend. The day she wakes up and realizes how she really feels about him should be quite interesting."

Amused, he said, "If I was a betting man, I'd say that day's not far off, if her reaction today was anything to go by. I guess I don't have to tell you Dan's crazy about her, too."

"I know," Janey replied. "That's what makes it so perfect." Reilly's smile died at that, and Janey didn't have to read his mind to know that he had to be thinking about his wife. *Don't!* she wanted to cry. *Don't get that sad look in your eyes.* But it was too late. She'd already lost him to the past.

Regret squeezing her heart, she forced a smile. "Well, I guess I should catch up with the rest of the family—they'll be wondering where I am. I just wanted to thank you for being so understanding with Mom. And for taking care of Dan."

Quietly wishing him good-night, she hurried out and couldn't for the life of her understand why she was suddenly so sad.

Over the course of the next few days, word of Dan's surgery spread throughout the county, and the phone at the office never seemed to stop ringing. Worried about Dan themselves, Krista and the rest of the office staff juggled the phones and tried to reassure worried patients who were no longer sure who their doctor was.

"No, Dr. Michaels hasn't retired," Krista said patiently into the phone as Reilly quickly pulled on his lab coat the third morning after the surgery. "He should be back in the office in about six weeks. Yes, Dr. Jones is here. He'll be seeing all of Dr. Michaels's patients while he's recovering from his surgery. We're still running a little behind schedule, but we're asking all patients to come in at their appointed times. That's right, dear. We'll see you at eleven."

Hanging up, she rolled her eyes at Reilly. "I hope you had your Wheaties this morning, Doctor. It's going to be a zoo again today."

That proved to be an understatement of gargantuan proportions. Not wasting any time, Reilly saw his first patient ten minutes before her appointed time and was off schedule the rest of the day. Everyone wanted to know about Dan, of course, and his prognosis, and although that was something Reilly would have never discussed with anyone in

L.A., he could hardly refuse to do that in Liberty Hill. Dan was like family to every one of his patients, and they were truly worried about him. Some of them even came in in tears, concerned that he was dying, and it was all Reilly could do to convince them that Dan really was going to be fine.

That took time, of course, and with twice as many patients to see as he normally did, he didn't have a prayer of getting back on schedule. He didn't even try. As Krista had predicted, the place was a zoo, and all he could do was take the influx of patients one by one and give them the time they needed to get to know him and talk about Dan.

It was going on noon when he grabbed the chart for the patient in examining room three and stepped inside to find himself face-to-face with the most beautiful woman he had ever seen in his life. Tall and decidedly pregnant, she had the striking features of a model and a face that looked more than a little familiar, though Reilly would have sworn he'd never met her before in his life.

Frowning, he studied her delicate features, the sweep of her brow and her deep-blue eyes, and suddenly he realized he'd seen an older version of that face just last night. "You're Sara McBride's daughter! And Nick's wife."

Smiling, she didn't deny it. "Everyone says I look just like Mom, but I think Janey's the one who got her pretty smile." Holding out her hand, her blue eyes twinkled up into his. "I'm Merry Kincaid. You must be Dr. Jones. I'm sorry I didn't get to meet you when you moved into Nick's cabin, but Dan has me on bed rest, so I've been sticking close to home. I've heard a lot about you, though."

"I won't put you on the spot by asking if it was all good," he said dryly. "I guess you know, though, that I acted like a jerk to your sister when she tried to welcome me to town."

"So I heard," she retorted. "Did you apologize?"

He had to give her credit—she didn't beat around the bush. But then again, neither did Janey. It had to be a family trait. "Yes, I did," he replied. "She didn't make it easy for me, but I can't blame her for that. I acted like a jackass. It won't happen again."

Her eyes searching his, she couldn't miss his sincerity. "Good," she said, satisfied. "See that it doesn't. So how's Dan doing? I talked to Janey last night, and she said he's progressing nicely, thanks to you."

"He was lucky," he said modestly. "If his recovery goes as expected, he should be back to work in six weeks." Glancing through her chart, he looked up and smiled. "Just about your due date, right?"

"So you think he'll be back in time to deliver the baby?" she asked eagerly. "Not that I don't want you to do it," she quickly amended, "but Dan's always been my doctor and this is my first baby and I'm a little bit nervous—"

That was more than a little obvious. Amusement glinting in his eyes, Reilly said gently, "I understand, Merry. You don't have to apologize. Dan is your doctor, and it's only natural that you want him to deliver your baby. If it's possible I know he'll be there for you. If he can't, though, I'll be happy to step in for him.

"And you don't have to worry that I'm an amateur just because I'm a heart surgeon," he assured her. "At one time I considered specializing in obstetrics, so I have plenty of experience delivering babies. I won't let you down if the baby decides to check in early."

Relieved, Merry felt tears well in her eyes and could do nothing but wipe them away as they spilled over her lashes and trailed down her cheeks. "I'm sorry," she choked out, flashing him a watery smile that unknowingly reminded him of Janey. "I'm okay. Really. I'm just so weepy. The least little thing seems to set me off these days. It's driving poor Nick crazy. Every time he so much as looks at me crooked, I blubber like a baby.''

From what he'd seen of Nick Kincaid, Reilly doubted that he'd have any trouble consoling a tearful, very pregnant wife. ''Your hormones are on a roller coaster right now, but they should even out once you have the baby. Just be patient. In another six weeks, Dan'll be back to work, you'll have the baby, and then the real fun begins. Life'll never be the same.''

He'd seen first-time mothers who were scared to death at the thought that their baby was going to change their life, but not Merry McBride. Her blue eyes shining with excitement, she was practically glowing at the thought of holding her baby in her arms. ''I can't wait. I just hope Dan will be there to share it with us.''

''He's in good shape for a man his age,'' he assured her. ''I'm not expecting any problems.''

After all, Dan had breezed through the surgery without a single problem. Now all Dan had to do was rest and give himself time to heal. How difficult could that be? Most patients welcomed the opportunity to lie around and recuperate, especially the hard workers like Dan. A vacation, even if it was spent mostly in bed, had to sound pretty appealing.

Or so Reilly thought until he stopped by the hospital later that evening and discovered that he wasn't, unfortunately, like most other patients. The second Reilly stepped into his room, Dan sighed in relief. ''Good. There you are. Now you can see about getting me out of here. I tried to get Janey to do something, but she's been stubborn.''

Seated next to her mother in one of the chairs at the foot of the bed, Janey only grinned. ''You know I can't do that, Dan. Only Reilly can release you.''

When he snorted at that, clearly displeased, Reilly struggled to hide a grin. "She's right and you know it." Nodding a greeting at the McBride women, he said dryly, "I guess I don't have to ask if he's been giving you a hard time."

"Oh, that's putting it mildly," Janey retorted, tattling on him without a qualm. "He actually wanted me to forge your signature. Can you believe it? I was shocked! I always thought he was one of those fine, upstanding citizens who never even so much as jaywalked. Boy, was I wrong!"

Far from embarrassed that he'd been found out, Dan grumbled, "You don't have to act as if I'm some kind of ax murderer or something. I just want to go home."

A smile tugging at her lips, Sara said, "Now, Janey, everyone knows what awful patients doctors are. It must be something they learn in medical school."

"It is not!" Dan growled.

"Then you're just naturally grumpy when you're not feeling well," she said soothingly, unperturbed. "It's okay, dear. We forgive you."

Torn between frustration and amusement, Dan had to laugh. "See what I have to put up with," he complained to Reilly with a mock frown. "I could have died the other night, but do I get any sympathy? Nooo! No one cares about me. They just come to visit so they can torture me. They couldn't do that if I was at home."

"I don't know why not," Janey drawled. "We can visit you there just as easily as we can here."

Fighting a smile, he struggled to hang on to his scowl. "But I could rest there. I can't do that here."

"You know it's too soon for that, Dan," Reilly said quietly, his smile fading. "You live alone. What if you needed help during the middle of the night?"

"I won't."

"You can't know that."

"Then I'd call an ambulance—"

"You might be too weak to get to the phone."

"I'll sleep with the damn thing. Anything to get out of here. The nurses are coming in every thirty minutes to poke me with a needle or take my blood pressure, and it's driving me crazy! How am I supposed to rest and regain my strength when I can't get any sleep?"

Sympathetic, Reilly could well understand his frustration, but he was caught between a rock and a hard place. "Look, I wish I could help you, but the only way I can consider it is if you hire yourself a nurse. If you get in trouble during the middle of the night, you've got to have someone there to help you."

Sara exchanged a speaking glance with Janey, then said quietly, "There is another option. He could come home with me and stay in the downstairs guest room. Since I don't work, I could watch over him during the day, and Janey would be there to handle any problems that might crop up during the night."

It was a logical solution, but Reilly still wasn't comfortable releasing Dan so soon after surgery. Hesitating when the older man looked at him expectantly, he said, "I don't know. I still think it's too soon. Janey works rescue—"

"I only work Tuesdays and Thursdays, and then, only until midnight," Janey said. "If you think that'll be a problem, I'm sure Red Hawkins would be willing to sub for me for the next couple of weeks. All I have to do is ask him."

"If there's going to be a problem, it'll crop up before next week," he retorted.

"So I'll just take the next week off and be home every night this week. If you release him in the morning, that'll give him another full night in the hospital. All you have to worry about then is the days, and Mom'll watch him like a hawk. If he so much as blinks wrong, she'll call an ambulance.''

It was a logical solution, one that would probably work. Reluctantly he gave in. ''I'd feel better if he spent at least two more days in the hospital, but,'' he added when Dan began to scowl, ''I know he'd be more comfortable at Sara's.''

''So?'' the older man asked when he once again hesitated. ''What's it gonna be? Are you releasing me or not?''

''All right,'' he sighed. ''I'll agree to an early release in the morning—''

''Thank God!''

''As long as you stay at Sara's and I can drop by there every evening after work to check on your progress,'' he continued without missing a beat. ''If you have the slightest twinge—I don't care if it's in the middle of the night and you think you dreamed the whole damn thing—I want to hear about it. Got it?''

Satisfied, Dan grinned broadly. ''Got it.''

Dan wasn't grinning nearly so broadly the next morning, however, when Sara arrived to pick him up at the hospital. Just moving from his bed to the wheelchair an orderly brought for him to ride to the front entrance wore him out. Pale and drawn, he hardly had the strength to stand as Sara pulled up in the drive next to him.

Alarmed, she hurried around to help him as he struggled to open the door to the car. ''Wait! Let me help you! Oh, Dan, are you sure you shouldn't stay another day?'' she asked worriedly as he let her assist him into the front passenger seat. ''You've got no business being out of bed.''

''I'm fine,'' he assured her faintly as he leaned his head back against the headrest and closed his eyes. ''I just need to catch my breath.''

Frowning, Sara wasn't buying that. "What you need is to get back in that chair and let me wheel you back into the hospital. You're weak as a kitten."

"I'll be fine as soon as I get to your house."

She wanted to argue. Damn him, what was he doing? Trying to kill himself? Last night, when she'd suggested he could recuperate at her house, it had seemed like a good idea. Now she wasn't so sure. He wasn't nearly as strong as she'd thought he was.

Hesitating, she studied his pale face and wasn't at all happy with what she saw. He didn't look like he had the energy to spit, let alone walk up the short flight of stairs to her front porch. "Maybe I should call Reilly. I'm not sure you can make it up the porch steps to the front door."

Forcing his eyes open, he smiled tiredly and took her hand. "Don't worry so," he chided softly. "I'm not going to die on your front steps. I'll just need a little help getting up them. Don't make me go back in there, Sara. I want to go home—either to your house or mine, but not the hospital. Please?"

She was a strong woman who could stand firm when she had to, but she couldn't resist that "please." Not when he could barely hold his head up and she'd come so close to losing him. "All right," she sighed, giving in with a tremulous smile. "But if you die on me, I'm never going to forgive you!"

Chuckling, he only squeezed her hand and closed his eyes with a tired sigh.

She tried to miss the worst of the bumps in the road on the drive home, but the ranch roads weren't the smoothest in the world, and it was impossible to miss every pothole. Dan groaned more than once, but there was little she could do except ease over the worst spots and get him home as quickly as possible.

"Thank God," she said when her house finally came into view. "Just a few more minutes and you can lie down," she promised him. "I've already got the bed in the guest room ready. All we have to do is get you inside."

She was chattering—she knew it, but there didn't seem to be anything she could do about it. She told herself it was because she was worried about him, but when she came around the car and slipped her arm around him to help him out of the vehicle, the pounding of her heart had nothing to do with worry. Startled, she froze as her eyes flew to his.

"What is it?" he asked huskily when she stiffened. "What's wrong?"

If her life had depended on it, she couldn't have told him. Her thoughts scrambled and her pulse pounding, she was sure she had to be having some kind of breakdown. That was the only explanation. Dan was her friend, *just* a friend. Oh, he still teased her about going out on a real date, but he was just joking. She knew how much he'd loved Peggy—she'd felt the same way about Gus. There could never be anyone for either one of them but the spouse they'd each lost.

So why, she wondered wildly, was her heart pounding like a runaway train just because she'd slipped her arm around him? What was going on? What was wrong with her?

"Sara? Are you all right? You look a little flushed."

Suddenly realizing she was staring at him as if she'd never seen him before, she felt heat pour into her cheeks and wanted to sink right through the porch steps. "It's nothing. I'm just worried about you. C'mon, let's get you inside."

Focusing on the task at hand, she kept a firm arm around his waist and urged him up the steps. It wasn't easy. There were only four steps, but after each one, he had to stop and rest. By the time they reached the top one, he was as pale as a ghost and dripping sweat.

Worried, she said, "I should call one of the boys. Joe can be here in two minutes—"

"No, I'll make it," he huffed, winded. "Let's go."

Stubborn as a mule, he made it the rest of the way to the guest room without stopping to rest, only to collapse when they reached the bed. Wanting to shake him for insisting on coming and furious with herself for giving in to him, Sara helped him under the covers, scolding him all the while. "You old fool. What are you doing? Trying to prove you're some kind of Superman? Look at you. You can't even hold your head up."

"Your cheeks are pink again," he pointed out, not the least perturbed by his weakness. "Just like a girl's. No wonder Gus fell in love with you the second he laid eyes on you. You must have been something to see."

Flustered, she didn't know if she wanted to thank him or berate him for bringing up Gus's name. "No, he was the one who was something to see," she said, and tried to steady her pounding heart with the image of Gus at eighteen and that day she'd met him just two weeks after her family had moved to town. She could see him as clearly now as she had that fateful day, but when her pulse continued to race, she was forced to admit that it wasn't for Gus.

Confused, alarmed, she stepped hastily away from the bed. "I—I've got s-some chores to do, and you need to rest. I'll check in on y-you in a little while."

Leaving a bell on the nightstand for him to ring if he needed her, she rushed out and hurried down the hall, her cheeks flaming. Her imagination was just playing tricks on her, she told herself desperately. It wasn't his closeness that had set her heart pounding. She was just worried about him, that was all. That was all it could be, she assured herself and tried to believe it. But as she strode into the laundry room to put a load of laundry in the washing machine, she couldn't stop thinking about how right it had felt to hold him close.

"Reilly! I'm so glad you're here. Dan's in the guest room. C'mon, I'll show you the way."

Her smile just a little too bright, Sara opened the front door to him and pulled him inside, chattering about Dan's condition as she led Reilly through the family room to the short hall that led to the guest room. "He was very tired when I brought him home this morning, but he's rested all day. Janey's in with him now. I was just about to bring him his supper. Have you eaten? Can I get you anything?"

"No…thank you. I had something at Ed's."

"I was going to offer you dessert, but if you ate at Ed's, I bet you had chocolate pie," she said, smiling. With a wave of her hand, she motioned him toward the open doorway to the guest room. "Go on in. I'll be right back."

She hurried off to the kitchen, leaving him to step into the bedroom alone, where he found Janey taking Dan's pulse. "So how's our patient doing?" he asked, arching a brow at the two of them. "Resting, I hope."

"How could I do anything else?" Dan grumbled with a weak smile. "Sara took the remote so I couldn't watch TV, then gave me this awful magazine about doing your own income tax. I've been so bored, I had to sleep just to have something to do."

Chuckling, Janey patted his hand. "Just think, Dan. Only six more weeks of this, and you can go back to work."

When he groaned, Reilly laughed and stepped over to the bed to examine him. "Don't look so down in the mouth. Give it another couple of days, and Sara will let you watch TV. I promise."

"Did I hear my name mentioned?" Sara said as she strode in with Dan's dinner tray. "He's been complaining about the TV again, hasn't he? Who would have guessed he was such a baby?" Shaking her head, she deposited the tray on the nearby dresser while Reilly finished his examination. "I'm just following doctor's orders."

"Oh, really?"

Caught red-handed, Reilly grimaced when the older man shot him a narrow-eyed look. "Now, Dan—"

"You took him on as a partner because he was the best," Sara reminded Dan as she moved to the foot of the bed to straighten the covers. "You can't complain now because he's doing his job."

Put that way, there wasn't much he could say. "Well, no, I guess I can't," he growled. "But that doesn't mean I have to like it."

When he sat there sulking like a two-year-old, Reilly expected Sara to smile. Now that the surgery was past, and Dan was obviously well enough to complain, she shouldn't have been so worried about him. But she was definitely nervous about something. She fussed around the room, straightening things, never staying in any one place for long. Her smile was forced, her cheeks pale, her body language decidedly stiff.

Glancing over at Janey, Reilly saw that she, too, was watching her mother, and she was as concerned as he by what she saw. Frowning, she started to ask her what was wrong, then obviously thought better of it. Glancing away, her eyes met Reilly's and he motioned for her to step out into the hall.

"Do you think this is too much for your mother?" he asked quietly when she joined him. "She seems awfully skittish."

"I know, and I don't understand it. She's been this way ever since I got home from work. At first I thought something was wrong with Dan, but you examined him. He's doing fine."

Reilly couldn't argue with that. His partner was, in spite of the weakness that was a natural result of the surgery itself, doing much better than he'd expected. "Maybe it's the pressure of taking care of him all day by herself," he suggested. "She's not used to having that kind of responsibility on her shoulders, and it could be more of a strain than she expected."

"But she doesn't usually let things like this rattle her," Janey replied in a low voice that wouldn't carry into the bedroom. "Zeke nearly cut off a toe with a chainsaw when he was a teenager, and she was as calm and cool as an E.R. nurse. She didn't even break into a sweat."

"Then what do you think's wrong? Maybe I should talk to her."

"No, I—"

"What are you two whispering about out there?" Dan suddenly called grouchily from the bed. "If there's something wrong, I want to know about it."

"Nothing's wrong," Reilly assured him as he stepped back into the bedroom. "Janey and I were just discussing—"

"The decorating committee," she supplied quickly, following him into the room. "There's a meeting tonight, and I was planning to go, but Mom's probably tired—"

"I am not!"

"But—"

"No buts," Sara said firmly. "I'm fine. Since Dan's being such a baby about the TV, though, I was wondering if it'd be okay for him to watch his favorite cop show. If that's okay with you, Reilly. It's only an hour, then we'd both turn in early.''

"I don't think one hour's going to hurt anything.''

Pleased, she said, ''Good. So there's no need for Janey to stay home and baby-sit the old folks—''

"Hey, speak for yourself!'' Dan yelped.

Her blue eyes suddenly sparkling with amusement, Sara struggled not to smile. ''I beg your pardon—I stand corrected. There's no need for you to stay home and baby-sit the *older generation*.'' Glancing at Dan, she arched a delicate brow. ''How's that?''

"Much better,'' he said with a grin.

"So you see,'' she told Janey, ''I've got everything under control here, dear. And the decorating committee could use your help. The festival's only a week and a half away, and with both Dan and me out, they're really shorthanded. I think you should go.''

Put that way, Janey really couldn't see that it was necessary for her to stay home. ''Well, if you're sure.''

"I could go with you, if you like,'' Reilly said impulsively. ''Then you wouldn't have to drive all the way into town and back by yourself.''

Later, Reilly couldn't have said where the suggestion came from. It just popped out of his mouth. He hadn't given any thought to going to the committee meeting tonight— he'd worked a long day and had planned to spend the rest of the evening catching up on his reading. But he had enjoyed himself the other night—up until the moment Dan had his heart attack—and the more he thought about spending the rest of the evening alone, the less the idea appealed to him.

Surprised, Janey hesitated. "Are you sure? I don't mind going by myself."

"No, I'd like to go," he said, and meant it. "I was just going to go home and read. I can do that anytime. Unless," he added quickly, "you'd rather go alone."

"Oh, no. I just didn't want you to feel like you had to go just because I was. This kind of thing must seem pretty tame to you after L.A."

"Actually, I enjoyed it more than I expected," he admitted. "I really would like to go."

"Then I'll get my coat."

They discussed whose car to take, finally deciding on Reilly's as they skirted around each other's feelings like two skaters who suddenly found themselves sharing thin ice. And they didn't even seem to realize it. But Sara and Dan did, and as the younger couple wished them good-night and left for the meeting, they waited only until they heard the front door close before they both turned to each other and smiled broadly.

"That just made my day," Sara said, pleased. "Do you think they realize what's going on?"

Chuckling, Dan shook his head. "I don't think either one of them has a clue."

Chapter 6

"You like *Dirty Harry?* And the Star Wars series? You're kidding!"

"Why? I think Clint Eastwood and Luke Skywalker are kind of cute. What's so odd about that?"

"You mean other than they're from different galaxies and their movies are set in time periods that are light-years apart?"

Her grin lighting her face, Janey chuckled as she enthusiastically slapped paint on yet another booth for the festival. "Yeah. So one used a .357 and the other a light-saber. They fought the bad guys and won. I like that."

His own painting forgotten as he watched her smile light up her eyes, Reilly couldn't help but grin. The lady was something else. She had a dab of red paint on her cheek, tendrils of her hair had slipped from the confining knot she'd scraped it back into and what little bit of makeup she wore had faded hours ago. Another woman might have rushed to a mirror to repair the damage, but Janey only pushed her hair back out of her way with the back of her hand, scratched her nose, inadvertently adding another smidgen of paint to the one on her cheek, and never once reached for her lip gloss.

And she had no idea how refreshing that was to him. Oh, the women in L.A. who had spent the past eight months chasing him had worn paint, too, only theirs had been war paint, the kind a woman painted on when she was on the prowl. Janey, like the movie heroes she liked, was, thankfully, from a whole different galaxy.

"Then you must like Indiana Jones, too," he said. His lips twitching with amusement, he added nonchalantly, "He's a relative of mine, you know."

Startled, she glanced up quickly from her painting. "You're related to Harrison Ford?"

"No. Indiana Jones. *Jones,*" he stressed, grinning. "Get it? His father and mine were brothers."

Groaning, she rolled her eyes. "Cute, Doctor."

"Thank you. I like to think I am."

"And modest, too," she added dryly. "How do you stand being so wonderful?"

Pretending to consider it, he confided, "You know, it's not easy. But everyone's got their cross to bear in life. I do what I can."

He spoke so earnestly that for a moment Janey thought he was serious. Then she caught sight of the self-deprecating twinkle dancing in his blue eyes. Laughing, she licked her index finger and marked an imaginary point in the air. "Score one for you, Doctor. That was good."

Chuckling, he said, "Like I said. I do what I can."

They turned their attention back to their painting, and Janey couldn't believe how much work they were able to accomplish together. She'd worked on the decorations for the Christmas festival for years and always enjoyed it—but never like this. And it was all due to Reilly. He was a different man from the brooding one she'd met when he'd first moved to town, and it was impossible for her not to like him. Laughing and joking, they painted decorations and never ran out of things to talk about.

Caught up in a spirited conversation about who was the best president of the last century, they never noticed the passage of time or when, by unspoken agreement, the rest of the committee members started putting away their paints and cleaning brushes. Then, suddenly, people reached for their coats and jackets and called good-night to each other.

In the process of explaining why he thought Nixon deserved to make the list of best presidents, despite Watergate, Reilly suddenly noticed that the place was clearing out fast. "Hey, it looks like it's time to lock up shop."

Surprised, Janey glanced up from her painting and gasped. "My God, is it ten o'clock already? Where did the time go?"

Reilly wondered the same thing. It seemed they'd only been there a few minutes, when, in fact, it had been three hours! Later he was sure he would have to give that some thought, but for now they had to get out of there. "I guess we'd better clean up and get out of here before they turn out the lights on us," he said. "Why don't you put the paint away while I clean the brushes?"

Quickly setting everything right, they grabbed their coats from the cloak room and hurried toward the front door, only to find Hap Clark waiting for them with a rueful grin on his face. The mayor of Liberty Hill and holder of the keys to the VFW hall, he couldn't lock up until everyone was out. "I was beginning to wonder if you two were going to talk politics until midnight. Did you ever come to a decision on Nixon?"

"Yes."

"No."

Chuckling, he followed them outside. "I thought as much. If you need a deciding vote, I vote for Truman. Now there was a president!"

They hadn't even considered Harry, and that started another discussion that could have easily lasted another hour. Unfortunately, they ran out of time when they reached the ranch fifteen minutes later.

Disappointed, Janey would have liked to continue the discussion over a cup of coffee and some of her mother's apple pie, but it was already going on ten-thirty, and they both had to work the following day. Like it or not, the evening was over.

When he braked to a stop in the circular drive in front of the house, Janey turned to thank him for the great conversation and the ride, but before she could even open her mouth, her eyes met his in the glow of the porch light, and everything seemed to change. Something shifted on the night air, something rare and elusive that she'd never experienced before, and suddenly, without warning, her heart was pounding and she couldn't seem to breathe properly.

In the sudden, hushed silence, she tried to tell herself that her imagination was just playing tricks on her. But Reilly felt it, too. She watched his smile fade, his eyes sharpen with sudden awareness, and just that quickly, tension throbbed between them. Her pulse skipping crazily, Janey couldn't have said how long she sat there, caught in the cool heat of his blue eyes, her mind a complete blank. It could have been seconds, minutes, eons. Then, she realized she was staring at him as though she'd never seen a man before, and hot color flooded her cheeks. What in the world was wrong with her?

Mortified, she jerked her gaze free of his and quickly

grabbed her purse, looking anywhere but at him. "Thank you for the ride. And for going tonight. We got a lot done."

"I enjoyed it. I was glad I could help."

In the hushed quiet that surrounded them, his voice was rough and seemed to reach out and stroke her like a caress. Goose bumps sliding down her spine, Janey fumbled for the door handle with fingers that were anything but steady. "I h-have to g-go, now," she stuttered. "G-good night."

She was out of the car like a shot, hurrying up the steps to the porch like the hounds of hell were after her. Reilly, always the gentleman, would have escorted her to the front door and unlocked it for her, but she didn't give him the chance. Jamming the key into the dead bolt, she sent the door flying back on its hinges. A split second later, she stepped across the threshold and shut the door behind her...and never knew that Reilly stared after her like a man who'd suddenly been struck in the head with a rock.

Soundlessly turning off the TV in the guest room with the remote, Sara glanced over at Dan to ask him how he'd liked the show, only to smile tenderly when she discovered he was slumped against his pillow and already sound asleep. Foolish man, she thought fondly as she rose from the easy chair in the corner and quietly crossed to the bed to check on him. For most of the day she'd been telling him he was trying to do too much too soon, but he'd always been so stubborn. And now he'd tired himself out. Maybe tomorrow he'd listen to her.

Reaching his side, she gently slipped his glasses off and laid them on the nightstand. He didn't so much as twitch an eyelash. Lying there with his white hair mussed and his face relaxed in sleep, he looked healthy and whole and strong, and she thanked God for Reilly's skill as a surgeon.

Without him there was a good chance that Dan wouldn't be there now.

Staring down at him, Sara felt something shift in the region of her heart and tried to convince herself that the tug of emotion she was feeling was perfectly normal. Over the past few days she'd experienced everything from fear to worry to the kind of relief that left even a strong woman weak at the knees. Anyone who'd come that close to losing a lifelong friend would have felt the same. If she was still a little shaky, she had every right to be.

But even as she tried to believe that's all it was, she couldn't forget that moment when he'd been in recovery and she'd been allowed to spend a few moments with him. He'd still been groggy from the anesthetic and barely able to keep his eyes open, but hers was the first name he'd said when he'd regained consciousness. And when he'd reached for her and closed his hand around hers, nothing had felt so right since Gus had died.

And that had nothing to do with the fact that they were old friends.

The thought came out of nowhere to steal the breath out of her lungs, and she immediately rejected it. No! she told herself firmly. She wasn't going there. She and Dan were just buddies, chums who'd fallen into the habit of going out to dinner or the movies or just watching TV with each other several times a week. The only feelings they shared were the affection of old friendship, nothing more or less, and only a foolish old woman would allow herself to think otherwise. She might be on the downhill side of sixty, but she liked to think she was neither old or foolish. She'd only loved one man in her life and that was Gus. That wasn't going to change at this late date. She was just imagining things.

But even as she tried to convince herself that nothing

had changed in her world, her fingers weren't quite steady as she reached out to adjust the pillow under Dan's head. Murmuring in his sleep, he shifted into a more-comfortable position, and without quite knowing how it happened, Sara found herself softly stroking his hair.

The second she realized what she was doing, she should have stopped. She certainly meant to. But it was so soft and it had been so long since she'd touched a man's hair. Transfixed by the silky texture of it, she ran her fingers gently through it and felt her heart constrict with an emotion she couldn't put a name to.

Suddenly, without warning, she heard the front door open and close, signaling Janey's return, and she jumped guiltily. What, dear God, was she doing? If Janey walked in right then and found her caressing Dan's hair, she'd think…it would look like—

Unable to finish the thought, Sara felt hot color burn her cheeks and bit back a rare curse. No one was going to think anything if she'd quit standing there mooning over the man like a teenager who'd just discovered boys!

"Mom?"

Janey's soft call from the hallway was all it took to galvanize her into action. Assuring herself with a quick glance that Dan was fine and sleeping soundly, she snapped off the light on the nightstand and hurried to the door. She'd barely stepped into the hall when she came face-to-face with Janey.

She could feel a flush warming her cheeks and prayed Janey wouldn't notice, but she needn't have worried. Her daughter seemed to be as flustered as she and more than a little distracted. Concerned, she frowned and quickly shut the door to the guest room so they wouldn't disturb Dan. "What's wrong?"

Janey would have sworn that her face was perfectly expressionless, but she didn't bother to wonder how her mother knew anything was wrong. For as long as she could remember, Sara had always seemed to know when things weren't quite right with one of her children. It was just a gift she had, and it was comforting to Janey to know that she was always there to share her problems with.

Normally, Janey wouldn't have hesitated to sit down with her in the family room and unburden her heart. They'd always been close, and nothing had ever come up that she couldn't discuss with Sara. Until tonight.

She was a thirty-seven-year-old virgin who'd only had two blind dates in her life. No man had ever shown an interest in her, yet, just moments ago, something had passed between her and Reilly that she couldn't explain, something that had set her nerve endings tingling and her body humming. And she didn't know what to make of it. How did she tell her mother something like that? How did she make her understand that all of her life she'd felt out of step with other women because she'd never dated, and now, at thirty-seven, she was feeling emotions she should have experienced in high school. *And she didn't know what to do!*

It was embarrassing, frustrating, scary. She wasn't normally an insecure person—she had all the confidence in the world when it came to her job and everything else in her life. Everything except this. What if she'd imagined the whole thing? she thought, horrified. What if she was the only one who'd felt the attraction? If Reilly somehow found out that she'd blown that moment in the car all out of proportion, she'd be mortified.

Cringing at the thought, she forced a weak smile that did little to reassure her mother. "I'm just distracted," she fibbed. "I was thinking about a patient." Deliberately changing the subject, she glanced past her to the closed door of the guest room. "How's Dan? Did he give you any problems tonight?"

Considering Dan's surgery had only been two days ago and he'd practically come out of the operating room demanding to go home, Janey didn't think the question was all that unusual, but suddenly she would have sworn her mother was blushing like a schoolgirl. Surprised, she arched a brow at her. "Mom? Is everything okay? Dan—"

"Is doing fine," she assured her softly as she motioned her to precede her down the hall to the family room. "He fell asleep during his show and didn't even hear me turn off the TV. After wearing himself out trying to be Superman today, I don't think we have to worry about him waking up during the night."

"His temp's okay? We can't take any chances with that. If he starts spiking a fever, there could be an infection."

"I took his temperature every hour, just as Reilly instructed, until he fell asleep. He's doing fine. So how was the meeting tonight? It was nice of Reilly to go since Dan and I couldn't. An extra pair of hands always comes in handy—especially this close to the festival. Everyone must have been painting like crazy."

Janey would have given anything to agree with her, but she couldn't have said what the other committee members were doing. All she'd seen was Reilly. "You know how it is," she said vaguely. "You sort of lose track of time and what's going on around you. Speaking of time, I'd better get to bed or I'm going to be beat tomorrow."

"Me, too," Sara said. "Help me lock up and I'll walk up with you."

Together they turned out the downstairs lights and checked to make sure all the doors were locked, then walked up the stairway that Janey's great-grandfather had built himself when he added on to the house sometime after the Civil War. With a soundless sigh, the house seemed to settle for the night as they wished each other good-night and went their separate ways at the top of the stairs.

Sleeping, after the long day they'd each had, should have been easy after that. Sara had a monitor in case Dan called for help in the middle of the night, so there was no reason for her to lie awake all night listening for him. And Janey really was exhausted. Painting had taken more out of her than she'd realized, and work started early in the morning.

But when they each crawled into their lonely beds a few minutes later and snuggled under the covers, sleep was irritatingly elusive. Lying in the dark, staring at the ceiling, they counted sheep and goats and cows, but nothing helped. Because the two men they were determined not to think of insisted on pushing their way into their thoughts, and there wasn't a damn thing they could do about it.

"Did you hear the news about Janey and Dr. Jones? They were so wrapped up in each other that Hap had to run them out of the VFW Hall last night."

"He kissed her."

"No, they were just holding hands…"

The news raced through the nursing home like wildfire the next morning, setting tongues wagging, and no one could have been more pleased at the unexpected turn of events than the group of patients affectionately called the "Busybodies." Comprised of a handful of gossip-loving old women and a couple of sweet, meddling old geezers, they loved sticking their noses where they didn't belong. Little escaped their notice—or attention—and there was nothing they enjoyed more than playing matchmaker, especially when one of the parties was someone they were particularly fond of. And there was no one they loved more on the staff than Janey.

"He's perfect for her, don't you think?" Abby Hart said dreamily as the group gathered in the TV room after breakfast. "So tall and handsome."

"You always did have a soft spot for a tall man," her sister Caroline retorted. "Give me a smart one anyday. And I think Janey's the same. She's no dummy, you know. It'll take a smart man to keep up with her."

"None of that means a hill of beans if there's no chemistry," Henry Perkins argued. "If the gal would just spruce herself up a little, she could have her young man eating out of her hand."

"Well, she could use a little makeup—"

"And a haircut—"

"Shh! Here she comes!"

Distracted by the call she'd just received from the nursing home's front desk, Janey rushed through the TV room and didn't hear a word they said. Hannah Starks's son, William, had come to visit his mother. It was about damn time! It'd only been a little over a year!

Breathless by the time she reached the front desk, she took only a second to catch her breath before she arched a brow at Renee Jackson, who was working the information desk. "Well? Where is he?"

Without a word Renee nodded toward the visitors' lounge and the man who paced the length of it with a jerky pace that clearly spoke of his impatience.

Janey took one look at him and recognized him immediately from the pictures that were plastered all over Hannah's room. Dressed in an expensive black business suit, with his collar buttoned down and his tie knotted tight enough to strangle him, he looked uptight and irritated, as if he was in the last place he wanted to be. He obviously couldn't wait to be away from there—and his mother—and Janey's heart broke for poor Hannah. She was a kind, loving woman who should have died weeks ago, but she hung on because of William, because she couldn't even consider dying without seeing him again, and he didn't seem to care two cents about her. Sometimes life just wasn't fair.

"He looks like a real prize, doesn't he?" Renee murmured in a nearly soundless voice that wouldn't carry to where William waited like a man who was late for a meeting with the president. "And just think, Janey—he's divorced. There's our chance to go steady."

"Then by all means—let's not let him get away," she said grimly. "We had a hard enough time getting him here." And with her chin set at a determined angle, she headed straight for him.

"Mr. Starks? I'm Janey McBride," she said pleasantly. "I spoke to you last week—"

That was as far as she got. Rudely ignoring her outstretched hand, he scowled down at her and said coldly, "I don't have a lot of time, Miss McBride. I have to be back in Seattle this evening for a political fund-raiser, so if you'd just show me to my mother's room, we can get this over with."

The CEO of a highly successful computer chip company, William Starks might have run his company like a dictator, but Janey had no intention of letting him do the same to her. Far from intimidated by him, she met his hard gaze with one of her own and stood right where she was.

"In a minute, Mr. Starks. First we need to get a few things straight. Your mother knows nothing about our conversation last week. For her sake it would be best if we kept it that way. She doesn't need to know that the only reason you're here is because I called you. That would only hurt her, and I'm sure you don't want to do that."

He didn't like that, but he'd walked in with a chip on his shoulder, and Janey didn't care. Hannah was her patient and the only one she was concerned about. "If you care anything at all about your mother," she continued, "you'll let her think this visit was all your idea."

His mouth compressed into a hard, flat line, he wanted to tell her to go to hell—Janey could see the angry resentment in his eyes—but he obviously realized that if he did that, it really would look like he was more concerned with himself than he was Hannah. So he reined in his temper and nodded curtly. "Fine. Where's her room?"

"In the east wing," she replied, satisfied. "If you'll follow me, I'll show you the way."

Outside the door to Hannah's room, Janey stopped and said quietly, "I'd like to go in first and prepare her for your visit. She hasn't had any visitors for a while, and the sudden shock might be more than her heart can stand. So if you'll just wait here, I'll call you in in just a second."

Not giving him a chance to reply, she swept inside to find Hannah lying in bed and staring lethargically out the window. She'd done little else for the past few weeks. Hiding her concern behind a bright smile, Janey said, "Good morning, Miss Hannah. I see breakfast wasn't to your liking this morning." On the table next to the bed sat her breakfast tray, which had hardly been touched. "Don't worry— I'm not going to scold you. I have something I think you'll like much better. How about a visitor? Do you think you're up to seeing someone this morning?"

For a moment, Janey didn't think she was going to respond. Then interest flickered in her eyes, followed by a hope that was almost painful to watch. "William?"

Smiling, Janey nodded. "He's waiting outside in the hall. I thought you might like to spruce yourself up a little before you saw him."

"Oh, yes! My rouge—I'm sure I need some color in my

cheeks. And my comb." Struggling to sit up straighter, she looked around with a frown. "Where is my purse? I never can remember where I put it."

Thrilled that she was so excited, Janey laughed. "Hang on. It's right here in the cabinet where it always is. Let me get you a mirror."

It only took a few moments to fluff her hair and add a glow of color to the delicate parchment skin of her cheeks and lips, then Janey stepped to the door. "Your mother's ready to see you now," she told William quietly. "Please, come in."

The wait hadn't improved his mood, and with a scowl he strode across the threshold, only to stop short when he spied the pictures of himself spread all around the room. The photos captured him at all ages, chronicling his life from boyhood to maturity in a collection of family snapshots that he had, no doubt, long since forgotten. Most of them had been taken when he was a boy and life had yet to carve his face with maturity, but there were some recent ones of him at social functions that Hannah had clipped from the Seattle paper, which she had delivered to her daily.

Watching him closely, Janey saw shock flash in his eyes and knew he hadn't had a clue that his mother had created a virtual shrine of him in her room. It was a humbling experience. Hesitating, he stood flat-footed, and in the blink of an eye, his entire attitude changed. His hostility vanished, as did his impatience, and when his eyes met his mother's, the hard line of his mouth actually softened into a crooked smile.

"Hello, Mother," he said gruffly. "How are you?"

The smile that bloomed across her face was so sweet, so loving, that just seeing it brought the sting of tears to Janey's eyes. "I'm better now that you're here," Hannah said, holding out a hand to him. "I've been waiting for you."

Reaching her in two strides, William took her hand, and that was all Janey needed to see. Pleased, she turned and slipped out into the hall, quietly shutting the door behind her.

To his credit, William Starks didn't rush his visit with his mother. He spent the rest of the morning and early afternoon with Hannah, and when he left, he promised her that he would be back the following week to see her, and this time he would stay the weekend.

Thrilled, Hannah couldn't stop talking about him. "He's such a good-looking boy," she told Janey later that afternoon. "Don't you think so? Just like his father." A fond smile playing about her mouth, she sighed in remembrance. "I'll never forget the first time I met Bill. My, he was something! So tall and handsome. I took one look at him and forgot my name." Grinning, she laughed softly. "We were married fifty years, and he never let me forget that."

It had been weeks since she'd reminisced about the past or shown any spark of interest in life, and now she was practically beaming with happiness. Checking her pulse, Janey grinned. "I don't think I've ever seen you so bubbly. I'm glad you had such a good day."

"It was wonderful, the best Christmas present I ever had. Thank you."

Surprised, Janey blinked. "I beg your pardon? Why are you thanking me? Your son—"

"Would never have come if it hadn't been for you," she finished for her with a knowing smile. "I don't know what you said to him to convince him to visit me, but I know you had to do something. That's why I want to give you this."

When she reached under her pillow and pulled out a small box wrapped in Christmas paper, Janey looked at it suspiciously. "What is it?"

Smiling, Hannah held it out to her. "An early Christmas present. Open it."

Janey didn't want to. She'd done what she could to convince William to visit Hannah because she cared for her. She wanted nothing in return, but she didn't want to hurt her feelings, either. Reluctantly she took the present and unwrapped it.

At the sight of the antique diamond brooch nestled on a bed of cotton inside the small box, she murmured, "Oh, Hannah, it's beautiful! But I can't possibly accept it. It's too valuable."

She tried to hand it back, but Hannah would have none of it. "You gave me the only thing I wanted—a visit with my son before I died. It would give me great pleasure if you would accept it."

Since it was put that way, Janey couldn't refuse her. "I'll treasure it always. Thank you." Leaning down to hug her, she chided, "But what's all this talk about dying? You don't have time for that. William will be back next weekend. I think you're going to be seeing a lot more of him now, so you have to stay strong and healthy. Okay?"

"Okay," she said with a smile. "I'll try."

There was no doubt that she would. Of all of Janey's patients, Hannah was the one who never gave up, the one who hung on despite the odds. She had a will that went soul deep, and it was that will that had kept her alive so far. Still, she and Janey both knew she was running out of time.

It was a quiet night, and Janey was glad of it. After Reilly had driven her home last night, it had taken her hours to fall asleep. She'd gone to work exhausted, and the day had not only been long, but emotionally draining. When her shift ended, she would have liked nothing better than to go home, fall into bed and sleep around the clock, but she couldn't. It was Thursday night, and that meant she had to spend the evening at the fire department, working rescue.

She could have called Red Hawkins as she'd planned to, and he would have been happy to take over for her as long as she needed him to. But her mother had talked to Reilly, who had reassured her that Dan was doing well enough that Janey didn't need to change her plans, so she'd reported to the fire department, as scheduled, and the powers that be must have known she needed a break. There hadn't been a single call yet, and her shift was half-over already. Two more hours and she could go home.

"Hey, Janey, how about a game of poker?" Scott asked. Seated at the game table, where he'd been playing solitaire, he grinned and shuffled the cards temptingly. "I'm feeling lucky tonight. How about you?"

Wanda, who'd just finished doing the dishes after the three of them had eaten a simple supper of soup and sandwiches, rolled her eyes. "Men," she sniffed. "I swear you're all blind as bats. Can't you see the woman's out on her feet. What happened, Janey? You have a rough day?"

"Actually, it's more a combination of two late nights and not enough sleep," she admitted. "I'll be fine once I catch up on my sleep."

"You want to go upstairs and stretch out on one of the bunks?" Wanda asked with a frown. "There's not much going on, and we'll call you if we need you."

Tempted, Janey almost took her up on her suggestion. There were bunks upstairs for the firemen and EMTs, and with no effort whatsoever, she knew she could be asleep in five minutes flat. The problem was, she wasn't one of those people who hit the ground running when she woke up. It took her a while to wake up, especially when she was as tired as she was now, and she couldn't risk not being fully alert if an emergency call came in.

"Thanks, but I'm okay. Maybe a game of poker will help," she added, grinning when Scott let out a whoop of delight. "It just might be my lucky night."

"Maybe. Maybe not," he drawled, winking at her as he shuffled the cards like a card shark. "I've got my rabbit's foot with me. You know what that means."

It meant that he was one lucky devil. They played three quick hands, and he won every one. "Where's that rabbit's foot?" Janey demanded, trying and failing to appear stern as he raked in his winning cache of M&Ms. "Nobody wins with a pair of threes. You must have marked the cards somehow."

"I did not! I swear—"

Caught up in their usual card-playing banter, they never noticed they had a visitor until Reilly cleared his throat. "I'm sorry to interrupt," he said, when the three of them looked up, startled, "but I need to talk to Janey for a minute, if that's all right."

Already pushing back from the table, Scott said, "Of course, Dr. Jones. Wanda and I need to check supplies in the ambulance, anyway. Take your time."

"No! Wait!" Her heart in her throat and a sick feeling of dread spilling into her stomach, Janey knew this wasn't a social visit. Reilly wouldn't seek her out at that time of night unless there was some kind of emergency. Suddenly horrified that something had happened to someone she loved, she pushed to her feet. "My mother...something's happened to my mother, hasn't it?"

"What? No! She's fine. As far as I know, your whole family's fine. So is Dan."

"Then why are you here?"

Even as she asked, she knew. Her heart sinking, she pressed her hand to her chest. "It's Hannah, isn't it? Oh, God, I should have known! She said she couldn't die until she saw William, so what did I do? I harassed the man until he showed up—and took away her last reason for living."

"My God, Janey," Scott exclaimed, scowling, "you can't think this is your fault!"

"You loved that old woman," Wanda said indignantly. "Don't you dare blame yourself. If not for you, she would have died a long time ago."

"She's right," Reilly said quietly. "You know she was fading fast, Janey. It wasn't her need to see her son that was keeping her alive. It was you."

Pain squeezing her heart, Janey knew they all meant well, and she appreciated it. But they didn't understand. *She* was the one who'd bullied and cajoled and finally pulled a guilt trip on William Starks to convince him to do the right thing and visit his mother. And now *she* was the one who was feeling guilty.

"I should have minded my own business," she murmured. Suddenly chilled, she turned away to hug herself. "She'd still be alive."

"Not necessarily," Reilly argued. "It was her time—her heart just gave out on her. But instead of dying with regrets, she had the one thing she wanted—a visit from her son. Thanks to you. You made her last hours happy ones."

When she just stood there, half-turned away from him and grief etching her face, Reilly said impulsively, "I'm on call at the hospital tonight, but I think I can take some time for coffee and pie at Ed's. How about you? You've had a shock. You could use a break."

"That's a good idea," Wanda chimed in, frowning at her worriedly. "Take the rest of the night off. There's no much going on, anyway, and if something comes up that Scott and I can't handle, we'll swing by Ed's and pick you up. Take your beeper.''

''And your purse,'' Scott said, digging it out of a closet to hand to her. ''If you don't hear from us in an hour, go on home. Jacob Hopper always comes in early on Thursdays, so he should be in by then. Between the three of us, we can take care of anything that crops up.''

Not giving her time to so much as open her mouth in protest, he handed her her purse, gave Reilly her jacket so he could help her on with it, then ushered her and Reilly out the front door of the fire station. Just that easily, she found herself walking to Ed's with Reilly by her side.

Chapter 7

"**Y**ou should have seen it. I was this young, still-wet-behind-the-ears intern working the emergency room of L.A. General for the first time, and I was scared to death. And I had a right to be! Talk about trial by fire. There was a full moon the first night I worked, and no one warned me that that really did bring out the crazies. My first patient was a seventy-two-year-old woman who thought she was Cleopatra and needed to be treated for a snake bite."

"Oh, no!"

Reilly grinned. "I didn't find out until later that she came in every Friday night, claiming to be some famous woman in history who needed help." Shaking his head over that, he chuckled. "She was a sweet old lady, just lonely for some attention. And then there was George Peabody."

Watching his eyes twinkle, Janey felt her own lips twitch into a smile. "I'm afraid to ask what his problem was."

"Well, I don't know if I'd call it a problem," he replied solemnly as he tried and failed to suppress a grin. "You see, he had these false teeth, and sometimes, when he was excited and talking too fast, they'd just fly out of his mouth—''

"You're making this up!"

Holding up his hand as if he was swearing an oath, he said, "If I'm lying, I'm dying. He brought in four people on different occasions who were struck by his flying teeth. It got so bad, the nurses starting wearing helmets with face guards whenever they saw him coming.''

"Yeah. Right.''

"Really,'' he insisted. "If you don't believe me, call L.A. General. Everybody there knows George Peabody.''

He was lying through his teeth and enjoying every minute of it, and Janey couldn't help but smile. She knew why he was doing it, of course. He was trying to take her mind off Hannah's death, and for a little while, at least, he'd done that. When he'd ordered coffee and a slice of Ed's famous chocolate pie for each of them, she'd been sure she couldn't eat a bite. But then he'd started telling her stories about his days in medical school, and somehow, she'd not only eaten her pie, but he'd actually made her laugh. And he didn't have any idea how much she appreciated that. "I don't think I need to make any phone calls,'' she said dryly, grinning. "I believe you.''

He would have gone on with more stories if she'd needed him to, but now that she'd gotten past the first shock of Hannah's sudden death, she realized that Reilly was right. Hannah had only lived as long as she had by sheer will. She was old and had suffered from heart disease for years, and it was that, and not her son's visit, that had killed her.

Before he could launch into another story, she said quietly, "Thank you.''

He didn't pretend not to know what she was talking about. "I know how difficult it is to lose a patient, especially one you've grown fond of,'' he replied. "I'm glad I could help.''

By unspoken agreement they decided it was time to go, and after paying for their pie and coffee, Reilly walked with her to the fire station at the end of the next block, where she'd left her car. "If you don't feel like driving, I can take you home,'' he said gruffly as she pulled her keys out of her purse. "You've had a rough night, and it's not that far out of my way.''

Staring up at him in the darkness, Janey was shocked by how badly she wanted to say yes. But he'd driven her home from the decorating committee just last night, and she hadn't forgotten that moment when he'd pulled up before her house and her heart had started to pound like a school-girl's. He'd just been being kind, and she'd let her imagination run away with her. Still mortified, she was determined not to let that happen again. Which meant she was driving herself home.

"Thanks for the offer,'' she said, "but I'm fine. Really.''

There was no doubt that she was back in control of her emotions. Although there was still a lingering sadness in her eyes, there was no trace of the tears he'd seen there earlier. Relieved, he should have wished her good-night and ended the evening right then. It would have been the right thing to do. But his mind suddenly shut down, and impulsively he took a step toward her and leaned down to kiss her on the cheek.

It was meant to be a simple kiss, the kind friends exchanged all the time without a second thought. But when his lips brushed the petal-like softness of her skin, suddenly, nothing was simple at all. Something kicked him in the chest, something awfully similar to what he'd felt last night, only stronger, and when he drew in a quick breath of surprise, his senses were instantly filled with the clean fresh scent of her. Between one heartbeat and the next, his body was humming.

Shocked, he only had to take one look at her to know that she felt the kick of that innocent kiss, too. She wasn't like the sophisticated women he'd known in L.A. who knew how to play games. She never thought to hide her emotions, and they were all written right there in her face, in plain view for him to see. Surprise, need, trepidation. Caught in his gaze like a deer in the headlights of an oncoming car, she hesitated, not sure whether to step closer or turn and run for her life.

And it was that, more than anything, that brought him back to his senses. Because he felt the same way, and that was the last thing he expected to feel for her or any other woman.

Hastily stepping back, he deliberately broke the spell that had fallen over both of them and did what he should have done in the first place. He took another step away from her and said gruffly, "Good night."

For a moment she didn't move, then she seemed to realize that she was staring at him as if she'd never seen him before. She blinked as though she'd just come out of a daze, and suddenly she couldn't look him in the eye. "It is getting late, isn't it? Thanks again for the pie. Good night."

She was gone before he could give in to the need to call her back, and he knew it was for the best. Because if she hadn't left when she had, he was afraid he would have given in to the unexpectedly strong need to grab her and kiss her. And that could have been nothing but a mistake.

He still loved Victoria. He would always love her. There was no place in his heart for another woman.

Over the course of the next few days, he told himself that over and over again, until it became a mantra in his head, but it didn't help. Every time he turned around, he ran into Janey, and it wasn't just at the hospital or nursing home. He stopped for bread at the grocery store, and there she was, picking up a few things for her elderly patients at the nursing home. She was in line at the bank and gas station, and when he dropped by Ed's for dinner because he was tired of cooking for himself, there she was with a nurse from the hospital. It was enough to drive a man crazy. And make him more than a little paranoid. It was almost as if fate was throwing them in each other's path.

And it didn't stop there. Every night after work he drove out to the McBride ranch to check on Dan, and every night he came face-to-face with Janey. To her credit she acted just as she always did. There were no stilted conversations or wary looks. She was at ease and friendly and treated him as if she'd known him all her life.

If he'd have been a less confident man, he might have wondered if he'd imagined the way her breath had caught in her throat when he'd kissed her on the cheek or the sudden sexual tension that had throbbed between them that night. But then his eyes would lock with hers, and he knew he hadn't imagined anything. He didn't have to touch her, kiss her, to feel the sparks that flew between them. They were there whenever they came within twenty feet of each other.

And it scared the hell out of him.

He didn't understand what was going on, dammit! Victoria had only been dead a little over eight months. He shouldn't even have been thinking about another woman. But he couldn't get Janey out of his head. Thoughts of her drifted in and out of his head at all hours of the day and night, and that made him feel incredibly guilty. How had this happened? How had he *let* it happen?

It had to stop, he told himself. He had to put some distance between them and avoid her until he was able to get his head on straight. But how was he supposed to do that when they worked together and his partner—and patient—was staying in her family home? It wasn't possible, dammit!

And then there was the Christmas festival, which was Friday night. Just last night Dan had asked him and Janey to take over the booth he and Sara had been scheduled to work, and Reilly hadn't been able to find a way to turn him down. So now he was committed to spending the entire evening with Janey, trapped inside the small confines of a booth, running the water-shooting gallery where festival goers would compete for stuffed animals. To make matters worse, *he* was the one who'd suggested that he and Janey might as well drive into town together since he needed to check on Dan before the festival started, anyway.

He must have been out of his mind, he decided. He couldn't, in good conscience, go back on his commitment to work the booth, but he could take steps to make sure that working the festival didn't turn into a semidate. And to do that he would have to fib a little. He hated doing it, but he had no other choice.

Refusing to even consider the possibility that he was panicking, he stopped at the nursing home on the way to his office Friday morning and tracked down Janey at the nurses' station in the east wing. "We need to talk about tonight," he said by way of a greeting.

In the process of going over her patients' charts to make sure there'd been no changes in their regular morning meds, she looked up in surprise. "Oh, good morning, Dr. Jones. You're out and about early this morning. So what did you want to talk about?"

Her smile was easy, her tone the same friendly one she used with just about everyone. And for some reason that irritated him to no end. It seemed as though there should have been more between them than *friendliness,* dammit!

Stiffening at the thought, he frowned and said bluntly, "I've got some late consultations at the hospital, so I think we're going to have to go in separate cars. That won't be a problem, will it?"

"No, of course not. What about Dan, though? I have to go home to change after work, so I can check in on him for you, if you like."

Feeling guiltier than ever, he almost told her the truth then—that there weren't any consultations, that he was just afraid that tonight would turn into something a lot more complicated than working a booth together at a festival if he picked her up and that he wasn't ready for that. He didn't know if he'd ever be ready for that.

But the words just wouldn't come. Disgusted with himself, he said instead, "He's doing much better than I expected, so I don't think it'll hurt anything if I don't check him tonight. Just to be on the safe side, I'd appreciate it if you could take his vitals, though. Unless there's some kind of problem, I'll meet you at the booth at seven."

"Then I'll see you then," she said with an easy smile. "It should be fun."

So it was settled. Reilly should have been pleased, but for some perverse reason, it irritated him that she had complied so easily with his request. Didn't she want to go with him? He'd thought she was as attracted to him as he was to her. He couldn't have imagined—

Suddenly realizing what he was doing, he swore silently. The woman was tying him in knots, and all she'd done was smile at him. He was working too hard—that had to be it. "Yeah," he growled. "See you then."

He turned and strode off, and never knew that Janey had been as shaken as he at the prospect of going with him to the festival. That would have been too much like a date, and she wasn't sure her heart could have taken that. She'd tried to put him out of her mind over the course of the past few days, to treat him as she would have any other doctor, but every time he walked into a room, she got this crazy feeling in her chest and the whole day just seemed to get brighter. And she didn't even want to think about the dreams she had at night.

Afraid she was going to give herself away if she spent too much time alone with him, she'd seriously considered calling in sick today so she would have an excuse to miss the festival tonight. In the end, though, she hadn't been able to bring herself to do that, and now she was glad she hadn't. The problem had taken care of itself. They would arrive in their own cars, work the festival together surrounded by other people, then go their separate ways afterward. What could be simpler?

Relieved, she put the coming evening out of her head. Mornings were the busiest time of the day, and she couldn't afford to be distracted. There were breakfast trays to deliver, morning medications to administer, vitals to be taken and baths to be given. Thankfully that gave her no time to think of Reilly.

She couldn't, however, put him out of her head the entire day. The Busybodies made sure of that. Convening in the sunroom that afternoon for a lively game of gin rummy, they were thrilled when Janey joined them for a break. She hadn't even sat down before they started questioning her about Reilly.

"So how is that good-looking Dr. Jones?" Abby teased. "Has he asked you out yet?"

"Didn't you hear?" Caroline retorted. "They're working the water-pistol booth together tonight."

"He's picking her up," Henry confided. His green eyes

dancing, he arched a brow at Janey. "So what are you wearing? Something pretty?"

"Something red," Abby decided, cocking her white head to the side to consider her. "With your coloring, you'd look great in red."

Surprised, Janey said, "Actually, I do have a new Christmas sweater I was thinking about wearing. It's red."

"But what about your hair?" Rebecca Flowers asked with a frown, studying the knot that Janey invariably twisted her hair up into every day. "You really shouldn't wear it scraped back that way, dear. I know it's convenient, but with your bone structure, you need something softer around your face. Why don't you let me trim it for you?"

"Oh, no," she said quickly. "I appreciate the offer, but I don't think I have time—"

"Of course you do," Abby scoffed with a wave of her hand. "You're on break. And it won't take you a second, will it, Rebecca? Henry, go get her scissors for her. She keeps them in her bedside table."

"She's really very good," Caroline confided to Janey when she tried to object. "Before she retired, people used to drive fifty miles to have Rebecca cut their hair. You can trust her, sweetie. She's a wonder with a pair of scissors."

Janey hesitated, not sure she wanted to go through with this. But Rebecca had been despondent since Hannah died, and this was the first time she'd shown any real interest in anything in days. What could it hurt to let her fix her hair? After all, she was only going to trim it.

Henry was back then, not only with Rebecca's scissors and comb but with a sheet that could be used as a protective drape, and they all turned to Janey expectantly. It was time for a decision.

"All right," she sighed, smiling weakly. "I guess I could use a trim. Where are we going to do this?"

Pleased, Rebecca pulled out a chair and patted the seat. "Sit right here, dear."

Already pulling the pins from her hair, Janey said, "I hope this isn't going to take long. My break's almost up."

"I'll just be a minute," Rebecca assured her as her friends settled in a half circle around them to watch the procedure. "Just sit still."

Janey didn't move so much as a muscle. Her eyes focused straight ahead on the picture window that looked out over the nursing home's small outdoor patio, she closed her eyes as Rebecca combed her long hair down the middle of her back. Waiting for her to trim the ends, she nearly jumped out of her skin when she suddenly felt the scissors at her neck, just inches below her left ear.

"What—"

Clip.

Horrified, she grabbed at the hand that held the scissors. "Rebecca! Oh, my God, I thought you were just going to trim it!"

Totally unconcerned, the older woman only patted the hand that held hers and said gently, "It's all right, Janey. Trust me. When I'm finished, you're going to love it."

Trust her? How could she trust her when she'd practically scalped her? But what other choice did she have? She'd already whacked off a huge hunk of her hair! She couldn't just leave it that way.

Groaning at the thought, she closed her eyes and fought the sudden sting of tears. "Just finish it, please," she said thickly.

The others, aware how close she was to crying, fell silent, and for long moments the only sound was the clip of Rebecca's scissors. And with each cut, Janey could feel the once-long strands of her hair fall whisper-soft to the floor, until finally, her neck was bare and there was nothing left to cut. Her heart pounding with dread and her eyes squeezed shut, she just sat there, afraid to even think what she must look like with short hair.

"Oh, Janey!"

At Abby's excited exclamation, her eyes flew open and her hand flew self-consciously to the nape of her neck. "Is it bad?"

"Are you kidding? It's wonderful!"

"Turn around and look."

"No, wait!" A broad smile lighting her face, Caroline held up a hand to stop her before she could turn around and see herself in the mirrored wall at her back. "Stay right where you are until I get back. I'll just be a moment."

She was, in fact, back in what seemed like a matter of seconds, carrying a small purple makeup bag. "Since you've gone this far, you might as well have a complete makeover to go with the new hairdo. It's probably been years since you've had one, and it'll make you feel wonderful."

She had, in fact, never had one, but Janey wasn't at all sure she wanted one now, especially when she hadn't even seen her hair yet. If it was awful, no amount of makeup in the world was going to be able to hide that. "I don't know, Caroline. This has already gotten out of hand, and I'm really not much into makeup. I think I should pass."

"You don't have to worry about me going overboard and making you look like that Mimi character on TV," Caroline promised. "You won't even notice it's there."

There was no doubting her sincerity, but Janey still hesitated. Everything was happening too fast. Without the weight of her hair twisted on her head, she didn't even feel like herself. That change alone was going to take some getting used to, and now they wanted her to wear makeup? When all she normally wore was mascara and lip gloss?

She wouldn't even recognize herself when she looked in the mirror.

But she was in for a penny, she thought ruefully. She might as well be in for a pound since she'd already gone this far. If she didn't like it, she could always wash it off.

"All right," she agreed with a sigh, wondering if she'd lost her mind. "But nothing heavy."

When the others started to grin, she couldn't help wondering if she'd made a mistake, but it was too late to change her mind. Lightning quick, Caroline had already smoothed on foundation. The deed halfway done, she had little choice but to suffer through the rest of it.

"Now, just a touch of color on your lips, and you're done," Caroline said a few minutes later. Stepping back, she surveyed her work like a painter examining a finished canvas for flaws, and it was all Janey could do to sit still during her perusal—especially when Abby, Rebecca and Henry were standing behind Caroline and grinning at Janey as if they were as pleased as punch with themselves.

Unable to withstand their scrutiny another second, she jumped to her feet. "I have to see," she said, and whirled to face the mirrors that lined the entire wall at her back.

Not sure what to expect, she went perfectly still at the sight of herself, her eyes wide with shock. Who was this stranger in the mirror? This woman who resembled Merry and her mother much more than she did the old, familiar Janey? Her eyes were still the same old brown they'd always been, only they seemed bigger, darker and full of life. And where had those sculptured cheeks come from? Her face had always been rounder than her mother's and sister's, but now she had cheekbones she hadn't even known she had. All because of a little makeup and a new haircut.

And what a haircut! Lifting her hand in wonder to the fresh-cut strands, she could only marvel at the change the new style made in her appearance. The Busybodies hadn't been kidding when they'd claimed Rebecca was a whiz with a pair of scissors. She'd cut her hair into a jaunty pageboy that just brushed the angle of her jaw, giving her a smart, sassy look she'd never had before. A smile curling the edges of her mouth, she felt like she was seeing herself, the true Janey, for the first time in her life. And she loved it. All this time, for all of her adult life, she'd worn it scraped back in a knot because she'd thought another style would only make her face look rounder. She couldn't have been more wrong.

"Well?" Abby demanded expectantly. "What do you think? Do you like it?"

"*Like it?* Are you kidding? I look almost…pretty."

That was an admission she hadn't intended to make, but the words just slipped out. She'd come to terms with the fact that she was never going to be as beautiful as her mother and sister years ago, and she'd have sworn she was okay with that. But now, seeing herself this way, looking so soft and pretty and feminine, she knew how the ugly duckling must have felt when it turned into a swan. It was as if her soul had suddenly burst free. She couldn't seem to stop smiling. Was this really her? Still not quite sure she could trust the image reflected in the mirror, she reached up to tentatively touch her hair again, the curve of her cheek, half-afraid she would return to the old Janey if she so much as breathed wrong. But the woman in the mirror smiled shyly back at her, never wavering.

Emotions bubbled up in her then like water in a fountain. Not sure if she was going to laugh or cry, she did both. Whirling, tears blurring her eyes, she enveloped first Caroline and Rebecca, then the others, in a fierce hug. "Thank you *so* much! This is just so incredible. I don't know what to say."

"You don't have to say anything," Rebecca said with a smile. "Just enjoy the festival tonight."

"Oh, I will! It's going to be wonderful!" A glance at the clock then had her gasping in horror. "Oh, Lord, where did the time go? I've got to get back to work."

Taking time to give them each one more hug, she promised to check in on them before her shift ended, then rushed back to the nurses' station. Her co-workers took one look at her and nearly dropped their teeth. Delighted, she only laughed and told them how a little trim had turned into a complete makeover. Before her shift ended, three other nurses tracked down Rebecca to see if she could do the same for them.

After that, the rest of the day passed in a blur. Patients and staff alike raved over the change in her, and everyone wanted to talk about it. By the time she was finally able to head home, it was going on six, and she was running late.

Rushing inside the house, her thoughts on everything she had to do before she could leave for the festival, she ran into her mother in the hall and completely forgot her new look as she said hurriedly, "Oh, there you are, Mom. Reilly's not going to be able to look in on Dan this evening, so I'll check his vitals before I leave for the festival. I've got to get dressed first, though. I thought I'd wear my new sweater and a pair of jeans. What do you think? Or should I wear my black slacks?"

Staring at her blankly, Sara hardly heard her. "Janey...my God! Your hair...what..."

Suddenly remembering her makeover, Janey stopped in her tracks, a slow, self-conscious smile spreading across her face as she lifted a hand to her shorn locks. "Two of my patients gave me a makeover. Do you like it?"

"Like it? Oh, honey, it's wonderful!"

Tears welling in her eyes, Sara hugged her, then drew

back to look at her again. "You're beautiful. But you've always been pretty—you just didn't know it. Wait till Merry sees you. And the boys. They're going to be so proud of you. I've got to call them—"

"Mom! Did you forget the festival? I have to get ready."

"Oh, my. Of course." Laughing, she hugged her again. "Let's go show Dan, then I'll help you get ready. The jeans will be perfect with your sweater."

Chattering like two schoolgirls, they hurried to the guest room looking more like sisters than mother and daughter and had no idea what a pretty sight they made. Sitting up straighter in bed, Dan grinned broadly. "There's nothing a man enjoys more than the company of a beautiful woman. And I've got two! Janey, what have you done to yourself? You look great!"

"I feel great," she laughed, her brown eyes sparkling. "If I'd known a new haircut could do this for me, I would have done it years ago." Crossing to the bed, she sat down on the side of the mattress next to him and arched a teasing brow at the stethoscope on the nightstand. "So what's this, Dr. Michaels? Treating yourself again?"

Caught red-handed, he had the grace to blush. "Just checking the old ticker."

"And how is it?"

"Great. In fact, it's my medical opinion that I'm well on the road to recovery and should be able to resume normal activity anyday now."

Not surprised that he'd come to that conclusion, Janey grinned. "Nice try, but you're not the doctor on this case, Doctor. You'll have to consult with Dr. Jones on that. In the meantime, he's tied up with some consultations this evening before the festival, so I volunteered to check your vitals."

Reaching for his wrist, she took his pulse, then blood

pressure and wasn't surprised to find both perfect. When he just grinned at her, he didn't need to say, I told you so. She could read the words right there in his twinkling blue eyes.

Pulling the stethoscope from her ears, she said, "Okay, so you appear to be healthy as a horse. I'll tell Reilly."

"Good girl," he chuckled, and kissed her on the cheek. "Now go on and get ready for your date. You're going to knock Reilly out of his socks."

She almost told him it wasn't a date—they were just working a booth together. But as she went upstairs and changed out of her nurse's uniform and into her new red sweater, it certainly felt like she was dressing for a date. Her pulse was pounding, her heart was in her throat, and there was a sense of excitement surrounding her that set the air humming. Nervous, she fiddled with her hair, making sure every carefully cut strand fell into place, and took an inordinate amount of time with the brick-red lipstick her mother had loaned her.

Unlike other women, she seldom spent much time before the mirror primping—it just wasn't her style. But as she checked one last time to make sure hair and makeup and clothes were just right, she realized she was acting like a sixteen-year-old getting ready for the prom. So this was what she'd been missing out on all her life. It felt wonderful. And scary.

She didn't realize just how apprehensive she was until her mother and Dan hugged her and wished her good luck and she climbed in her Jeep and headed for town and the festival. She looked the best she'd ever looked in her life— and it was all she could do not to turn around and race back home like a scared rabbit. She didn't know herself anymore, didn't know this new Janey in the red sweater who was so much prettier than she'd ever thought she could be. How would people react to her new look? How would Reilly react?

The butterflies in her stomach took flight at that, and once again she gave serious consideration to turning around and going home. But she reached the town limits of Liberty Hill then, and she couldn't, in good conscience, back out now. The booths had been assembled around the square earlier in the day, then strung with twinkle lights that now set the night aglow. The festival wasn't scheduled to officially start until seven, but that was really just a technicality. People were already milling about, waiting for the food and entertainment booths to open and the party to begin. Left with no choice, she found a parking spot.

Where the devil was she? Reilly wondered, scowling as he searched through the growing crowd for Janey. They were supposed to be in their booths and ready to go by 6:55, and there was no sign of her, dammit! Now what was he supposed to do? Run the whole booth by himself? He didn't think so!

Reaching for his cell phone, he was trying to remember her number when he heard a murmur spread through the gathering crowd like wildfire racing across an open prairie. Curious, he glanced up just in time to see a woman part the crowd without saying a word. Expecting her to be some kind of knockout dressed inappropriately for a small-town festival, he was surprised to note that the red sweater she wore was neither tight nor low cut. But there was something about the way it softly molded her breasts that caught his eye and every other man's within a two-block area. Curious, his gaze moved up to her face.

He couldn't have said how long he stared at her before recognition suddenly hit him in the face like a blast of ice water. Dear God, it was Janey!

Stunned, sure his eyes were playing tricks on him, he could do nothing but stare. This couldn't be Janey! What had she done to herself? She looked so…different. *Pretty!* Why had he never noticed before how pretty she was? There was a sparkle in her brown eyes, and her smile—it was just so sweet. Did she know what that did to a man? he wondered as she walked straight toward him. He just wanted to gather her close and cover her mouth with his—

"I'm sorry I'm late," she said breathlessly.

Caught up in the images that teased him, he jerked back to awareness to find her standing right in front of him. With no effort whatsoever, he discovered, he could have reached for her. "That's okay," he said, shaken. "You're just in time." Noting the way people in the crowd were staring at her, he said wryly, "You've caused quite a stir. I didn't recognize you at first."

Self-consciously, she touched the nape of her neck and the much shorter strands of her hair. "One of the patients at the nursing home wanted to cut my hair, and I thought she was just going to trim it. Everything just sort of got out of hand."

As unsure of herself as a sixteen-year-old who'd just appeared in public wearing lipstick for the first time, she couldn't quite look him in the eye. Why, she's shy! he realized, shocked, and found that incredibly appealing. "I think you look great," he said sincerely, trying to reassure her. "That hairstyle's perfect for you."

He would have said more, but they abruptly ran out of time when the town clock on the corner of the square struck seven and the crowd let out a cheer. All the booths opened, people surged through the narrow streets fronting the square, and the festival began.

His grin rueful, he raised his voice over the throng of

kids that suddenly rushed the booth, demanding water pistols. "Looks like it's time to get to work!"

"C'mon, Johnny, you can do it," Janey coaxed when Johnny Thompson, the son of one of her family's ranch hands, hesitated when it was his turn to try for a prize. "Don't be afraid. I'll show you."

Stepping out from behind the front counter of the booth, she found a box for the five-year-old to stand on, then guided the barrel of his water pistol at the paper bull's-eye at the far end of the booth. Her chin all but propped on his shoulder, she grinned and said softly in his ear, "All right, you're all set, tiger. Just squeeze the trigger, and I'll bet you can win a teddy bear."

Concentrating, his bottom lip caught between his teeth, he tried squeezing the trigger, but it was stiff, and he had little hands. Quickly moving to help him, Janey molded her hand around his, pulled the trigger and sent a stream of water shooting straight at the target.

"All right!" she cheered. "That kind of straight shooting deserves a teddy bear."

Handing him a stuffed bear that was nearly as big as he was, Janey couldn't remember the last time she'd had such a good time. The crowd waiting to get in on the game was a big one that had kept her and Reilly hustling all evening, and they'd hardly had time to exchange more than a few words, but she wouldn't have traded that time with him for anything. The booth was small and they kept brushing shoulders, but she'd laughed more tonight than she had in years. The night itself seemed to sparkle. She told herself she couldn't stop smiling because she was feeling good about herself and the spirit of Christmas was in the air, but she knew there was more to it than that.

And so did Reilly. Watching her with Johnny, he, too,

felt the magic in the air, but he knew the cause of it had nothing to do with Christmas and everything to do with Janey herself. She was the one who made people smile, the one who made them feel special, and he couldn't take his eyes off her. He liked her new look, but he'd liked her before. There was no pretension to her, and he didn't think she had a clue how special that made her. He liked her, dammit, as a person, as a woman, and that was tearing him apart.

He wasn't supposed to be enjoying himself this much so soon after Victoria's death, especially with another woman. But how could he not? He'd never known anyone quite like her. She had to be thirty-seven or thirty-eight, yet she was blooming right before his eyes. Watching her was fascinating. Over the course of the evening, her brothers and their wives, friends and extended family all came over to their booth to hug her and tell her how incredible she looked, and he couldn't think of a better person for it to happen to. She had to feel like Cinderella.

Given the chance, he could have stayed there all night with her, but the evening just seemed to fly by. All too soon the crowd began to thin and before he was ready for it, it was time to shut down everything and go home. Disappointed, he didn't want to let her go, but once they cleaned their booth, there was no longer any reason to prolong leaving.

"Come on," he said gruffly. "I'll walk you to your car. Where'd you park?"

"Behind Myrtle Henderson's antique store," she said, falling into step beside him. "And I was lucky to find that. The streets were so packed I thought I was going to have to park at the nursing home and walk over."

Her car was just where she'd left it and sat all alone in the dark behind Myrtle's shop. Taking her keys from her, he unlocked the driver's door for her and opened it for her, but he still couldn't bring himself to let her go. Before she could slip behind the wheel, he stopped her simply by catching her hand in his.

It was the wrong thing to do—he knew that the second his fingers closed around hers. Even in the darkness he saw the surprise in her eyes and felt the sparks that jumped between them whenever they got within touching distance. Suddenly, in spite of the coldness of the night, the air around them was hushed and intimate and warm with expectation.

A smart man would have released her immediately and stepped back to clear his head. Reilly couldn't bring himself to do that. Not yet. Not when her hand was in his and she was this close and so pretty in the starlight. He just needed a few more minutes with her, he told himself, and tightened his hand around hers. "I really had a good time tonight."

"Me, too," she said huskily. "I can't remember the festival ever being this much fun before. There was just something in the air…."

"I know," he murmured, moving closer with a single step. "It's still there. Feel it?"

Her eyes dark and fathomless and her fingers clinging to his, she stared up at him and nodded soundlessly, and any chance Reilly had of resisting the need she stirred in him was lost. With a quiet groan he pulled her closer and kissed her softly parted lips the way he'd been dying to for days.

Chapter 8

At the first touch of his mouth against hers, everything inside Janey went still—even her heart. Her thoughts reeling, she told herself she was dreaming. She had to be. This type of thing just didn't happen to her. Even in the privacy of her dreams, she didn't dare let herself imagine attracting a man like Reilly. He might enjoy talking to her, she told herself, but that was as far as it went. He would never actually be interested in her as a woman. Would he?

Then why is he kissing you, Janey?

Confused, her heart starting to slam against her ribs, she drew in the spicy scent of him, felt his mouth hot on hers and was forced to admit this was no dream. A sob rising in her throat, she could have given anything to melt into his arms and kiss him back with all her heart. *But she didn't know how!*

And that mortified her. She was thirty-seven years old, for God's sake! She'd only had two blind dates in her life, and both of those had ended with handshakes and sighs of relief all the way around that the evening had finally been over. She hadn't cared then that she hadn't known how to kiss those men—she hadn't liked them any more than they'd liked her.

But Reilly was different. She liked him. And there was something about him that stirred a longing in her soul that she'd never known before. A longing, she admitted with a hastily swallowed sob, that she didn't have a clue how to deal with.

And he had to know that.

Embarrassed, hurt that she felt so inept as a woman, she pulled back to look up at him with searching eyes. She knew she was feeding her own insecurities, but she couldn't help wondering if this new desire to kiss her had anything to do with her makeover. "Why did you do that?" she asked huskily.

His blood hot and his head not quite clear, he frowned. "Do what? Kiss you?"

When she nodded, Reilly would have thought the answer was obvious, but he was learning with Janey not to take anything for granted. Every time he thought he knew who she was, she surprised him. "I like you," he said with a shrug. "We had fun tonight, and I had a sudden urge to kiss you, so I did. Is that a problem? Because if it is, you'd better tell me now. Because I'd like to take you to dinner tomorrow night, and if I get another chance tonight, I thought I might kiss you again."

His tone was teasing, but Janey only had to see the gleam in his eye to know he meant every word. Her heart suddenly thundering, she threw up a quick hand against his chest when he would have reached for her again. "Wait!" she cried, panicking. "There's something I need to tell you."

She expected him to step back. He didn't. Instead he laid

his hand over hers on his chest with a tenderness that was almost her undoing. "So speak."

The rough timbre of his voice was like a slow, intimate caress across her nerve endings and sent a shiver of awareness rippling across her skin. Shaken, she tugged at her hand. "Please," she said faintly. "We need to talk, and I can't do that while you're touching me."

A more sophisticated woman would never have made such a remark and given herself away so easily, but Janey couldn't worry about that. Not when she was out of her league and couldn't fake experience she didn't have.

Something of her desperation must have gotten through to him. Studying her for a long moment in the faint light from the streetlight on the corner, he abruptly released her and frowned in concern. "What is it?"

How, she wondered wildly, was she going to tell him? Heat climbing in her cheeks, she turned away, searching for words, but they weren't easy to find. When she finally faced him again, she still wasn't sure what she was going to say until she opened her mouth.

"I'm not like other women you know," she said quietly. "I'm not like other women *I* know. I didn't date in high school or college. That's a part of adolescence that I missed out on. While other kids were going steady and learning how to kiss, I was staying home on Friday nights and reading. You need to know that before this goes any further."

Studying her, Reilly could see the admission wasn't easy for her to make. But it was what she *didn't* say that had him staring at her warily. "You said you didn't date in school. What about afterward?"

Lifting her chin, she met his searching gaze head-on. "I've had two blind dates since college. They were both disasters."

Stunned, Reilly didn't pretend to misunderstand what she

was saying. There'd never been anyone in her life. Ever. No boyfriends when she was in high school or college, no men when she returned to Liberty Hill and began working at the nursing home. She'd never had a boyfriend to teach her how to kiss or make out…or make love.

Dear God, she was a virgin!

Janey saw the shock he couldn't quite manage to hide, and if he'd only found a way to joke about the situation, everything might have been okay. It wasn't as if she didn't have a sense of humor about her condition. She knew there weren't many thirty-seven-year-old virgins walking around, but she certainly wasn't the last of the dinosaurs.

If his expression was anything to go by, though, Reilly didn't find the situation the least bit amusing. And Janey didn't have to have experience with a man to know why. If he was going to have a woman in his life, he had no use for a virgin. Which meant he had no use for her.

Up until then the evening had been the most magical of her life, but suddenly she had more doubts about herself than she could stand. Tears stung her eyes, and it was all she could do to keep her voice steady as she said quietly, "If you'd like to withdraw your invitation to dinner tomorrow night, I'll understand."

"I didn't say that!"

"You didn't have to." Keeping her head high and her tears at bay, she made a move to step past him. "It's late. I need to go home. Good night."

He didn't try to stop her, and Janey was thankful for that. Because if he'd said so much as a single word to her, she would have horrified them both by crying. And that was something she was determined not to do. So she slipped into her Jeep and never looked at him as she backed out of her parking space and turned her car toward home.

It wasn't until she'd left Reilly far behind that the tears began to fall.

Long after Janey drove away, Reilly stood in the darkness behind Myrtle Henderson's store and cursed himself for a jackass. To say that he'd handled the situation badly was the height of understatement. What the hell had he been thinking of? She was a virgin, dammit, not some kind of monster from outer space, which is how he'd treated her. No wonder she'd run for home. After this he'd be lucky if she ever spoke to him again.

Go after her, a voice urged in his head. *Talk to her and explain that she just caught you flat-footed.*

He should have. It was the right thing to do. Not only was he attracted to her, but they'd become good friends, and he needed to make her understand that his feelings for her weren't going to change just because she was a virgin. One had nothing to do with the other.

He knew that, accepted it…and couldn't have gone after her if his life had depended on it. Not when he was still reeling from the punch of an innocent kiss. She hadn't even known what she was doing and she'd still managed to turn him inside out. And that scared the hell out of him.

So instead of heading for the McBride ranch, he went home and settled in front of the fire with Victoria's picture, just as he had every night since she'd died. But tonight when he stared down into her laughing green eyes, she wasn't the one he saw. Instead it was Janey who pushed her way into his thoughts. If he lived to be a hundred, he didn't think he'd ever forget that moment when she'd realized he thought she was pretty. She'd looked like a young girl discovering her womanhood for the first time, and just watching her realize how attractive she was had been incredibly seductive.

He wasn't the only one who'd been fascinated by the change in her. He'd seen the way the local cowboys had eyed her tonight, and there wasn't a doubt in his mind that they were going to be coming after her the first chance they got. They'd rush her and probably scare her, and just the thought of anyone doing that to her infuriated him.

She was so special, dammit, and the first man in her life needed to be just as special. She needed someone who was patient and gentle, someone who would give her the time to discover her sensuality at her own pace, not his. Someone who wouldn't push her into giving more of herself than she wanted to give. Someone who would care about her and be willing to let her experiment and grow without trying to bind her to him with emotions. Because like all first boyfriends, he would eventually get left behind, and he had to know how to let her go.

None of the men he'd seen watching her tonight had had that kind of sensitivity. Rough and macho, they'd all been the caveman type, and just the thought of her getting mixed up with someone like that when she was so much more vulnerable than she realized sickened him. She could get hurt if she wasn't very, very careful.

So what's wrong with you? the voice in his head demanded in a rough growl. *Why can't* you *be her first boyfriend?*

Caught off guard by the question, he just sat there, stunned that he was actually considering the suggestion. Why not? he thought with a frown. He cared about her and had to admit that the idea appealed to him. After all, it wasn't as if there was any chance of him getting hurt. Victoria was the only woman he would ever love. And because of that, he could protect Janey and guide her, and then when she was ready to fly and leave her first boyfriend behind, he could let her go. And still remain friends with her. He hoped.

Just that easily the decision was made. Satisfied that he had everything worked out in his head, he put Victoria's picture back on the mantel and went to bed. Five minutes later he was asleep, but it wasn't Victoria he dreamed of. It was Janey and her beautiful shy smile as she'd first approached him earlier that evening and he hadn't recognized her. Only this time, in his dreams, she walked straight into his arms.

Tears streaming down her face, Janey didn't have a clue how she made it home without running off the road. She crossed over the centerline several times, but she had the road to herself, thankfully, and she could only assume her angels were watching out for her. If they'd been watching out for her just as diligently when Reilly came to town, her heart wouldn't be breaking now.

Swallowing a sob, she parked in her usual spot in the drive and told herself she wasn't going to think about him. Not after the way he had hurt her. If he let something like virginity scare him away, then he wasn't the man she thought he was and she didn't need or want him in her life.

That didn't, however, make the hurt any less. Pain squeezing her heart, she wiped at the tears that welled in her eyes and was relieved to see that the house was dark except for the light her mother had left on in the foyer for her. She knew Sara and Dan would both want to know all about the festival and everyone's reaction to her new look, but she didn't think she could bear it if she had to face them tonight. Tomorrow would be soon enough for that.

How she made her way upstairs without waking her mother or Dan she never knew. What little control she had over her emotions seemed to vanish as she climbed the stairs, and try though she might, she couldn't stop crying. By the time she reached her room, she was shaking with silent sobs, and with a muffled cry she threw herself on her bed and buried her face in her pillow. Within moments, it was soaked from her tears.

Later she couldn't have said how long she cried. It seemed like forever. Eventually she cried herself to sleep, but the release didn't help. An hour later she woke again. The second she remembered those moments in Reilly's arms and his face when she'd told him she was a virgin, the tears were back, more painful than before.

Considering everyone's reaction to her makeover, it should have been the happiest night of her life, but she'd never been more miserable. She must have slept some after that, but she couldn't be sure. It seemed like all she did was cry.

By the time the sun came up the next morning, her eyes were red and swollen, her throat scratchy from all the tears she'd shed. Groaning at the sight of herself in the mirror, all she wanted to do was hide away for the rest of the day, but she couldn't. Her mother would come looking for her if she didn't show up for breakfast, and she didn't want her to see her the way she was. So she washed her face with cold water and thanked God that Caroline had given her enough makeup yesterday to hide the dark circles under her eyes. Unfortunately the makeup couldn't cover up all the ravages from her marathon crying session, but it did help.

Dressed in jeans, boots and a turtleneck sweater, she faced herself one last time in the mirror and had to admit that she looked better than she'd expected. Oh, her eyes were still red, but if anyone noticed, she could always claim she'd caught a cold in her eyes. As long as she didn't cry, Dan and her mother would never suspect anything out of the ordinary had happened last night.

It should have been easy. She was all cried out; she didn't have a single tear left in her. Or so she thought until she went downstairs and found her mother and Dan sitting down to breakfast. They looked up and smiled at her with so much love and affection that something just seemed to twist in her heart.

"There you are," her mother said, pleased. "Just in time for breakfast. I hope you're hungry. I made pancakes for all of us."

"I was just telling your mother that I didn't even hear you come in last night," Dan said with a wink. "So how was the festival? Did you have a good time? I bet you had all the young bucks tripping over themselves to talk to you. Sit down and tell us all about it. You must have knocked Reilly out of his shoes."

She should have just laughed and joked about having to fight the men off with a stick, but the words stuck in her throat and she couldn't have laughed if her life had depended on it. To her mortification, tears welled in her eyes again, and try though she might, she couldn't blink them away.

"I'm sorry," she choked, turning hurriedly away. "I'm not hungry, after all."

Swallowing a sob, she bolted for the stairs and didn't see Dan's bewilderment as he looked helplessly at Sara. "What'd I say? You know I'd never do anything to hurt that girl. I love her."

"I know," she said, patting him reassuringly on the shoulder. "Janey knows that, too. She wasn't upset by what you said—it has to be something else. I'll go talk to her."

Her expression somber, Sara hurried up the stairs, unable to imagine what in the world was wrong. Out of all her children, Janey was the strongest, the one who could handle practically anything, which was why she was such a good nurse. That didn't mean she didn't have a soft side. She was kind and caring and protective, and when she lost a patient, she grieved deeply. But she didn't usually wear her heart on her sleeve. When she cried she did so in the privacy of her own room. The only time Sara remembered her crying in front of anyone was at Gus's funeral twenty years ago.

Something had to be horribly wrong for her to break down in front of Dan. Worried, Sara reached her room and knocked gently on the door. "Janey? May I come in, dear? I'd like to talk to you, if that's okay."

For a long moment her only answer was silence. Then just when she was about to turn away, Janey pulled open the door. Her face red from crying, she said huskily, "I'm sorry I'm not very good company."

"Don't you dare apologize," Sara scolded gently. "There's no law that says you have to be good company. Something's obviously upset you. I was hoping I could help."

The tears welled again at that, and there was nothing Janey could do to stop them. When she was a child, her mother had been there for her at every major crisis of her life, but this was a problem she couldn't help her with. No one could. "I wish you could," she said tearfully as she turned toward the wall of windows that overlooked the mountains to the west. "But this is something I have to work out myself."

"All right," Sara said quietly. "But sometimes it helps just to have someone to talk things over with. I'm here for you if you need me."

She hadn't thought she could tell her. She hadn't thought she could tell *anyone!* But as her mother turned to go, she blurted out, "Reilly kissed me last night after the festival."

Her gaze still fixed on the mountains in the distance, she

heard her mother shut the bedroom door behind her, then cross the room to join her. She, too, stared out the window at the snow-covered mountains in the distance. "So Reilly kissed you," she said as casually as if they were discussing the weather. "And that made you cry? Why? Didn't you want him to?"

"No. I mean, *yes!*" Not sure even now what she'd wanted, she struggled to find the words to explain. "It wasn't that I didn't want him to kiss me. I just didn't…I couldn't…I didn't know…"

"What, dear?" Sara pressed when she floundered. "Just say it."

"I've never had a boyfriend, Mom," she said tearfully. "There are a lot of things I haven't done before, and kissing's just one of them. Do you know how difficult it was for me to tell him that?"

Her heart aching for her, Sara could just imagine. "It's not anything to be ashamed of," she said gently. "If there was no boyfriend in your life, that was your choice. You could have had a man any time you wanted one."

Janey knew Sara was only trying to make her feel better, but it was impossible for her mother to understand what being in her shoes was like. Sara was beautiful, and like all beautiful women, she took it for granted that she only had to smile to get a man's attention.

It wasn't that easy when you weren't pretty, Janey wanted to tell her. You didn't even have the confidence to smile—because if you did, what would you do if no one noticed? So over the years, when friends were getting ready for New Year's Eve and Valentine's Day with the men in their lives and she'd sat home night after night, year after year, she'd never felt she'd had any choice at all.

"It wasn't that I was ashamed," she said huskily. "I

have nothing to be ashamed of. But I've always felt different, and last night only reinforced that. Reilly—"

When she hesitated, unable to go on, her mother jerked her gaze away from the mountains to frown at her in concern. "What about Reilly? What did he do when you told him the truth?"

"Nothing," she said thickly. "He just looked shocked. He'd already asked me out to dinner for tonight, but I knew he really didn't want to go. That's when I told him I wouldn't hold him to the invitation. Then I came home."

"And he didn't try to stop you?"

She shrugged. "I don't know if he did or not. I drove off and never looked back." For the first time in what seemed like days, the corner of her mouth twitched into a slight smile, but it faded quickly when she pictured again the look on Reilly's face when she'd told him she was a virgin. "I don't think he'll ever ask me out again, Mom. I'll be lucky if he even speaks to me."

There were, Sara knew, men who were only interested in sex and had no use for a virgin, but she didn't think Reilly Jones was one of them. From what she'd seen and heard about him, he respected women too much for that.

"I think you're underestimating him," she said. "Once he gets over the initial surprise, he'll come around. Just give him time. In the meantime, the worst thing you can do is lie around the house feeling sorry for yourself. Why don't you go get the Christmas tree today? That'll lift your spirits."

She really wasn't in the mood, but Janey had to agree that lying around the house all day would do nothing to improve her mood. She needed a distraction, and she couldn't think of a better one to keep her busy the entire day.

"Maybe I'll do that. I could use the exercise, and the

weather's good." Pleased, she pulled her mother into a fierce hug. "Thanks, Mom. You don't know what a help you've been."

"That's what I'm here for, sweetheart," she laughed, returning her hug. "Now get out of here before somebody calls you to go into work for them. While you're gone, Dan and I'll start stringing popcorn."

She didn't have to tell her twice. Giving her one last hug, Janey grabbed her jacket and keys and hurried out the door. "String a lot," she called back over her shoulder. "I'm going to get a monster of a tree!"

He woke up before dawn and lay there for what seemed like hours, feeling like a heel.

Lying flat on his back staring up at the log rafters above his bed, all he could think of was last night and Janey. It had taken incredible courage for her to bare her soul to him the way she had. She'd probably never told another man that in her life. And he hadn't said a word. It hadn't been his finest hour.

"Jackass!" he muttered.

Now that he'd had time to come to terms with the fact that she was a virgin, he was even more appalled by his own behavior. He should have said something, *anything*, but he hadn't. And in his silence she'd read an insult he'd never intended.

He had to talk to her, had to apologize. Today. Because if he didn't find a way to make this up to her, she might never speak to him again. He didn't know when she'd become so important to him, but he wouldn't, couldn't, lose her friendship.

Throwing off the covers, he grabbed the first clothes he could reach and dragged on a green-plaid flannel shirt and jeans, then stomped into his boots. It was still early, barely nine o'clock, but he didn't even give the time a thought as he strode out the door. If Janey and her mother were still eating breakfast in their pajamas, they'd just have to forgive him. He had to see Janey now!

The wheels of his BMW barely touching the pavement and the needle of the speedometer never dropping below seventy, he made it to the McBride homestead in record time. But even as he strode up to the front door, he knew he'd made a wasted trip. Janey's Jeep was nowhere in sight.

Where could she have gone so early on a Saturday morning? he wondered as he jabbed the doorbell. If her night had been anything like his, she probably hadn't slept much...

If she'd come home at all. She was upset. Maybe she just went off by herself instead.

He stiffened at the thought and muttered a sharp curse under his breath. No! She wouldn't have done that. She was too level-headed to take off by herself just because she'd gotten her feelings hurt. She wouldn't worry her family that way. There had to be another explanation.

But even as he reasoned that she'd probably just gone into town to the grocery store or something, worry knotted his gut as he impatiently rang the doorbell again. Dammit, where was everyone?

Just when he thought no one was home, Sara pulled open the door and made no attempt to hide her surprise at the sight of him. "Reilly! I wasn't expecting you this morning. Are you here to see Dan?"

"Actually, I wanted to talk to Janey," he replied. "But I noticed when I drove up that her Jeep was gone. She did come home last night, didn't she?"

He looked so worried that Sara couldn't help but feel sorry for him. He obviously wasn't feeling any better than Janey this morning, and that was probably no more than he deserved. He'd messed up. She had to give him credit, though. He was here to make amends, which was more than a lot of men would have done. Her smile kind, she nodded. "She would never do anything that stupid, Reilly. She did come home last night. I won't pretend she wasn't upset, but I'm sure you already know that."

"It was all my fault," he said miserably. "I acted like an idiot. That's why I have to see her. I need to apologize."

Sara agreed. The problem was, she wasn't sure Janey would. Hesitating, she studied him through narrowed eyes. "I'm not sure she wants to see you this morning, but I'm going to tell you where she is because the two of you need to make peace. There's one condition, though. Don't hurt her again. She's a wonderful person, and she doesn't deserve that."

"Trust me, I know that," he said huskily. "I don't want to lose her friendship."

There was no doubting his sincerity. Satisfied, Sara said, "She's gone to get our Christmas tree."

"At the lot in town?"

If Sara needed any proof that the man was a city boy, she just got it. Smiling, she said, "No. It's always been a family tradition to find one here on the ranch and cut it down. Before she left, Janey said something about going up to Wild Horse Canyon. Go on past the house and take the right fork when you come to a Y in the road. Wild Horse Canyon is ten miles past that.

"Don't worry, you can't miss it," she assured him when he frowned. "It's where the road ends. Oh, and Reilly," she said quickly when he started to turn away, "the keys are in my Explorer if you want to take it. You might not make it if you don't."

When she glanced pointedly at his BMW, which definitely hadn't been built for rough, rocky roads, he had to grin. "I'll do that. Thanks."

Within ten minutes of leaving the homestead behind, Reilly thanked his lucky stars that Sara had loaned him her truck. Otherwise, he would have already had to turn back. He'd never seen such a horrible road in his life. Rutted with deep chug holes and rocks that looked as big as boulders, it was little more than a rough track cut through the wilderness that made up the western section of the ranch.

And the higher he drove into the mountains, the rougher the terrain became. He couldn't, however, complain. Not when the scenery was so spectacular. According to the Explorer's odometer, he was only a few miles from the homestead, but if it hadn't been for the road itself, he could have easily thought he was a hundred miles or more from civilization. There were no power lines, no telephone poles, no chimneys or rooftops. Instead, spread out before him was the pristine beauty of snow-covered peaks glistening like jewels in the bright morning sunshine for as far as the eye could see.

When he'd first left the homestead behind, his only thought had been to find Janey as quickly as possible. He'd gripped the steering wheel until his knuckles had turned white and cursed the fact that the poor driving conditions forced him to reduce his speed to a crawl. But as he finally reached the Y in the road and took the right fork, as Sara had directed, the quiet solitude of his surroundings brought an unexpected peace to his soul.

His grip eased on the steering wheel, the tension in his shoulders lessened and he found himself looking for wildlife. He didn't have to look far. A deer, startled by the sound of the truck in the hushed quiet of the gradually thickening forest, bolted gracefully across the road a hundred yards in front of him, its white tale raised in alarm as it disappeared into the trees.

Instinctively slamming on the brakes, Reilly never knew how long he sat there in the middle of the road with a grin on his face. But it was when he spied an eagle gliding high on the thermals overhead that emotions he couldn't put a name to squeezed his heart. He felt as if he'd been set down in the middle of a national park, but this was actually where Janey had grown up. Incredible.

After the turnoff, the path grew steeper and narrower, twisting and turning as it wound its way back into the trees, and it soon became obvious that that particular trail was seldom used. Overgrown with underbrush and fallen tree limbs, there was only one set of tracks in the primitive, muddy roadway, and those belonged to Janey's Jeep.

Marveling that she would come all this way by herself for a Christmas tree, Reilly glanced down at the odometer and frowned. According to Sara's directions, he should have reached Wild Horse Canyon by now, but the trail continued on into the trees. Had he taken a wrong turn somehow and ended up on the wrong road? But Sara had only mentioned one road—the same one he was supposed to drive to the end of. The only problem was, where was the end of the road?

He came across it so fast that he almost overran the clearing where Janey had parked her Jeep. One second the trees were closing in on him, shrouding the road in shadows the sunlight could barely penetrate, and the next, the path ended in a clearing that seemed to be carved out of the very side of the canyon wall.

His heart pounding, he slammed on the brakes, then realized after a closer look that he hadn't been as near to the edge as he'd first thought. Relieved, he pulled over next to

Janey's Jeep and cut the engine. He'd made it. Now all he had to do was find Janey.

When Sara had told him where she'd gone, he'd thought finding her would be easy. After all, how difficult could it be? She was out in the middle of nowhere with a chainsaw. All he had to do was listen, and the sound of her saw would lead him straight to her.

But when he stepped out of the Explorer, there was no growl of a chainsaw to tip him off as to her location. Instead, silence swirled around him, surrounding him, and the only sound he heard was the low moan of the wind through the trees.

Dammit, where was she?

Chapter 9

Wild Horse Canyon was rough and dangerous and not the kind of place Janey usually went to alone. But it had always been one of her favorite parts of the ranch and the perfect place to find a Christmas tree. Hiking through the canyon, she drew in a deep breath of pine-scented air and lifted her face to the morning sky with a sigh of contentment. She would have to do something especially nice for her mother as a thank-you for suggesting she go look for the Christmas tree today. A hike through the mountains was just what she'd needed to clear her head and take her mind off Reilly.

Pain lanced her heart just at the thought of last night, but she quickly pushed aside the memory and reminded herself why she was there. She had to find a tree, a big one that would take hours to decorate so she'd have no time to think of anything else for the rest of the day. Climbing deeper into the canyon with her chainsaw at her side, she pushed on.

"JAN-EEEEY!"

Surrounded by ancient lodge pines in a place where eagles nested, Janey heard the whisper of the wind through the trees and lifted her head sharply, listening. For a moment she'd have sworn someone was calling her name. But when she held her breath and listened again, the only sound she heard was the sigh of the trees as the breeze swirled through them.

"You're losing it, Janey," she muttered to herself. "That's what happens when you spend half the night crying."

Shaking her head over her own imaginings, she stomped through the underbrush, creating enough noise to scare off a herd of elk, then had to laugh at her own paranoia. "There's nobody out here, silly, but you and the animals. Chill out!"

"Janey!"

This time the call was much clearer, and there was no question that she was no longer alone. Shocked, she nearly dropped her chainsaw. "Reilly? Is that you?"

"Keep talking," he yelled. "I'm coming!"

Her heart in her throat, she heard him crashing through the trees off to her right and called, "Over here. I'm just to the south of a dead pine that points straight up to the sky like a finger."

Even as she guided him to her, she wondered what the devil she was doing. She didn't want to see him, didn't want to talk to him. Not yet. Not when her emotions were still so shaky and just the sound of his voice made her heart pound crazily in her breast. She needed time to heal her bruised heart, time to let her pride come to her rescue so when she did face him again, he'd never know just how badly he'd hurt her.

But it was too late for that, and all too soon he broke through the underbrush practically right in front of her, and time ran out. She saw in a single, all-encompassing glance that he hadn't slept any better last night than she had. He looked tired and somehow wonderful at the same time. With a will of their own, her eyes roamed over his broad shoulders, his chiseled jaw, the deep-set dimples that framed his mouth when he smiled hesitantly, and her heart just seemed to turn over. All too easily she remembered the feel of his arms around her and the heat of his mouth on hers.

"Your mother told me where you were," he said huskily when she couldn't seem to find her voice. "I hope you don't mind. I needed to talk to you."

Why, she wanted to ask, *when you didn't have anything to say last night?*

Holding her tongue, she didn't say a word, but he heard her, nonetheless. "I hurt you last night," he said gruffly, "and that's the last thing I meant to do. You surprised me. And please understand," he added earnestly, "I'm not making excuses. I should have told you immediately that your virginity was not something you had to apologize for or ever make excuses for, because it changed nothing. But my mind went blank, and by the time I realized how much my silence must have hurt you, it was too late."

His eyes meeting hers unflinchingly, he took a step forward, and although his hand reached out to her, he made no attempt to touch her. "I'm sorry," he said sincerely. "You said last night that you're different from other women, and you are. But in the best way possible. Could you please forgive me and let us start over again? I want to be your friend."

It would have taken a heart of stone to refuse his entreaty, and Janey just couldn't be that cold. Not when she enjoyed his company as much as he seemed to enjoy hers.

Her smile hesitant, she held out her hand. "Apology accepted."

His eyes locked with hers as his fingers engulfed hers, and for just a second she felt the same spark she had last night when he'd pulled her into his arms and kissed her. Her blood warming under his touch, she couldn't have said how long they stood that way, hand in hand, not daring to so much as breathe. Then Reilly released her and all she felt was disappointment.

"I was going to ask you to go with me to Colorado Springs to do some Christmas shopping, but your mom said you were up here looking for a Christmas tree," he said, nodding at the small chainsaw she'd set on the ground beside her. "I never knew anyone who cut their own Christmas tree before."

"When you live on a ranch with thousands of trees on it, it seems kind of dumb to go buy one," she said with a grin. "Anyway, you can't find one as fresh on a lot as you can in the mountains."

"Hey, you don't have to convince me. I think it's great. Do you mind if I stick around and help you?"

He looked so eager that Janey couldn't have turned him down if she'd wanted to, which she didn't. Still, she hesitated. They'd cleared the air about her virginity, and he claimed it didn't change anything between them, but she didn't see how it couldn't. Especially after the way he'd kissed her last night. Did he mean that he no longer wanted to kiss her now that he knew she was a virgin?

"I'd love for you to stay and help," she said honestly, "but there's something else we need to discuss about last night—"

"If you're worried that I'm going to grab you again and kiss you," he said quietly, "you can relax. That's something we'll work up to."

Confused, she frowned. "Work up to? But I thought—"

"What?" he asked with a slight smile when she hesitated. "That I wouldn't want to kiss you again because you're a virgin? I told you—*that* doesn't change anything. Except next time you'll know it's coming."

Janey knew she shouldn't have asked, but the word just popped out. "How?"

For an answer he leaned over and kissed her on the cheek. "One," he counted huskily. "When we get to ten, I'll kiss you again the way I did last night—and teach you how to kiss me back."

Her heart thudding crazily, Janey looked up at him with wide, searching eyes and tried to convince herself that he was just amusing himself. His heart still belonged to his dead wife and probably always would. If she wanted to avoid a lot of heartache in the future, she'd be wise to tell him to keep his kisses to himself.

For a second she almost did. The words were right there on her tongue, but she couldn't say them. Not when the wonder of last night's kiss was still so fresh in her mind. Right or wrong she wanted him to kiss her again, to hold her again, to show her for the first time in her life what love songs were really about. And if, in the end, she got hurt, she was willing to bet the heartache would be worth it. Because until he'd come into her life, she hadn't really been living. Now she was, and she loved it.

"Then if we're ever going to get to ten, I guess we'll have to spend a lot of time together," she said with a shy smile. "So you'll still stay and help me find a tree?"

For an answer he picked up the chainsaw. "Lead the way. This is your neck of the woods, not mine."

After that, the morning took on a glow that Janey couldn't begin to describe. The sun was brighter, the sky bluer, the cold snap of the mountain air crisper. She couldn't seem to stop smiling, and neither could Reilly. As they traipsed through the woods in companionable silence, she would glance over and find him watching her with a smile on his face that warmed her all the way to her toes. It was wonderful, scary, exhilarating.

They came across a dozen or more trees they could have chosen as a Christmas tree, but for one reason or another they always found a reason to pass them by. Arguing good-naturedly, they concluded that the trees were either too tall or too short or didn't have strong enough limbs to carry all the decorations the McBrides had collected over a lifetime.

Janey had had the very same discussion with her mother every Christmas for most of her life, but picking out a tree with Reilly was somehow different. He made her laugh…and made her want the day to last forever. It couldn't, of course, and all too soon they came across a noble fir they couldn't walk away from. Tall and stately and thick with branches that were just the right size, it was perfect.

Janey took one look at it and knew their search was over. "That's it," she said, stopping in her tracks.

Reilly had to agree. It was the kind of tree that belonged on a Christmas card. Holding the chainsaw, he lifted a masculine brow at her. "Do you want to do the honors or shall I?"

"I'll cut," she replied, mischief dancing in her eyes as she took the saw from him. "You get to carry it."

"No problem," he said, chuckling. "As long as you point me in the direction of the car. I haven't got a clue where we are."

Janey could well understand that. If she hadn't grown up there and wandered over every inch of the ranch as a child,

she would have been turned around, too. After a while all
the trees and canyons started to look alike.

"The cars are about a mile due south of here," she said
with a grin. Struck by a sudden thought, she cocked her
head and lifted a delicately arched brow at him. "How'd
you get up here, anyway? You didn't—"

"Drive my BMW over that path you call a road?" he
finished for her when she looked horrified. "No, thank
God. I planned to, once your mother told me where you
were, but she was kind enough to offer me her Explorer.
Remind me to send her some flowers. I owe her."

He wasn't the only one. Janey planned to give her a hug
and a kiss herself for sending Reilly after her. "I'll do
that," she promised. "But first we've got to get this baby
home."

It wasn't easy. The ground was too rocky and the forest
too thick with trees for Janey to drive her Jeep farther into
the canyon, so they had to carry it out by hand. By the
time they huffed and puffed and carried it back to the car,
they were both winded—and grinning like idiots.

Exhilarated, Janey fairly danced with glee as they loaded
it onto the top of her Jeep and tied it down. "All right! We
did it! There were a couple of times there when I thought
we were going to have to leave it behind."

Still trying to catch his breath, Reilly gasped, "Was that
before or after we stopped for the tenth time?"

"After," she laughed. "Are you okay?"

Caught in the warmth of her smile, he couldn't think of
the last time he had been so all right. Tomorrow he would
probably be as sore as an old bear with a thorn in its paw,
but given the chance, he would have done it all over again
in a heartbeat if it meant he could spend this time with
Janey.

He'd thought he lost her. After the blunder he'd made

last night, he'd thought any chance he had of having a relationship with her was irreparably harmed. He should have known better, he realized now with a sigh of relief. Time and again he'd seen what a kind heart she had. She wasn't the type to hold a grudge.

Staring down at her, an emotion he couldn't put a name to squeezing the spot where his heart had once been, he wanted to reach for her, to wrap his arms around her and hold her close, to kiss her the way he had last night and lose himself in the sweetness of her. But he couldn't. He'd made her a promise, and he had every intention of sticking to it.

That didn't, however, mean he had to deny himself completely. Giving in to temptation, he leaned down and kissed her on the cheek. "Two," he murmured, and had the satisfaction of watching her brown eyes grow large with surprise.

Her breath catching in her throat, Janey put her hand to her cheek before she could stop herself, and captured the tingling heat of his kiss against her palm. "What was that for?"

"Nothing," he replied, smiling. "I just wanted to kiss you again. Is that okay?"

She should have said no. Now that she'd had a little time to think about it, she realized that she couldn't possibly let him continue to kiss her whenever the mood struck him, even if it was only on the cheek. Because ten kisses on the cheek would lead to a very heated one on the mouth, and just thinking about that made her heart turn over in her breast. She was too vulnerable where he was concerned, she told herself, and for her own peace of mind, she needed to slow things down between them before she did something stupid—like start to think that she could make him forget his dead wife.

But even as she recognized the wisdom of that, she looked into his beautiful dark-blue eyes and couldn't bring herself to lie and say she didn't want him to kiss her. That was exactly what she wanted and she couldn't pretend otherwise.

Color singeing her cheeks, she nodded. "I'm just not used to men doing that. No one ever has."

"Then they were all idiots," he said simply, and opened her car door for her so they could drive back to the homestead.

He meant it, Janey thought as she carefully turned around and headed back to the house. He really thought all the men who'd never thought to kiss her on the cheek were idiots. Grinning, she smiled all the way home.

"If you'll hold the door for me, I'll get this monster inside for you," Reilly said as they reached the house and he joined her on the drive and began to help her untie the ropes they'd used to secure the tree to the roof of her Jeep. "Where's your Christmas tree stand? I'll help you set it up."

He'd already gone beyond the call of duty by hunting her down in the canyon and helping her carry the tree back to the car. She shouldn't have taken further advantage of him. But instead of thanking him for his offer and politely sending him on his way as she should have, she said, "Would you like to stay and help me decorate it? Mom and Dan have been stringing popcorn while I was gone and have probably eaten half the popcorn. Mom loves to cook while I put the tree up. We put Christmas music on the stereo and build a fire in the fireplace, then spend the rest of the afternoon trimming the tree.

"You don't have to stay until we finish, of course," she added hastily. "That'll take hours. In fact, if you only want

to stay for a little while, that's okay, too. I'm sure you must
have things to do. Oh, I forgot! You were going Christmas
shopping in Colorado Springs, weren't you? Forget I said
anything—''

Fascinated by the way she tried to find excuses for him
not to stay, Reilly couldn't help but grin. Did she have any
idea just how cute she was? She was so earnest, so flustered, like a teenager asking a boy over to her house for
the first time and tripping over every other word because
she was afraid he'd say yes only because he somehow felt
obligated.

''Hey,'' he chuckled, stopping her rambling simply by
pressing his fingers gently against her mouth. ''Will you
stop?''

He'd meant to tease her, to lighten her obvious nervous-
ness with a joke that would ease the tension, but the second
his fingers settled against her mouth, he knew he'd made a
mistake. With no effort whatsoever, he could feel again the
softness of her lips under his when he'd kissed her last
night.

It'd just been one little kiss, he tried to tell himself as
he swallowed a groan. It shouldn't have been the stuff of
fantasies. But even as he tried to shrug off the memory,
deep inside his chest, he felt his heart skip a beat. Not that
that was anything to worry about, he assured himself
quickly. He wasn't made of stone—he expected his body
to react to her. But he knew how to keep his emotions under
control. Nothing was going to get out of hand as long as
he kept his head, which he had every intention of doing.

Reminding himself to take it slow and easy, he forced
himself to drop his hand and grinned crookedly. ''I *want*
to stay, Janey.''

''Oh. Well, then…good!'' Blushing, she couldn't quite

hide how pleased she was. "Then let's get started. I'll get the tree stand."

Long after Sara had sent Reilly after Janey, she couldn't help wondering if she'd made a mistake. She should have called Janey on her cell phone first and asked her if she wanted to see him before she'd told him where she was. But reception in Wild Horse Canyon wasn't always clear, and it had just seemed the right thing to do.

But over two hours had passed since Reilly had left, and there'd been no word from either him or Janey. Worried, Sara wanted to kick herself for interfering. She should have minded her own business.

"She's okay," Dan said gruffly, not taking his eyes from the popcorn he was still stringing. "Quit worrying."

Startled out of her musings, Sara jumped guiltily. "How did you know?"

"I've only known you, what? Thirty-five or forty years?" he said dryly. "I think I know by now when you're worried about one of the kids."

"It's not that I'm worried," she fibbed. "Well, maybe a little. I just want Janey to be happy—"

Whatever she was going to say next was lost when the front door was suddenly thrown back on its hinges and Reilly struggled inside with the heavy end of a huge Christmas tree. "Merry Christmas, everyone. Where would you like this, Sara?"

"In the corner by the fireplace," Janey answered for her with a grin from the opposite end of the tree as she trailed in after Reilly. "That's where we always put it."

She was practically beaming, the sparkle in her eyes giving her the kind of beauty that had nothing to do with makeup or the cut of her hair. Her heart expanding with

love, Sara sighed in relief. "There you two are! I was starting to worry."

"We had a little trouble getting the tree back to the car,"
Janey explained. "It's huge! But I guess you can see that,"
she quipped as they struggled to set it upright on its stand.
"Reilly's going to stay and help us decorate."

"Good," Dan retorted, eyeing the huge fir with a skep-
tical lift of a bushy, gray brow. "We're going to need more
popcorn."

"I'll help you with that," Sara quickly assured him.
"We'll let Sara and Reilly take care of the actual decorating. We're too old for that, anyway."

Caught off guard, Dan sputtered, "Old? Who are you
calling *old?* I'm not! And I know you're—"

Rolling her eyes, Sara sent him a hard look that would
have stopped a Mack truck in its tracks. Frowning, Dan
scowled right back at her...then suddenly got it. "*Oh!*
Well, yes, of course," he backpedaled, grinning. "I'm not
supposed to be doing much, and Sara's not as spry as she
used to be. Just the other evening she was complaining that
she just can't get around like she once did. Her bones creak,
and her energy's gone by two in the afternoon if she doesn't
take a nap—"

"I'm sure they get the picture, Dan," she said dryly.
"You don't have to go on."

"Oh, I don't mind," he insisted, mischief dancing in his
eyes. "They should know what's down the road for them.
After all, none of us is going to get out of here alive. If
they live long enough, they're going to have to deal with
liver spots and cataracts and gas—"

"I don't have liver spots! Or gas!"

His lips twitching, it was all he could do to keep a
straight face as he arched a brow at Janey. "You know
that's why they call us old farts, don't you?"

"Dan!"

Chuckling, more than content with the reaction he'd gotten, he returned his attention to his popcorn stringing and said to himself, but loud enough for everyone else to hear, "Some people think we talk too much, too, though, I don't see it myself. It's a free country. Everyone has the right to express themselves."

Barely resisting the urge to laugh, Sara wanted to kill him for nearly giving her away, but she needn't have worried that Janey had caught on to the fact that she was throwing her and Reilly together. She was so happy that Reilly was staying that she didn't know if she was up or down and wouldn't have noticed if the Pope himself had walked into the room.

"I got the decorations out while you were gone, dear," she told her, "so you and Reilly can get started whenever you like. While you're doing that, I'll make some snacks. You both must be hungry after lugging that tree around."

Leaving the tree to them, she bustled into the kitchen, and within minutes, mouthwatering scents were filling the house. Cheese dip, chili, nachos, and Mexican hot chocolate with cinnamon. Helping Reilly separate the dozens of strings of twinkle lights it would take to light the huge tree, Janey grinned as Reilly sniffed the air in appreciation. "I told you Mom loves to cook while I put up the tree. If you don't like Mexican food, don't worry. Before the afternoon's over with, she'll make pizza and hot wings and God knows what else."

"You might want to pace yourself," Dan added with a knowing smile, "or you're going to be absolutely miserable by the end of the day."

They weren't, Reilly soon discovered, kidding. Ten minutes later Sara hustled into the family room with a tray loaded with chips and dips and nachos spiced to set your hair on fire, and it was all delicious. Enjoying himself, he filled up. Thirty minutes later, just as Janey and Dan had warned him, Sara went back to the kitchen and returned with meatballs in a marinara sauce that was, hands down, the best he'd ever tasted.

"These are fantastic!" he told her, reaching for another in spite of the fact that he wasn't the least bit hungry. "You couldn't have just cooked these."

"They were in the freezer," she admitted with twinkling eyes. "I like to keep things cooked up. You never know when you're going to need them."

Just the thought of what else she might pull from her freezer had him groaning and throwing his hands up in defeat. "No more. Please. I'll be so full I won't be able to help Janey with the tree."

In the process of stringing lights through the thick branches on the back side of the tree, Janey stuck her head around to tease, "It's so nice of you to remember what the objective of this exercise is. I could use another pair of hands."

Chuckling, he went to help.

Satisfied that she'd fed them all well, at least for the moment, Sara took the easy chair next to Dan by the fire and settled down to help him string popcorn and oversee the decorating. "You really did get a beautiful tree, dear," she told Janey. "We haven't had one that big in years."

"Not since Joe dragged that Douglas fir home when he was in high school," she said, grinning. "That was the ugliest tree I've ever seen in my life."

"Just because it was a little dry—"

"*Dry?*" she scoffed. "C'mon, Mom, it was dead and you know it. The needles were turning brown."

"Which was why she spray painted it green one night

while everyone was asleep,'' Sara confided to Reilly, chuckling. ''She thought it was just awful.''

Enjoying the reminiscing, Reilly could just see Janey sneaking down the stairs in her nightgown in the middle of the night with a can of spray paint. ''Why didn't you just go get another tree if that one was so bad?'' he asked Janey, grinning broadly. ''You certainly had plenty to choose from.''

''It was Joe's year to pick the tree,'' she said simply. ''You can bet when it was my year to pick, I didn't get a dead one.''

''No,'' her mother agreed, biting her lip to keep from laughing. ''It just had a crooked trunk and kept falling over. Every time I turned around, I was buying lights for it, because the old ones kept breaking when it fell.''

Left with no choice, she had to agree that her tree hadn't exactly been perfect, either. ''Okay, so it had a little problem with balance,'' she admitted. ''But once we figured that out and put a rock under the tree stand on one side, it was fine.''

''As fine as Joe's was once it was painted,'' her mother agreed sagely.

Brown eyes met blue, and Janey and Sara both had to laugh.

''Sounds like a draw to me,'' Dan decided. ''How about you, Reilly? What do you think?''

Caught off guard, he blinked. ''What? You want to drag me into this? Oh, no, you don't! I'm no dummy. I know better than to get involved in a discussion between mother and daughter. I plead the Fifth.''

''A wise man,'' Sara chuckled. ''Now that we've got that settled, how about some brownies? I'm hungry.''

For an answer, everybody groaned.

* * *

They spent the rest of the afternoon laughing and eating and decorating the tree with ornaments that had been in the family as long as anyone could remember. After dozens of strings of lights were strung through the tree, setting it aglow, a long rope of brightly colored glass beads was draped from limb to limb like a necklace gracefully adorning a woman's neck. Bulbs and old-fashioned ornaments were added, and with them, stories were told about the family and Christmases past and days that were long gone.

Listening to the history of the McBrides, Reilly couldn't help but be entranced. In many ways Janey's family was much like his. She was close to him in age, and her childhood, with all its hopes and dreams, hadn't been all that different from his despite the fact that she'd grown up on a ranch and he'd been very much a California kid of the sixties.

The resemblance ended there, however.

He was first-generation Californian—his parents had been born and raised in Illinois, and their parents before them in states even farther east. So he didn't have the kind of family traditions that came from living and dying and working the same piece of ground year in and year out, generation after generation. And he envied Janey that. Her family history was all around her, her ancestors as familiar to her as if she'd actually grown up with them. She not only knew where she and generations before her had been born, she only had to walk through the small cemetery east of the homestead to know where she and the rest of her family would one day be buried.

In today's world, where no one seemed to put down roots anymore because they were too busy moving around the country in search of the almighty dollar, he found that— and Janey—incredibly fascinating.

Watch it, the voice of reason cautioned in his head.

Don't get too taken with the lady. You're only her first boyfriend. Remember? You're just helping her get her feet wet so she won't be afraid of the water, then you're history. If you allow yourself to forget that, you're the one who's going to be in over your head. Then who's going to get hurt?

A smart man might have listened to that and taken it under advisement, but he wasn't worried. He still loved Victoria. How could he get hurt?

So when they finished the tree just as dinnertime rolled around and Janey invited him to stay to eat one more meal, it seemed a shame to end the evening. He stayed and thoroughly enjoyed himself. Then somehow, before he knew it, it was going on ten o'clock at night, Janey was walking him to his car, and he didn't know where the day had gone.

"You don't have to walk me out," he said when she slipped on a jacket and stepped outside with him. "It's too cold."

"I don't mind," she said huskily, huddling in her wool jacket as they reached his car. "And I wanted to thank you for all your help today. I had a wonderful time."

Her eyes shining in the muted glow from the porch light, she looked up at him with the sweetest smile on her face and had no idea what kind of alarm bells she set off inside him. He should have heeded the warning, but he couldn't hear anything but the rush of his blood in his veins. With a will of their own, his eyes dropped to the innocently provocative curve of her mouth, and need kicked him hard in the gut. Swallowing a groan, he just barely resisted the need to haul her into his arms.

Right then and there he should have thanked her for the day, gotten in his car and driven away. But before he could stop himself, he murmured, "So did I." It seemed the most natural thing in the world to lean down and once again kiss her on the cheek. "Three." It was only then, when he felt the softness of her cheek under his lips and saw the happiness shining in her eyes, that he realized he'd been waiting hours for just that moment.

Janey had, too, and she hadn't had a clue. Feeling slightly dizzy with anticipation, an ache she couldn't understand squeezing her heart, she looked up into the dark depths of his midnight-blue eyes and wanted so much more than a kiss on the cheek from him. How, she wondered, had he done this to her so easily, when she didn't even know what to expect next? And when were they finally going to reach ten?

There was a lot to be said for putting a sparkle in a woman's eye, Dan decided as, in spite of her objections that he needed to rest, he moved to help Sara collect the dirty glasses and dessert plates from the coffee table. He'd watched Reilly flirt and tease with Janey all day, and he didn't doubt that right that very moment he was kissing her good-night. And Dan envied him that. It had been too long since he'd kissed a woman he loved good-night. And that was years ago, when he still had Peggy. He'd never kissed Sara, though he'd wanted to for years. Maybe it was time he did something about that. Making a snap decision, he stepped in front of Sara and took the tray of dirty dishes from her.

Focusing on what she was doing, she automatically reached for the tray again. "You shouldn't be carrying that. Reilly said you're supposed to rest at least another week before you even think about doing anything physical—"

That was as far as she got. A split second later he reached for her and had the satisfaction of watching her blue eyes widen in surprise. Before she could do anything but gasp, he kissed her full on the mouth.

Shocked, Sara felt the ground tilt beneath her feet and

instinctively clung to him, her thoughts in a whirl. He'd lost his mind, she thought as her senses began to blur. Being out of bed for the first full day, helping string the popcorn and visiting with Reilly, it all must have been harder on him than she'd anticipated. He was exhausted and didn't know what he was doing. That was, she decided, the only reasonable explanation. After all, they were just friends.

But when he finally let her up for air, the emotions rushing through Sara had nothing to do with friendship. Her heart was pounding, her knees were weak, and she couldn't seem to think clearly. Still caught close in his arms, she looked up at him in confusion. "What are you doing?"

"Reilly isn't the only one taken with a McBride woman," he growled. "Why are you so surprised? I told you that years ago."

It was true—he had asked her out several years after Peggy had died, but Sara hadn't really taken him seriously. How could she? He was one of her best friends, for heaven's sake!

"I thought you were just going through a lonely spell. You only asked that once, so I assumed you just did it on a whim and lost interest when you came to your senses."

"That won't happen until the day they put me in the ground," he assured her gruffly, and kissed her again.

Her head spinning, she should have stopped him. This was all happening too fast. She had to have some time to herself to think, which she couldn't seem to do when he was kissing her. Then she heard Janey at the front door.

Later, she never remembered moving, but between one heartbeat and the next, she pulled free of Dan's arms and put half the distance of the room between them. By the time Janey stepped into the family room, she'd turned to quickly start picking up dirty glasses again.

"Oh, there you are, dear," she said, flustered, and didn't

notice Janey's cheeks were as pink as hers. "I was just telling Dan that it's been a long day, and he shouldn't overdo it."

"She's right, Dan," Janey told him when he moved to pick up the tray of dirty dishes on the coffee table. "I'll help Mom with that. Why don't you go to bed? You do look a little flushed."

Swallowing a silent groan, Sara didn't dare look at Dan when he hesitated. If he said anything...

"Maybe you're right," he finally told Janey gruffly. "I guess I tried to do too much too soon. I never did know how to take things slow. I'll try not to make that mistake again."

Not misunderstanding his veiled message, Sara released a long, soundless breath she hadn't even realized she was holding. It was going to be all right. Janey didn't seem to have a clue what he was talking about, and he was all but openly assuring her that she didn't have to worry about him kissing her again. She should have been pleased. They could go back to being just friends and forget that any of this had ever happened.

But even as she assured herself that was what she wanted, she couldn't help but remember how long it had been since she'd been in the arms of a man she cared about. She'd forgotten how wonderful it could be.

Chapter 10

The minister had a packed house and was in his element. Outside, it was cold and wet and miserable, but the spirit of Christmas filled the church, and when the congregation raised its voice in song, it sounded like the angels themselves had descended from Heaven to praise the Lord.

Seated next to her mother on one side and Zeke, Lizzie, and Cassie on the other, Janey couldn't stop smiling. She told herself it was because it was Christmas and this year, as always, she had a lot to be thankful for. Everyone was well and happy, and when Merry had her baby sometime within the next few weeks, there would be another baby in the family to love. Work was going well, and she was feeling good about herself. Those things alone were enough to make anyone happy.

But even as she closed her eyes to thank God for her blessings, she couldn't stop herself from peeking across the aisle to where Reilly sat directly across from her. She hadn't expected to see him at all today, but there he was, his dark-blond head bowed in prayer, looking wonderful in a navy suit that did wonderful things for his eyes. He appeared to be listening attentively to the minister's every word, but Janey knew he was as aware of her as she was of him. From the moment he'd slipped into the pew and realized she was seated across from him, he'd been sneaking as many peeks at her as she had at him. And every time their eyes met, they both smiled.

This time was no different. As soon as the prayer was over, Reilly lifted his head and glanced over at her, and just that easily, they were both grinning at each other like a couple of toddlers playing peekaboo.

After that, the rest of the service passed in something of a haze. Janey stood when she was supposed to and sang the hymns that were as familiar to her as the sound of her mother's voice, and every time the minister said, "Let us pray," she closed her eyes obediently. But if anyone had asked her what the sermon was about, she couldn't for the life of her have said.

After the service Janey wasn't surprised when Reilly stepped across the aisle. "Hello," he said huskily. "It's a beautiful morning, isn't it?"

He spoke to everyone, but it was Janey his eyes lingered on. Her heart thumping pleasantly, she said with a smile, "Actually, it's sleeting outside."

"Then I guess we should all get going before the roads get nastier," he said. "Be careful on the way home."

And before she could guess his intentions, he leaned over and kissed her gently on the cheek, right there before God and her family and half the congregation of the Liberty Hill Methodist Church.

Her heart turning over in her breast, Janey heard him softly whisper, "Four," and almost moaned at the feel of his warm, moist breath in her ear. Surprised by the kiss, her brothers glanced back and forth between the two of them with a frown, but she never noticed anyone but Reilly. He was right, she thought, feeling like she was walking on air as she and the rest of her family followed him outside into the cold, icy drizzle. It was a beautiful day.

"Did you hear about the kiss? Everybody's talking about it."

"She's walked around with a smile on her face all day. Isn't it wonderful to be in love?"

Sighing dreamily, Margaret Lester said, "I remember when Otto courted me. I couldn't stop smiling, either. That was the best summer of my life."

"I have to admit, I had my doubts at first," Abby Hart confided as the Busybodies and Lester sisters gathered in the solarium Monday afternoon to discuss the latest course of events concerning Janey's romance. "Dr. Jones seemed so unhappy. I thought he was still in love with his dead wife."

Caroline Saunders nodded her white head. "So did I. But he certainly seems happier now. I saw him in the hall a few minutes ago, and he was actually whistling!"

"That's because he's expecting to see Janey—"

Striding into the solarium for her afternoon break just in time to catch her name on the lips of the octogenarians gathered around the table in the far corner, she arched a teasing brow at them when they jumped guiltily. "All right, what's going on? I heard you guys talking about me. What'd I do?"

"Nothing!"

"We were just talking about...about..."

"About the jitterbug and how it's making a comeback," Rebecca Flowers said hurriedly when Margaret drew a blank. "And we were wondering if you knew how to dance."

"The jitterbug?" Janey asked, and had to laugh at the very idea. "Lord, no! I was never very good at dancing. I guess I don't have any rhythm."

"Then today's your lucky day," Abby said, beaming. "Henry was just saying it's been ages since he's danced. He can teach you."

Henry Perkins looked as shocked as Janey, but he quickly recovered and winked at her. "I promise not to step on your feet."

"It's not *my* feet I'm worried about," she said with a chuckle. "I appreciate the offer, Henry, but—"

"But you don't think you can do it," he finished for her, his green eyes twinkling merrily. "Give me five minutes, and I promise I'll change your mind."

She shouldn't have agreed. She really did have two left feet and had always felt less than graceful whenever she was forced to dance at weddings and special occasions. But Henry was one of her favorites, and she hated to disappoint him. "All right," she sighed, giving in. "Five minutes. Don't say I didn't warn you."

Pleased, Henry didn't give her time to change her mind. Quickly pushing tables and chairs out of the way, he cleared an open spot for a dance floor, then hurried over to the portable stereo set up against the far wall and flipped through the old albums stacked there. Before Janey had time to get nervous, the catchy beat of an old familiar big-band song was blaring from the speakers.

"We're going to start with two steps," Henry told her and demonstrated them for her. "Just listen to the beat and let me guide you. Ready?"

She wasn't, but he didn't give her time to object. Grinning, he took her hand in his, placed the other one on his narrow shoulder and, with no warning, swung her into the music.

Her head spinning, Janey gasped and tried to concentrate on the simple steps he'd showed her. One—two. One—two. But she'd barely got them down pat when he suddenly raised his arm and twirled her like a ballerina.

"Oh!"

Winking at her, he pulled her back to him and immediately fell back into the first two steps he'd taught her. With a will of their own, Janey's feet followed suit, and just that easily she was dancing a simple version of the jitterbug. She couldn't have been more stunned if she'd suddenly found herself in-line skating through the middle of town.

"My God, I'm dancing!" she laughed, amazed. "How did you do that?"

"I told you," he said, grinning broadly. "You start with two steps. Once you've got that down, you throw in a few twirls, a little imagination, and you're jitterbugging. Hang on, gal. Here we go."

Laughing, she did as he said and hung on.

Reilly heard the music long before he knew where it was coming from. It drifted down the hall like the lilting melody of a Pied Piper, calling to all who would listen, sparking memories and smiles with its infectious beat. Already on his way toward the solarium in search of Janey, Reilly had to smile as a dozen or more of the nursing home's ambulatory patients headed down the corridor in the same direction. There was just something about that music that was impossible to ignore.

Someone was obviously celebrating something, he decided as laughter and applause burst from the solarium. It was probably somebody's hundredth birthday, and Janey had organized a party for them. Knowing her, she'd probably paid for a cake and refreshments herself—that was just the kind of thing she'd do. He'd just stop in for a few minutes and join the fun.

Stepping across the threshold into the large recreational room, he expected to find her passing slices of cake around and pouring punch. Instead, she was in the spindly arms of a man old enough to be her grandfather and laughing in delight as he twirled her to the hot swing of Benny Goodman.

Stunned, Reilly stopped in his tracks, a broad smile slowly spreading across his face. This was a side of Janey he hadn't seen before. And he had to admit, he liked it. Her brown eyes sparkling like diamonds, she was in her element and having the time of her life. Enjoying himself immensely, Reilly could have stood right where he was the rest of the afternoon and just watched her dance.

Her partner, however, seemed to be running out of gas. Eighty if he was a day, his energy had started to fade, though he was trying his best to keep going. Slightly winded, he gave the dance everything he had, but he was already a step behind the beat. Giving in to impulse, Reilly stepped forward to cut in just as Janey began to twirl.

Between one heartbeat and the next, he'd taken over for the old man, and he did it so smoothly that Janey didn't know the switch had been made until she finished her twirl and found herself face-to-face with him. "Reilly! How—"

"Your partner looked as if he could use a rest," he said with a grin. "Do you mind?"

"No, of course not."

"Good," he chuckled, and sent her spinning away from him, then back toward him with a lift of his hand.

Later, neither of them could have said how long the song lasted. Reilly grinned down into Janey's smiling face and time ceased to exist. There were just the two of them and the energetic, contagious beat of the music. Their feet moving, hearts pumping and breath tearing through their lungs, they weren't Fred and Ginger, but they didn't care. The song built to a crescendo and ended with a blare of horns. Reilly gave her one last twirl, and they collapsed in each other's arms, laughing breathlessly.

Their elderly audience clapped wildly, and to the delight of everyone there, Reilly leaned down and brushed a lingering kiss to Janey's cheek. "Five," he murmured in a low voice that only she could hear. Just that easily he sent her heart tripping into double time.

Happier than she could ever remember being, she wanted to tell him just how much he had changed her life, but there was no time for any private conversation. The patients surged up to them then, surrounding them, eager to talk about the dance and the past and the days when they themselves had stayed out dancing every Saturday night until the wee hours of the morning. And before she knew it, Reilly had to slip away to return to his rounds.

How she worked after that, Janey never knew. Reilly came across her thoughts at the most unexpected times, and with no effort whatsoever she found herself recalling every moment she'd had with him. Their trek through Wild Horse Canyon, the fresh, clean scent of his cologne, the pine needles that got caught in his hair, decorating the Christmas tree. But most of all she remembered the way he made her feel when he held her in his arms. As if sunshine sparkled in her veins. It was wonderful, exhilarating, intoxicating.

Life had turned into one surprise after another, and it was all because of Reilly. The very fact that he was in her life at all was a surprise, but it was more than that. *He* was the surprise. Who would have thought he was the type of man to count kisses? Or jitterbug in the middle of the afternoon in front of half the nursing home? She never knew what to expect from him next, and she loved it.

Because she was falling in love with him.

And that terrified her. She could be walking right into heartache, and there didn't seem to be anything she could do about it. She told herself not to take him seriously, that he was still in love with his dead wife and she was going to get hurt if she wasn't careful, but it was already too late for that. She had no defenses where he was concerned—he'd slipped past her guard the first time he kissed her.

Still, knowing how vulnerable she was where he was concerned, she should have tried to slow things down. It would have been the wise thing to do. But when she went out to her car after her shift was over and found a note under her windshield wiper, she forgot all about her good intentions and began to smile.

"Let's have dinner together at my house after work. I'll make spaghetti."

There was no signature, but she didn't need one. Even if she hadn't recognized the nearly illegible writing from the instructions he made in patients' charts, she would have known the note was from him. There was just something about it that had his name written all over it.

Grinning, she read it again—and knew there was no question that she was going.

Dressed in a bra and half slip, Janey frantically searched through her closet and couldn't find a thing to wear. Frustrated, she swore softly. How could she have a whole closet full of clothes and have nothing to wear? It made no sense! Where was her black knit dress?

"It has to be here somewhere," she mumbled to herself as she flicked through the dresses hanging at one end of her closet. "You've just overlooked it."

"Janey?" Knocking briefly at her bedroom door, Sara stuck her head inside. "There you are, dear. Good, you're still getting ready. I just wanted to tell you that Dan's going with us. I called Reilly, and he okayed it as long as we came straight home, afterward. He doesn't want him to get too tired."

Distracted, Janey never took her eyes from the clothes on the rack in front of her. "Going with us?" she repeated absently. "Where?"

"To Ed's, silly," her mother laughed. "It's Monday night. Remember?"

She hadn't. Swearing softly under her breath, Janey wanted to kick herself. How could she have forgotten? She and her mother went out to eat every Monday night at Ed's Diner, come rain or shine. It had become a ritual over the years, one they both took for granted and never forgot. Until now.

"You forgot," Sara said, smiling teasingly.

She couldn't lie. "Yeah. It's been a hectic day. And Reilly invited me to dinner." Guilt swamping her at the idea of abandoning their usual plans for a spur-of-the-moment date, she said quickly, "Don't worry. I'll call him and explain—"

"You'll do no such thing!"

"But we already had plans."

"So we'll go next Monday if you don't have a date," Sara said easily. "It's no big deal, honey. Dan and I will still go. He's been cooped up in the house, and the change of scenery will do him good."

Janey knew she was only trying to make her feel better, but that only increased her guilt. "When I was growing up, you always told me it was rude to make plans with one person, then bail out on them if you were invited somewhere else later. How is this any different?"

Sara had to smile at that. Out of all her children, Janey was the one who had always asked her to explain herself, to make her understand when she couldn't see the wisdom of something. "It isn't, but it is," she said, sinking down onto the edge of the bed for a heart-to-heart. "Yes, we had previous plans, but those plans are really just part of a routine we've fallen into over the years. It's nice when we can do it, but I'd never expect you to give up your own social life for me. Especially since someone special has come into your life. I want you to go out, to have fun. You're young and single and you should be doing those things.

"And don't you dare feel guilty about leaving your poor old mother at home alone," she added with a frown.

Janey had to smile at that. "You're not old."

"No, I'm not," she agreed proudly. "I have my own life, my own friends and interests, and plenty to keep me busy. There's only one thing I want right now, and that's for you to find happiness. So please don't worry about me. I'm just fine."

There was no doubting her sincerity. Love squeezing her heart, Janey blinked back tears. She'd always known she'd been blessed with one of the best mothers in the world, but she was only now beginning to realize just how incredibly special she was.

"Thanks, Mom," she said huskily, giving her a quick hug. "So will you help me get ready for my first real honest-to-goodness date? I can't seem to decide what to wear."

Grinning broadly, Sara laughed and hugged her back. "I'd love to, sweetheart. Let's see what you've got."

When Janey sailed out of the house thirty minutes later, Sara watched her leave with tears in her eyes. She'd come so far in the last few weeks. Dressed in a winter-white angora sweater and matching wool slacks, her makeup soft and subtle, she had a confidence in herself as a woman that she'd never had before, and Sara was thrilled for her. She was finding her way, discovering what she wanted out of life, and she couldn't have been happier for her. Or sadder.

She was losing her daughter.

Oh, she knew she would never really lose her—any more than she'd lost the rest of the children when they'd moved out and eventually married. But she and Janey had a special closeness. For so long it had been just the two of them there in the house together, and now life was changing, much faster than she'd ever expected. She had a feeling that nothing was ever going to be quite the same again, and she wasn't sure if she was ready for that.

Lost in her musings, she didn't realize Dan was watching every nuance of her expression until he took her hand in his and squeezed it comfortingly. "Hey, don't look so down. You've still got me. Well, at least until tomorrow," he quipped with a crooked grin. "Wanna fool around? It could be the last chance we get."

Caught off guard, Sara had to laugh. She'd driven Dan into town earlier for an appointment with Reilly, who was so pleased with his progress that he'd announced he was well enough to go home in the morning. He was still under orders to take things easy and rest, which meant no strenuous activity. And no *fooling around.*

Not that Dan was serious about that, she assured herself. He was just trying to tease her out of a blue funk. Wasn't he? Not as sure as she would have liked to be, she pretended to consider. "I guess this is our last night together, isn't it? Wouldn't you know it, though—Reilly said you're not supposed to exert yourself. Darn! I guess we'll have to wait."

Not the least surprised by her response, he grinned in

appreciation. "Then we'll have to go with plan B and go to Ed's, instead. If that's all right with you, of course."

Flashing him a smile, she slipped her arm through his. "I thought you'd never ask, Doctor. Let's go."

If there was one night of the week that was slower than the others at Ed's, it was Monday night. The special, which was always a comfort food from Ed's childhood, was corned beef and cabbage, and that wasn't a favorite with a lot of the locals. It was, however, with Sara and Janey, which was why the two of them had started eating there on Monday nights in the first place.

That didn't mean, though, that the place was deserted. There were plenty of items on the regular menu to bring people in, and just about every table was occupied. Ed, however, had been watching for Sara, and as soon as he saw Dan was with her, he quickly cleaned the one empty table left and seated them himself.

"I don't have to ask what Sara's having," he said gruffly, "but I've got a feeling your diet's changed, Doc. So what's it going to be? Baked fish or the turkey breast without gravy and stuffing?"

"Neither," he retorted with a quick frown. "I'll have the corned beef, too."

Sara stiffened at that. "Oh, no, you won't!"

"Now, Sara—"

Far from perturbed, Ed didn't bother to get involved in the discussion. Instead, he jotted Sara's order down on his notepad, then growled, "And fish for the doc, no tartar sauce. I'll be right back with your orders."

Winking at Sara, he turned and strode off, not the least concerned that Dan was muttering curses at his back.

Biting her lip, Sara tried her best not to smile, but she was fighting a losing battle. Scowling, Dan grumbled, "I don't know what you're laughing at. You get to order what you want.''

"He's only trying to protect you from your own bad habits,'' she said with a chuckle. "You know what Reilly said. *No fat.*''

"So what'd he do?'' he demanded. "Call everybody in town and tell them to watch my diet for me?''

Sara wouldn't have put it past him. When it came to his patients, Reilly was extremely protective. "So what if he did? I seem to remember you doing something like that once with Trudy Goodyear. You called all her girlfriends and told them not to let her have any more candy at their bridge club meetings because she was trying to lose weight and didn't have any willpower.''

"But I'm not an airhead like Trudy. I've got plenty of willpower!'' Amused, Sara arched a brow at him. "Oh, really? Since when is corned beef on a low-fat diet?''

She had him there and they both knew it. Grinning sheepishly, he said, "Okay, so maybe I got a little carried away. I'm just feeling so good, and I can't remember the last time I had corned beef. So I thought, what the heck? What can it hurt?''

"It's that attitude that landed you in the hospital in the first place, Dr. Michaels.''

"Said the tortoise to the hare.'' Glancing pointedly at the huge plate of food Ed set before her just then, he drawled, "You were saying, Miss Corned Beef?''

Another woman might have found herself put in her place, but not Sara McBride. Enjoying herself immensely, she merely smiled. "Unlike someone else at this table, *I* don't have a problem with my cholesterol.''

Neatly trumped, there was nothing else Dan could do but laugh and concede defeat. "Game, set and match to Mrs. McBride.''

* * *

Sara couldn't remember the last time she'd had such a wonderful time. But then again, she and Dan had always enjoyed each other's company, and that hadn't changed with the passage of time. They'd been friends for so long that they knew each other's strengths and shortcomings, likes and dislikes, and could usually even finish each other's sentences.

As she pulled into her own garage an hour later with him at her side, she tried to convince herself it was for the best if their relationship remained just as it was. She counted on him so much to be there for her as a friend that she didn't ever want to risk losing that.

Not that there was much chance of things changing between them, she assured herself as she unlocked the door and he followed her inside. True, he had kissed her, but only that one time. He'd shown no inclination to do it again, so despite his claims to the contrary, he'd obviously decided he wasn't romantically interested in her, after all. And that was all right. She wasn't the kind of woman who expected men to fall at her feet. If a part of her secretly longed for him to kiss her again, that was nobody's business but her own.

"You're awfully quiet," Dan said as she flipped on the lights to the Christmas tree and shrugged out of her coat. "You're not still worried about Janey, are you?"

Abruptly dragging her attention back to her surroundings, she felt heat climb into her cheeks and prayed that in the muted light of the tree, he couldn't see her blush. "What? Oh, no. I'm sure she's fine."

"Then what's wrong?"

"Nothing. It's just a senior moment."

They each had times when their minds went blank and there was no one home for a second or two, and they usually laughed about it. This time, however, Dan didn't even crack a smile. His eyes searching hers, he lifted a hand and cupped her cheek in his palm. "Are you sure that's all it is?"

His touch was warm, tender, intimate. And even though he never touched her heart, he tugged on her heartstrings with nothing more than the soft caress of his fingertips against her cheek. "Oh, Dan," she sighed, and just that easily, tears welled in her eyes.

Dan liked to think he was a strong man. He'd survived his wife's death, bypass surgery and the loneliness of loving a woman who didn't appear to want anything more from him than friendship. But when she looked up at him with tears in her big blue eyes, she brought him to his knees. His defenses shattered, his only thought to comfort her, he reached for her, his mouth already lowering to hers as his arms slipped around her to draw her close.

He meant to give her just a kiss—just one. But when she melted in his arms and kissed him back the way he'd been dreaming of for more years than he could remember, every other thought flew right out of his head. Sara. She was all he thought of, all he dreamed of, and he had to tell her. Even though the thought of losing her scared the hell out of him. She had to know how he felt about her.

Searching for the right words, he pulled back, but only enough to focus on her face. "I love you," he rasped. Dear God, how he'd needed to say those words! "I've loved you for years."

Stunned, Sara whispered, "You have?"

He nodded. "I didn't tell you because I knew you weren't ready to hear it, but I can't keep it to myself any longer. We're not young kids anymore. There's no way to know how much time we've got left. I want to spend that time, however much it is, with you—as your husband."

Her heart overflowing with wonder, Sara could only stare

at him. He loved her. All this time he'd loved her, and she'd never realized—or let herself see that she loved him, too. But she did. It flooded through her like the sun breaking through the clouds, and she didn't know if she wanted to laugh or cry.

Questions hit her from all sides. How? When? Where did they go from here? Could she really marry him?

She wanted to. So much that it scared her. It had been so long since she'd loved this way. What if she lost him the way she lost Gus? How would she stand it?

Tears once again spilling into her eyes, she reached for his hand. "I love you, too," she said huskily. "And I want to say yes. But I have to think. And talk to the children. I know that's probably not what you want to hear right now—"

He stopped her with a kiss. A sweet, loving, understanding kiss that was nearly her undoing. "It's okay," he said in a rough, sandpapery voice she loved. "Do what you have to do. Just don't make me wait too long, okay? We've waited long enough as it is."

If she hadn't loved him before, she would have then. Knowing him, he would have married her that very night if she'd have said the word, but he was still willing to give her the time she needed to come to terms with everything. "I think I can manage that," she promised with a smile and leaned up and kissed him on the mouth.

Janey approached Reilly's front door with a sure, confident stride, but inside she was shaking like a leaf. And that embarrassed her to no end. She was nearly forty years old, for heaven's sake! Okay, so the big four-o was still a couple of years away, she amended. She was still close enough to it that she shouldn't have been a nervous wreck at the thought of having an intimate dinner for two at a man's home. Especially a man like Reilly. He was always so gentle with her, so careful. He would never do anything that would make her feel uncomfortable.

It was just that she didn't know what to expect.

And it was that, more than anything, that had butterflies fluttering in her stomach as she lifted her hand to knock on his door. Maybe she shouldn't have come, after all. She was all dressed up for a date, but she didn't know if that's what he'd intended when he left the note on her car. He just might have been lonely and wanted company. She should have worn her jeans—

Suddenly horribly afraid she'd misunderstood everything, she started to turn, her only thought to leave before he even knew she was there. But it was too late. Not waiting for a knock, he pulled open the door, and she couldn't do anything but smile weakly. "Hi."

"Hi, yourself," he said with a smile. "You're right on time. Dinner's just about ready. Come on in."

He wasn't surprised when she hesitated. He'd seen the panic in her eyes when he'd opened the door. She'd been right on the verge of changing her mind and making a run for it, and he couldn't say he blamed her. While he'd waited for her, he'd wondered at least a dozen times what had possessed him to leave that note on her windshield.

But now, seeing her there on his front porch, dressed all in white like an angel, he knew. She was such a contradiction in terms—strong and vulnerable, confident and shy—and she didn't have any idea how she enchanted him. Dancing with her earlier had been so much fun that he'd just had to see her again.

Given the chance, he would have pulled her into his arms right then and kissed her, but he didn't want to make her any more nervous than she already was. So he smiled easily and stepped back from the door, making sure not to crowd her. "I hope you like baked chicken. It's not anything fancy, but I was running late because I had an emergency consultation at the hospital after I left the nursing home this afternoon."

As he'd hoped, he only had to mention medicine to get her to drop her guard. Distracted, she stepped across the threshold. "Chicken's fine. What about this consultation? Was it with another heart patient?"

He nodded. "A preemie with a defective heart valve. The primary care physician wanted my opinion on open-heart surgery."

"On a preemie?"

"Yeah. Come on in the kitchen while I check the chicken and I'll tell you all about it."

Within seconds they were talking medicine and thoroughly enjoying themselves. The chicken was done, a salad made, and they sat down at the table in the cabin's small dining area without the least awkwardness. Animatedly discussing her work with preemies while she was still in nursing school, Janey never noticed the candles Reilly had lit right before she arrived or the soft music playing on the stereo. And he did nothing to draw her attention to the intimate setting. He was, he liked to think, a patient man.

But, Lord, he wanted to kiss her! And he didn't think he was ever going to get the chance. Then when they retired to the living room after they finished their meal and she sank down onto the sofa, he couldn't resist the need to be close to her. Joining her on the couch, he half turned to face her and his knee just brushed hers. It wasn't until he rested his arm along the back of the sofa and reached out to touch the soft strands of her hair, however, that she stiffened.

"It's getting late," she blurted out. "I should be leaving."

Given the chance, she would have bolted right then, but Reilly only leaned over and nuzzled her cheek. "Easy," he murmured. "This is just number six."

Her heart threatening to pound right out of her breast, Janey frowned in confusion. If this was just another kiss, why did it feel so different? Her skin tingled under his lips as he pressed a lingering kiss near her ear, and suddenly it was difficult to keep her eyes open. With no idea how it happened, she found herself melting against him. "What happens after number ten?"

"Let's find out," he suggested huskily, and quickly kissed her four more times. "Seven. Eight. Nine. Ten."

It all happened so fast, she only had time to laugh softly in surprise before he slipped his arms around her and purposefully lowered his mouth to hers. "Reilly!"

"Just relax," he rasped. "All I'm going to do is kiss your bottom lip. That's all, sweetheart. Okay? Just your bottom lip."

Already aching for something she didn't understand, she should have said no. But then his mouth closed sensuously over her bottom lip, tugging gently, and deep inside her a fist of need tightened in her belly. Shocked, she pulled back to look up at him with eyes that were wide with surprise. "How did you do that?"

Laughing softly, his breath caressing her sensitized mouth, he grinned. "So you liked that? Let's try it again."

He didn't rush her—she could have stopped him at any time. Or at least that was what she told herself up until the second his mouth touched hers. Then her mind clouded, her senses stirred to life, and she couldn't think of anything but Reilly and the feelings he stirred in her so easily. Enchanted, she slipped her arms around him and let him take her where he would.

Lost in the honeyed taste of her, Reilly was as caught

up in the moment as she. He meant to keep his kiss restricted to her mouth, but she was so soft, so yielding in his arms that for several long, heated moments, he forgot she was an innocent who didn't have a clue how desirable she was. Desperate to taste her all over, he dropped a trail of kisses from her mouth to her ear, and down the sensitive side of her neck.

"Oh, Reilly!"

"That's it, sweetheart," he groaned when she gasped and moved against him, her mouth hot and eager as it sought his. "You're so responsive. So sweet. Just let me show you."

His only thought to touch her, to drive her slowly out of her mind and kiss every inch of her, he slipped his hand under her sweater. Her skin was like silk—soft and smooth and oh, so warm. And just a touch only made him want more. Without a thought he swept his hand over her and found her breast.

And went too far.

Chapter 11

At the first stroke of his fingers on her breast, Janey felt heat streak through her like a bolt of lightning and wanted to curl into his touch. How could she have known that having his hands on her would feel so wonderful? Her blood sang through her veins, setting her body throbbing, but even as she moaned softly, alarm bells clattered loudly in her head, refusing to be ignored.

"No," she muttered against his mouth, and couldn't be sure if she was protesting his touch or the voice of reason that demanded to be heard.

That's when she knew she was in trouble.

Swallowing a sob, she moved then because she had to, because she'd only just now learned to kiss him and she wasn't ready for anything more. And because if she didn't move within the next few minutes, she wouldn't want to.

"No!" she cried, pushing free of his arms while she still could. "I can't. I'm sorry, but I can't!"

Scrambling up from the couch, she looked wildly around

for her coat and finally spied it hanging on the old-fashioned wooden coatrack by the front door. In two strides she reached it. "I have to go. It's late. Thank you for dinner...for everything..." Another sob welling in her throat, she turned blindly away and jerked open the door.

Her whispered good-night swallowed by the cold wind that rushed inside, she ran out into the night. Before Reilly could do anything but swear, she drove off as if the devil himself was after her, leaving behind a silence that was swift and harsh and condemning.

"Idiot! Jackass! Talk about an insensitive clod! Why didn't you just rip her clothes off and jump her and be done with it?"

Cursing himself roundly for rushing her, he strode over to the door and slammed it shut with a force that nearly rocked the cabin on its foundation. Dammit all to hell! He should have stopped her, should have apologized for losing control and giving in to the need she stirred in him just by breathing.

But she wasn't the only one shaken by what had nearly happened between them. When he'd decided to be her first boyfriend, he'd been sure he could teach her to kiss and make out and discover herself as a woman without letting his emotions get out of control. After all, he still loved Victoria. But just now, when he'd held her in his arms and caressed her breast as he'd kissed her, the only woman he'd been thinking of was Janey and what she did to him. Something was happening between them that he'd never expected. He was falling in love with her.

This wasn't supposed to happen, he told himself. It couldn't. He couldn't fall in love with Janey, not without betraying Victoria. *She* was the one he had promised to love...*until death did them part.*

Guilt swamped him at that, and with a muttered curse he

blew out the candles scattered around the living room and strode into the kitchen to do the dishes. Just because Victoria had died didn't mean his love for her had died—or that the commitment he'd made to her was lessened in any way, he told himself furiously. When he'd married her, he'd married her for life. That hadn't changed. He wouldn't let it.

But when he returned to the living room once he'd finished the dishes, then settled down in front of the now-dying fire, it wasn't Victoria's perfume that lingered in the air to tease him. It wasn't Victoria he could taste on his tongue. And it wasn't Victoria he ached for. And that only increased his guilt. Desperate to protect his heart, he grabbed her picture and stared down at it, trying to recall the deep love that they had shared. She was his first love, his only love, and he needed to believe it was always going to be that way. But although the woman who stared back at him from the photograph was Victoria, his mind's eye kept drifting to Janey, and he couldn't forget the way she'd run out of the cabin. Somehow she'd carved a place for herself not only in his life, but in his every waking thought, and in the process, pushed Victoria to the back of his mind and heart. And he didn't know what to do about it. How had he let this happen?

Packing the small suitcase he'd brought with him from the hospital to Sara's, Dan glanced around for any items he may have overlooked, but the guest room was neat as a pin. Still, he lingered, pain stabbing him in the heart. He hadn't thought leaving would be this difficult. After all, it wasn't as if he would never be back or see Sara again. Even if she turned down his marriage proposal, their friendship would continue. They would be in and out of each other's homes and lives, just as they had always been, and life would return to normal.

He should have found comfort in that. Instead, that was the last thing he wanted. A man didn't ask a woman to marry him so they could live in separate houses and go on with their lives the way they always had, dammit! He wanted to go to bed with her at night and wake up in the morning with her, to see her at her best and worst and cherish her for the rest of their lives.

But she needed time.

He tried not to let that hurt him—or scare the hell out of him—but it wasn't easy. He couldn't stop worrying. What if she needed time to find a way to turn him down?

"Ready?"

Turning at the sound of Sara's quiet question, he hesitated at the sight of her standing in the open doorway to the guest room. No, he wanted to tell her. He wasn't ready to leave. He didn't want to go anywhere until she gave him some kind of inclination of what her answer to his proposal would be. That didn't mean she had to give him a yes right now—he just needed to know she was leaning toward a maybe so he would have something to hold on to.

But he'd promised her she could have some time, and he was a man of his word. Resigned, he forced a smile that didn't reach his eyes. "Let me check the bathroom one more time to make sure I didn't leave anything, then we can go."

That only took a second, and before Sara was ready to let him go, she was behind the wheel of her Explorer driving him home. And it was tearing her apart. There was so much left unsaid between them, so many emotions threatening to overwhelm her, and she didn't know what to do. She loved him. She hadn't planned to, but there it was.

Now she had to figure out what she was going to do about it.

Marriage would change her entire life. And although part of her wanted that with all of her heart, she had to admit that another side of her found that terrifying. She'd been alone for so long, and in the years since Gus's death, she'd grown independent. She wasn't used to answering to a husband anymore. She and Dan got along beautifully now, but they weren't married. Should they really try to fix something that wasn't broken?

More unsure than she'd ever been in her life, she reached his house, then parked and followed him inside. "Do you need me to do some grocery shopping for you?" she asked, frowning at the stale air of the closed-up house. "You've been gone so long, you probably haven't got a thing worth eating in the refrigerator. I should have thought of that earlier and we could have stopped on the way home."

"It's okay, Sara," he said gruffly when she would have stepped into the kitchen to check the refrigerator and pantry. "I have plenty of stuff in the freezer. I'll be fine."

Her eyes searching his, she knew he was right. He was one of those self-sufficient men who knew how to cook and clean and take care of himself. He'd been doing it for years, ever since Peggy had died. But being able to take care of yourself and being happy were two different things, and she knew that he was going to miss her as much as she'd miss him.

"Then I guess I'll be going." Her eyes misting with tears at the thought, she gave in to impulse and raised up on tiptoe to give him a soft, gentle kiss that said everything she couldn't say. "I promise I'll have an answer for you soon," she said huskily. "I really do love you. I just need a little more time."

He understood, just as she'd known he would, and pulled

her back into his arms for one last lingering kiss. When he finally let her up for air, love was shining in both their eyes. "You know where I am when you want to talk," he told her. "Any time of the day or night, all you have to do is call me."

Those words echoed in her ears all the way home, warming her heart as nothing else could. Ever since Gus had died, Dan had always been there for her, and that wasn't going to change now that he loved her and wanted to marry her.

Reassured, she arrived home with a smile on her face, but it faded the second she stepped inside and the loneliness of her own existence rose up before her. She'd grown so used to Dan being there that she'd forgotten how quiet the house was during the day when Janey was at work and she was there alone. She usually didn't even turn the TV on until the evening news came on.

Grimacing at the thought, she reminded herself that she wasn't some pitiful old widow woman who holed up in her house and felt sorry for herself. She had a full life. When she wasn't doing something with her friends or Dan, she was cooking or canning or working in the garden in the spring and summer. And church, of course, was all year round.

Then there was Janey. She was there for breakfast each morning, and they had dinner together the nights neither of them had plans. Sometimes they were both so busy that they just saw each other in passing, but just knowing Janey lived there in the same house and would be home eventually made her feel less alone.

But Janey has Reilly now, a voice whispered in her ear. *One day soon she could decide to leave and get a place of her own, and then where will you be? Sad and lonely and living in this great big old house all by yourself, that's where!*

No! she wanted to cry. It wouldn't be that way. She'd adjust to living alone. She'd do just fine. And even if she didn't, she couldn't marry Dan just so she wouldn't be alone. That wouldn't be fair to him or herself.

But even as she acknowledged that, she knew that if she did decide to accept his proposal, it wouldn't be because she was afraid of being alone. She loved him. The strength and wonder of that love still amazed her. She wanted to be with him for the rest of her life, but she didn't live in a vacuum. Marriage to Dan didn't just affect her—she had her children to consider, and they didn't even suspect that the two of them loved each other, let alone wanted to get married. How would they feel about her marrying another man? She wanted to believe that they would all be happy for her since they were so fond of Dan, but she couldn't be sure. What if they felt as if she was somehow betraying Gus? Then what would she do?

With the answer eluding her, she couldn't help but worry as she went about her morning chores. It wasn't supposed to be this way, she thought as she changed the sheets on the bed in the guest room, then strode into the laundry room to wash them. A wonderful man had asked her to marry him. She should have been walking on air and planning a wedding, not worrying herself to death.

"Mom?"

Her thoughts and hearing drowned out by the sound of the washing machine, she didn't realize she had a visitor until Joe waved his hand in front of her face. Startled, she nearly jumped out of her skin. "Joe! My goodness, you nearly scared me to death! What are you doing here? I thought you were going Christmas shopping this morning."

"I am," he said, grinning as he switched off the machine

so they could hear each other without shouting. "I stopped by to see if you could give me an idea on what to get Janey, but you looked as though you were a million miles away. Everything okay? How's Dan?"

"Great," she assured him, flashing a smile that wasn't quite as bright as she'd have liked. "I just got back from taking him home. Reilly's really pleased with his progress."

"And what about you?" he asked, studying her with knowing eyes. "Are you pleased he was well enough to go home?"

"Well, of course I'm happy that he's back on his feet. I was really worried about him at first."

"But now you miss him, and he hasn't even been gone an hour."

She couldn't have denied it even if she'd wanted to— Joe knew her too well. "I know. It's silly, isn't it? It's just that I got so used to him being here that the house seems empty without him."

She could have let the subject drop with that and distracted Joe with questions about Christmas gifts for Angel and Emma. But since he'd already guessed how much she missed Dan, the timing just seemed right to tell him everything.

Nervous, not sure where to begin, she struggled to find the right words. "There's something I need to tell you, honey."

"All right," he said with a frown when she hesitated. "It sounds serious. You're not sick, are you?"

"Oh, no!" she said quickly. "It's nothing like that. I'm fine. Everything's fine! It's just that…I don't know how to say this—"

"Spit it out, Mom," he retorted with a chuckle. "If everything's fine and nobody's dying, then it can't be that bad. Say it.''

"Dan and I are in love with each other and he's asked me to marry him.''

The words came out in a rush, not the way she intended at all, but she needn't have worried that she'd shocked Joe. Grinning broadly, he snatched her into his arms for a bear hug. "It's about damn time! So when's the wedding?''

That wasn't quite the reaction she'd expected. Confused, she stared up at him with wide, hopeful eyes. "You're okay with this? I was afraid you might think I was betraying your father.''

"What?'' Stunned that she would think such a thing, Joe hugged her again, this time more gently. "Mom, Dad's been gone a long time. I've never expected you to live the rest of your life alone. Especially when you have a chance to find happiness with a good man like Dan. He's been crazy about you for years.''

"You knew?''

Grinning at her shocked tone, he nodded. "Dan's not very good at hiding his emotions. It was written all over his face whenever he looked at you.''

So everyone had known. And she'd never realized. "I must have been incredibly blind. Why didn't somebody tell me?''

"Because you weren't ready to see it,'' he said simply. "Now you are. So when's the wedding?''

That wasn't something she'd allowed herself to think about, not yet. But Joe's reaction had lifted a huge load off her shoulders, and she had no reason to think that the other kids would respond any differently. Suddenly the possibilities for happiness were endless, and she couldn't stop smiling. "I'll let you know,'' she promised, hugging him again. "First I have to tell Dan.''

*   *   *

Reilly couldn't remember the last time he'd had such a hell of a day at work. Nothing seemed to go right. Three different patients had allergic reactions to the prescription drugs he prescribed for them, and the waiting room was packed to the rafters with patients suffering from the latest flu bug making its way through town. If patients weren't sniffling or coughing, they were complaining about headaches and back aches and looking to him for a quick fix. Unfortunately, there wasn't one.

Swamped, he'd been running behind schedule almost from the moment the office opened its doors that morning, and things only went downhill from there. By the time he was able to slip away for his rounds at the nursing home, he was an hour late and in a bear of a mood. He caught a glimpse of Janey going about her duties at the far end of the east hall, but she was busy and didn't see him, and that only frustrated him more.

She was all he could think of. He'd lost track of the number of times he'd picked up the phone to call her, only to change his mind before he could even punch in her number. He'd upset her last night by rushing things—she needed some time to come to grips with the change in their relationship. He knew that, accepted that, and still had to fight the urge to track her down, sweep her up into his arms and carry her off to someplace quiet and secluded so the two of them could be alone together.

Would she even talk to him? he wondered glumly. He had a sinking feeling that he'd ruined everything, and he didn't know what to do.

"Dr. Jones? My blood pressure is all right, isn't it? I've been feeling a lot better since you changed my pills."

Jerked back to his surroundings by Henry Perkins, Reilly looked up from his thoughts to find the old man frowning at him worriedly. Only then did he realize he must have scared him to death with his scowl. "You're doing great," he assured him gruffly as he quickly unwrapped the blood pressure cuff. "I was just thinking about something else. Sorry."

"That's okay," Henry said easily. "Janey's been distracted all morning, too. I was worried about her. Is anything wrong?"

When he arched a bushy gray brow, encouraging Reilly to confide in him, he had to grin. Oh, he was good. And smooth as silk. With a touch of concern in his eyes and his tone pitched to just the right degree of worry, the old man was the picture of a caring friend who just wanted to help. Reilly didn't doubt that he did truly care for Janey, but he couldn't let himself forget that Henry was also a member of the Busybodies. By quietly going about his business and innocently visiting with people, he unobtrusively collected bits and snippets of gossip like other people collected stamps. Anything was grist for the gossip mill and shared with Abby Hart and the others, who were better than CNN at spreading the latest news.

"Nice try, Henry," he said, chuckling, "but you'll have to ask Janey that. I don't have a clue."

If he was disappointed, he didn't show it. "Oh, well then, I guess you two aren't having problems. That's good." When Reilly merely looked at him, refusing to comment one way or the other, he grinned. "Maybe I'll have better luck with Janey."

"Maybe so," Reilly said with a laugh. "But I wouldn't hold my breath if I were you."

His examination finished, he sent Henry on his way to find Janey and was half tempted to go with him. But he needed some advice before he approached her, and there was only one woman he knew who was wise enough to help him. That was Sara McBride. If he finished his rounds early, he could drive out to the ranch and talk to her before Janey got off work. The decision made, he hurried down the hall to his next patient.

After talking to Joe, Sara spent the rest of the morning and afternoon alone, thinking. She loved Dan. She didn't know why it had taken her so long to realize how she felt about him, but now that Joe had assured her that he and the rest of the children would totally support whatever she wanted to do, she knew she wanted to spend the rest of her life with him. Before she could tell him that and accept his proposal, however, she had to first make peace with her lost love—Gus.

They'd had twenty years together, but now, looking back, it seemed like only hours. Hours of laughter and loving and raising a family together that had ended almost before they'd begun. One day they'd been newlyweds, so much in love that their feet hadn't even touched the ground, and the next, twenty years had passed, and he was gone. Just that quickly all the laughter had gone out of her life. Oh, she'd still had the children to love and bring her joy, but it had never been the same without Gus.

He'd been her partner, her lover, the one she could share her hopes and dreams with, and she'd missed him terribly. But he was part of her past, her youth, when everything was possible. And she had to let him go.

Tears flooded her eyes, but it wasn't with sadness. Because she realized now that the love she felt for Dan was separate from what she felt for Gus, and one didn't take away from the other. She loved them both, in different ways, at different times in her life, and that was all right.

All this time, she thought with a tearful smile, she'd been so torn by the fact that she loved them both. How could she have been so foolish? Gus would never have begrudged her a chance to find happiness, and given the chance he would have picked Dan for her himself. After all, they'd been best friends. And if the situation had been reversed, she knew in her heart Dan would have done the same thing. How could she have been lucky enough to love two such good men in a single lifetime?

She'd intended to wait until that evening when they had dinner together to tell him she would marry him, but suddenly she couldn't wait that long. She needed to see him now, to tell him how much she loved him and that she wanted whatever time they had left together to be wonderful. Quickly wiping the tears from her face, she hurried upstairs to her bedroom to change. When a woman was going to accept a man's proposal, the least she could do was wear something a little more appropriate than jeans and an old flannel shirt.

Her heart racing, she went through her closet like a madwoman, selecting first one item, then rejecting it for another, before she finally settled on a royal-blue wool dress that exactly matched the color of her eyes. Her cheeks were already tinged with a blush, her eyes sparkling, so all she needed was a couple of swishes of mascara and some lipstick and she was ready. Unable to stop smiling, she grabbed her purse and keys and ran down the stairs like a twenty-year-old.

The doorbell rang just as she reached the bottom step, and her first thought was it was Dan. Somehow, he'd known she'd needed to see him. But even as she hurried toward the front door, common sense kicked in and she knew it couldn't possibly be him. Reilly hadn't cleared him to drive yet, and even if he had, Dan had promised to give her time. He wouldn't go back on his word. Which meant her visitor was someone else.

Hesitating with her hand on the door, she was half

tempted not to answer it. She wanted to see Dan, not visit with an uninvited guest. And it wasn't as if the person on the other side of the door even knew she was at home—her car was in the garage and the house was quiet. If she just waited a few moments they'd think she was gone and leave.

And she'd feel like a heel.

"Your mother raised you better than that, Sara," she muttered to herself. "What if it's someone in trouble? Open the door and be nice."

Resigned, she knew her conscience would never let her do anything else. Opening the door, she half expected to find Helen Guthry, a nosy neighbor from down the road, on her front porch, wanting to gossip. Instead, she found herself face-to-face with Reilly.

Shocked, she started to smile. "This is a pleasant surprise," she began, only to stiffen as she realized that he wasn't in the practice of stopping by the house in the middle of the day unless Janey was there. "What's wrong? Is it Janey? Dan? Oh, God, something's happened!"

"Oh, no!" he quickly assured her. "They're both fine, as far as I know. I just needed to talk to you about something, but you look like you're on your way out," he added, noting the purse she'd slung over her shoulder. "I should have called first. We can do this another time."

He started to turn away, but Sara never even considered letting him go. He was obviously troubled about something. Pulling open the door, she smiled kindly. "I was just going into town to see Dan, but that can wait. Come in. Would you like something to drink? Coffee? Soda? It won't take me a second to make you something."

He hadn't meant to put her to any trouble, but five minutes later, he was seated across from her at the old kitchen table, drinking the best coffee he'd ever tasted. And somehow, talking to Sara in the same kitchen where countless McBrides must have discussed their problems with the women in their lives turned out to be easier than he'd expected.

"When my wife died," he said quietly, "I felt like my entire life had been ripped apart in a heartbeat. Victoria was the other half of me, the best part of me, and suddenly she was gone. I was so lost without her I didn't know what to do. I'd never been more miserable in my life."

Understanding softening her eyes, Sara reached across the table to pat his hand. "I've been there," she told him huskily. "It's the loneliest place in the world."

Hurt, muted some by time, squeezed his heart. "Then you know what it's like. Nothing matters. Not family or friends or work. You can't sleep or eat and the pain never seems to go away, even though everyone tells you it will."

"'Just give it time,'" she quoted with a grimace, repeating the advice everyone had rushed to give her. "'Give it time and you won't feel so lonely. Just give it time and you'll be able to remember him without it hurting.' God, I hated it when people used to say that! I could never understand how they thought they knew what I was supposed to feel when they'd never lost their husband. They didn't have a clue what I was going through."

"The pain was so awful, I thought I'd never love anyone again," he confided. "I didn't want to risk that kind of hurt again. Then I met Janey."

A slow, pleased smile spread across Sara's beautiful face. "And everything changed."

He couldn't deny it. She'd changed everything. "I'm falling in love with her," he said huskily. "And I feel so damn guilty, it's tearing me apart. Victoria hasn't even been dead nine months. How can I already love someone else?"

"Because you didn't die, too," Sara said simply. "Because you're human and have feelings. Don't ever feel guilty about loving someone, Reilly. It's the most beautiful thing in the world. And true love is so rare. I never had the chance to know your Victoria, so I don't know what kind of woman she was, but I can't imagine you loving anyone who would be so jealous and possessive that she'd want you to spend the rest of your life alone, grieving for her. If she truly loved you, she'd be happy that you'd found someone else to love.''

"But it's too soon!"

She smiled. ''Is it? Love has its own time frame. Some people only need eight months. Others—like me—need twenty years. That doesn't mean that you loved Victoria any less than I loved Gus. It just took me longer to let go.''

Caught up in his own thoughts, it was several seconds before her words registered. Stunned, Reilly just looked at her. ''Are you saying what I think you're saying?''

She nodded, her blue eyes twinkling. ''I've fallen in love with Dan, and he's asked me to marry him. So you see, I know exactly how you're feeling. When I realized I loved him, I felt guilty, too, like I was somehow betraying Gus. But Gus is gone. And as much I loved him and treasured the years we had together, it's time for me to starting living again. With Dan. If Victoria could talk to you, I bet she'd tell you the same thing. Go on with your life, Reilly. You've found someone to love. Don't let that go.''

The heartfelt emotion in her eyes touched a cord deep inside him, releasing the last lingering strains of guilt he hadn't, until then, been able to let go of. Peace settled over him, and for the first time since Victoria died, he felt a joy he hadn't felt for a very long time. He loved Janey, and there was nothing wrong with that.

''Thank you,'' he told Sara huskily. ''You don't know how much you've helped me.'' Rising to his feet, he waited

until she did the same, then pulled her into his arms for a
surprise hug that lifted her off her feet.

"Reilly!"

Laughing at her gasp of surprise, he only hugged her
again. "You're a good woman, Sara McBride. When I get
you for a mother-in-law, I'll be one lucky man."

"See that you remember that," she instructed him with
a teasing grin. "Now that we've got that settled, would it
be terribly rude of me to cut this short? You're not the only
one planning a wedding. Dan's getting married and he
doesn't even know it yet."

"You haven't told him you're accepting his proposal?"
he asked incredulously. "Good Lord, what are you waiting
for?"

"The right time, and I think this is it. If you don't mind
showing yourself out, I've got a marriage proposal to accept. That's where I was headed when you arrived."

"Why didn't you tell me? We could have talked later."

"Sometimes later never comes," she said wisely. "And
this was important. Take good care of Janey. She deserves
the best." Tears of happiness shining in her eyes, she gave
him a quick kiss on the cheek. "Lock up for me, will you?
I've got to go."

"Tell Dan I said congratulations," he replied with a grin,
and with a gentle push, sent her hurrying out the door.

Depressed and lonelier than he had been in years, Dan
threw down the medical journal he was trying to read and
rose to pace the length of his den. He couldn't concentrate,
dammit, and it was all Sara's fault. Why was it taking her
so long to make up her mind? Maybe she really was trying
to find a way to let him down easy.

"No!" he growled. He refused to accept that. She loved
him—he'd bet his life on it! It was just the idea of marriage

and all the changes it would bring to her life that was giving her pause, and that was understandable. She'd been on her own for a long time. She just needed some time to adjust.

Clinging to that thought, he picked up his journal and settled back down to read, but he was fighting a losing battle. His concentration shot to hell, all he wanted to do was call Sara and assure her that everything was going to be all right.

"Don't be a baby," he muttered to himself. "She'll be here in a couple of hours for supper, anyway. You can wait until then to talk to her."

Resigned, he forced himself to ignore the phone, which was within easy reach, and keep his eyes focused on his reading. Not a single word registered. Then the doorbell rang.

Surprised, he frowned and pushed to his feet. Who could that be? Most people still thought he was at Sara's, and that was just fine with him. Until she gave him an answer, he wasn't going to be very good company.

Scowling, he strode through the house to the front door and jerked it open, only to blink at the sight of Sara standing there. "Hey, you're early!"

"I'm not interrupting anything, am I?"

"No, of course not. I was just thinking about calling you." Pleased, he started to reach for her when she stepped inside, only to notice her somber expression. And just that easily, he knew she'd come to turn him down.

Pain lanced his heart, but he never so much as winced. *Keep it light,* he ordered himself sternly and quipped, "If you've come to turn me down, you should know that my doctor has warned me that I can't handle the stress of any disappointments."

"Oh, really?"

Raising his hand like a Boy Scout taking a pledge, he

said, "Scout's honor. I wouldn't lie to you about a thing like that."

Another woman might have been fooled by his light-hearted, teasing tone, but Sara knew him better than most. Her early arrival worried him and he'd already assumed the worst—she'd come to turn him down. Love flooded her heart. How, she wondered, could he think that any woman could turn him down?

Tears stung her eyes, but she quickly blinked them back. No, this wasn't the time for tears. He would misread them, and she was too happy for that, anyway. So she cocked her head at him and retorted with a grin, "I've talked to your doctor and have no memory of him saying any such thing. So don't think you're going to pull a fast one on me when we're married, mister. I know you."

"A fast one!" he sputtered, pretending to be insulted. Then her words registered. Going perfectly still, he just looked at her. "What did you say?"

"I've talked to your doctor—"

"Sara!"

At his warning tone, her smile softened, and the tears she'd sworn she wasn't going to shed flooded her eyes. "When we're married," she said huskily. "You do still want to marry me, don't you? Because I want to marry you—"

That was as far as she got. "Thank God!" he groaned, and reached for her.

Later, neither of them could have said how long they'd been in each other's arms when they drifted to the couch. There, in between kisses, they talked about the future and the life they planned to spend together, and they couldn't seem to stop touching and caressing. Happier than either had been in a long time, they could have stayed there for the rest of the day and night and been perfectly content.

When the phone rang, Dan almost didn't answer it. The only person he wanted to talk to was in his arms. He'd just let the machine get it and call back whoever it was later.

But even as he tried to ignore the persistent ringing, he knew that he couldn't. Someone might need him. "I'd better get that," he told Sara ruefully. "Wait right here."

Striding into his study, he snatched up the phone and growled, "Hello?"

"Dan? Thank God!" Merry breathed out in a rush. "I tried calling you at Mom's but nobody was home, then I remembered Mom said you were going home today, and I was so worried, I didn't know what to do. I want you to deliver the baby but I know you're not supposed to work yet but the baby's not going to wait—"

"Whoa, whoa, honey," he cut in. "Are you saying you're in labor?"

"Yes," she sobbed. "And I want you to deliver my baby. Is it okay? Can you do that? I know Dr. Jones is a good doctor, but he's not you and I want you there—"

She would have rattled on, but Dan stopped her with a quiet shush. "It's okay," he said gently. "Of course I'll deliver your baby. Reilly and I will do it together. Where's Nick? He's there with you, isn't he? Good. Your mother's here with me. I'll call Reilly, and we'll meet you at the hospital. Okay?"

She sighed tremulously, and even over the phone he could hear the tension drain out of her. "Okay. Thanks, Dan."

"Don't mention it, sweetheart. I wouldn't miss this for anything. I'll see you at the hospital." Hanging up, he hurried into the den, a broad smile lighting his face. "It looks like we're going to have to talk about the wedding later,'' he told Sara. ''Merry's having her baby.''

''What?'' Alarmed, she jumped to her feet. ''Is she okay? Is Nick with her? We've got to get to the hospital!''

''We certainly do,'' Dan chuckled. ''Because I'm delivering the baby!''

Chapter 12

Merry's birthing room was like Grand Central Station. Janey hovered close by, and Zeke and Joe wandered in and out, giving their sister encouragement and love. Lizzie and Angel would have been there, too, but they were at home, watching the children.

Impressed, Sara couldn't help but marvel at the way things had changed since she'd had her babies. Back then, no one had been allowed in the labor or delivery rooms but the husband, and even then, the majority of fathers-to-be preferred to spend their time in the waiting room, pacing. Gus, thankfully, had been right there by her side the entire time, and she was glad to see that Nick was there for Merry, as well. Not leaving her side for a second, despite the fact that she'd been in labor for four hours already, he held her hand and wiped her brow and murmured loving encouragement to her with every contraction.

"You're doing just fine, Merry, dear," Dan said as he checked the monitors. "It won't be long now."

Panting to help relieve the pain, Merry had to laugh. "You said that two hours ago, Dan. Define *long*."

Grinning, he chuckled. "Oh, no. First babies can be notoriously unpredictable. I learned a long time ago that they won't be rushed unless it's their idea."

"Sounds to me like he's giving you the runaround, Mer," Zeke told Merry with a grin. "Make him give you a time so we can narrow down the betting."

"You're betting on my baby?"

"Don't get your grundies in a bundle," Joe said. "The winner buys the baby a special present with the pot. Right now we've got enough to get junior a good used car."

"Good Lord!" Reilly exclaimed, keeping a close eye on Merry as Janey gave her some ice chips, then began to check her vital signs. "How much is a ticket for this pot?"

"There's no standard amount," he said with a shrug. "Whatever you want to put in. Nick started it off with a thousand."

"It's my first kid," Nick said proudly.

"Then put me in for fifty bucks," Reilly said. "I haven't delivered that many babies, but I'd say this one's going to put in an appearance at 9:36."

"Done," Zeke said promptly. "How about you, Dan? You want in? Give us a time."

"Ten-o-five," he retorted, grinning. "That okay with you, Merry?"

Glancing at the clock, she groaned. "What's wrong with eight o'clock? That's a nice round number. And only ten minutes away. I like it. Can't we strive for that?"

Exchanging glances, Dan and Reilly shook their heads sympathetically. "Sorry, honey," Dan said. "You've got two more centimeters to go. That's not going to happen in ten minutes."

It wasn't what she wanted to hear, but she didn't cry

about it. She only sighed ruefully and waited for the next contraction. Feeling for her, Sara stepped over to the bed and took her hand. "While we're waiting, dear, I have some news that might help distract you. And since the entire family's here, this seems like a good time to tell everyone."

"Uh-oh," Zeke said, his blue eyes dancing. "Sounds serious. What's going on, Mom? You didn't sign us all up to sell magazines for the church again, did you? Because I'm telling you right now, I'm not calling Martha Hoffsteader again. Last time she chewed me out royally for calling her when she was watching *COPS* on TV. My ears burned for a week."

Grinning, she had to laugh. "No magazines, I promise. This is something much more important than that."

Her smile lighting her face, she held out her hand to Dan and linked her fingers with his when he joined her. Turning back to her family, she said huskily, "Dan and I are getting married."

For a moment the only sound was the buzz and whirl of the monitors hooked up to Merry and her unborn baby. Then Sara's words registered, and her children reacted just as she'd prayed they would. Joyously.

"What? That's fantastic!"

"Oh, Mom! When did this happen?"

"When's the wedding? You are having one, aren't you?"

"Of course she's having one!" Joe retorted, grinning broadly. "When you've waited twenty years to get married again, you don't run off to the justice of the peace."

Merry gave her the first hug, then she was passed to Joe and Janey and Zeke for hugs and kisses. Then it was Dan's turn to be congratulated and welcomed into the family.

Laughing, he accepted kisses and hugs from the girls and slaps on the back and handshakes from the boys and Nick.

Distracted by the celebration, no one but Merry noticed that her contractions had intensified. Her teeth clenched on a groan, she tried to smile through a particularly strong one, but the pain was too much for her. Reaching for Nick, her fingers clutching tightly around his, she moaned softly as silent tears slid down her pale face.

Their smiles fading, Janey, Reilly, and Dan were at her side in a heartbeat. "Okay, folks, that's it," Reilly said, frowning at the monitors. "It looks like it's going to be an early evening, after all. The baby's decided he's waited long enough."

"Joe and Zeke, you can wait in the hall, boys," Dan told them. "No one but mama, daddy, and granny allowed inside now."

"What about Janey?"

Grinning, Janey answered for herself. "I'm here as a nurse. I'll let you know when the baby gets here."

Snorting, the *boys,* as Dan called them, were left with no choice but to make a quick exit.

Things happened fast and furious after that. All her concentration focused on her breathing, Merry hardly noticed the quick preparations Janey and the other delivery room nurse made. Then, before she expected it, she heard Dan say excitedly, "He's crowning, Merry! Push!"

He didn't have to tell her twice. With an instinct as old as time, she bore down...and pushed her son into the world.

"Oh, Merry! He's beautiful!"

"Just like his mother!"

"Don't forget his daddy," Janey said with a grin. "He's no slouch himself."

Nick never noticed the compliment. With tears running

down his face, he leaned over and gave Merry a long, loving kiss.

Her own eyes misting, Janey glanced away to give them privacy, emotions she'd never felt before tugging at her heartstrings. Cradled in Merry's arms, the baby was so sweet and beautiful, and for the first time in her life, Janey let herself imagine what it would be like to have a baby of her own. Her heart constricted, tears stung her eyes, and before she could stop herself she found herself looking for Reilly.

The second her eyes met his, something passed between them, something that caught at Reilly's breath and wrapped tightly around his chest. His heart slamming against his ribs, he told himself not to get caught up in the emotion of the moment, but it was too late for that. There was just something about delivering a baby that made people go goo-goo, and he was no more immune to it than anyone else. He watched Merry and Nick together, saw the love that throbbed between them as they admired the baby they'd made together, and all he could think of was that he wanted what they had—with Janey.

He loved her so much. Now that he'd let his barriers down and gotten past the guilt that had torn him apart, he could freely admit that he loved her with every fiber of his being. And he wanted to give her a child. *His* child. Just thinking about it brought a broad smile to his lips. That was something he'd never shared with Victoria, but he would with Janey. Some things were just meant to be.

But as much as he wanted to share that with her right there and then, he couldn't. This was Nick and Merry's moment, not his and Janey's, and not the time to think of another child when a beautiful baby had just been born and deserved his moment in the sun.

The baby was cleaned, then weighed and measured, then

promptly given back to his mother, who was glowing with happiness. Janey slipped out into the hall to give her brothers the good news, and within moments they were all back, and the hugs and kisses started all over again. To Merry's delight, she was the one who had come the closest to guessing the time the baby would put in an appearance, so she was the one who was awarded the pot of money. Laughing, she assured everyone that it wouldn't be used for junior's first car. Instead, it was going to be the beginning of his college fund.

It was a time of celebration, of family, of an engagement and a new baby, and now that he was no longer needed to assist Dan, Reilly knew it was time for him to leave. His work here was done and he had things to do at home. So while the family was gathered around Merry and the baby, he moved to Dan's side and said quietly, "I've got to go, Dan. I just wanted to tell you congratulations on everything. I know you and Sara are going to be very happy together."

Beaming, Dan shook his hand. "I haven't been this happy in a long time. But don't leave just yet. We're all going to go over to Ed's in a little while to celebrate—just for a little while," he said quickly, before Reilly could remind him that he was supposed to be taking it easy. "We'd love for you to join us."

Tempted, he hesitated, then shook his head. "I'd like to, but I've got something I need to do, and I can't put it off. Thanks, anyway. Maybe next time."

Understanding, Dan let him go, and Reilly took advantage of the others' preoccupation with their family celebration to slip quietly outside to his car.

During the four and a half hours he'd been in the hospital waiting for Merry's baby to put in an appearance, darkness had fallen, and the temperature had turned chilly. There was a hint of snow in the air, and twinkle lights decorated just about every house and business, but Reilly hardly noticed. Driving through the narrow streets, his mood was somber as he turned toward home.

Nestled under pines that stood as tall and straight as soldiers in the night, the cabin was dark and quiet, yet still somehow welcoming after a long day. The second Reilly stepped inside and turned on the lights, his eyes found the end table next to the couch...and Victoria's picture. Drawn like a magnet to it, he crossed the living room and reached for it as he sank down onto the couch.

She'd always been a beautiful woman, but never more so than on her wedding day. Tracing her smile, Reilly could remember all too clearly that moment when she'd started down the aisle to him on her father's arm. She'd had a glow about her that had dazzled everyone in the church. Reilly had taken one look at her and forgotten to breathe.

Looking back on their marriage, he knew now he'd taken it all for granted. Love, happiness, happily ever after. He'd thought they had forever, when they'd really only had mere moments out of a lifetime together. He'd hardly had time to pledge his love to her before he found himself staring numbly down at her grave as the minister prayed that she would rest in peace for all eternity.

He'd felt robbed, cheated, and he'd driven away from the cemetery that day convinced that his life was over. Oh, he hadn't died like Victoria had, but he might just as well have. She'd taken his heart with her when she'd died—and his reason for living. All he'd wanted to do was go somewhere and die so they could be together again. He'd stopped caring about life, himself, his patients. If it hadn't been for Tony urging him to get out of L.A., he didn't doubt that he'd be in serious trouble by now.

He owed Tony more than he could possibly know. He was the one who'd told him about Dan needing a partner to eventually take over his practice. Because of Tony, he'd come to Liberty Hill—and started to live again.

"Tony put me on the right path," he told Victoria's picture. "But it was Janey who saved me, Vic. She pushed her way into my life even when I didn't want her to and made me like her. Then she turned right around and made me love her."

That didn't mean he didn't still love Victoria. She was his first love and had carved her own special place in his heart. But he couldn't keep looking over his shoulder and clinging to what might have been. Life was in front of him, not behind him, and he wanted to share it with Janey.

Which meant he had to let Victoria go.

There was a time in the not too distant past when he would have thought he'd never be able to do such a thing without ripping his heart out. But Sara McBride had been right. Victoria would never have wanted him to be alone when there was someone out there he could love. She would want him to be happy, and he knew he would be with Janey. She was everything he wanted and more.

The decision made, he strode over to the desk in the corner and placed Victoria's picture in the bottom drawer, which he seldom used. He wouldn't, he knew, look at her picture again for a long time. And that was all right. Because he didn't need her picture anymore to remind him of her and the love they had shared.

Caught up in making sure Merry and the baby were okay, Janey didn't notice that Reilly had left until her mother suggested they let Merry rest and all go to Ed's to continue the celebration. She glanced around, intending to make sure Reilly knew he was included, only to discover that he was gone.

"Where's Reilly?"

In the process of helping Sara on with her coat, Dan said, "Oh, he left a little while ago. I tried to get him to stay, but he said he had something he had to do at home."

Disappointed—and concerned that he may have somehow felt awkward staying to celebrate when he was the only one there who wasn't a part of the family—she frowned. "Maybe he felt like he was intruding. I think I'll run by his place and talk to him before I go to Ed's."

"All right, dear," her mother said with a smile. "I'm sure we'll be there a while, so take your time." Still walking on air from everything that had happened that day, she gave Merry, Nick and the baby each a kiss, then sailed out with her hand in Dan's, beaming like a new bride.

Following the rest of the family out the door, Janey couldn't have been happier for her mother. After all the years she'd been alone, she deserved this time with Dan and the joy the two of them had found together. She just wished she could find the same thing for herself—with Reilly.

She was, however, afraid to hope. She knew how he felt about Victoria, knew that he never planned to love another woman, and she didn't know how to get past that. How could she hope to compete with a memory? Should she even try? Even as she asked the question, she knew she had to.

The evening had been an emotional one, and more than once she'd found herself blinking back tears. She told herself it was because she was so happy for her mother and Merry, and that was the truth. But part of her felt as if she was standing on the outside looking in while everyone else found happiness, and that hurt. She'd done that all of her life, but no more. She wanted love and marriage and happily-ever-after, and she wanted it with Reilly. Whether he wanted it with her was still to be determined, but she had to try.

The lights shining in his windows called to her, and she headed straight for the cabin. Later, she never remembered parking next to his BMW, but thirty seconds later she found herself on the porch at his front door. Feeling as if she was standing on the edge of a precipice and one wrong step could be her last, she drew in a long breath to try to calm her suddenly pounding heart, then knocked on the door.

She was the last person he expected to find on his doorstep. "Janey!" Surprised, he pulled the door wider, a pleased smile spreading across his face. "What are you doing here? I thought you'd be celebrating with the family at Ed's."

"I might drop by there later." Stepping inside, she started to ask if he was busy, only to just then notice the way the furniture was haphazardly scattered around the living room. "What's going on?"

Caught in the act of rearranging his life, he shrugged sheepishly. "I know this will probably seem crazy to you, but I just realized that when I moved in, I arranged the furniture exactly the same here as it was in my house in L.A. So I decided to rearrange it."

"At nine o'clock at night?"

"It seemed as good a time as any," he replied, chuckling. "Want to help?"

The offer wasn't the least bit romantic, but it made her heart sing. Happiness spreading through her like liquid sunshine, she grinned and reached for the buttons of her coat. "Sure."

Janey thought they were just rearranging the living room, but over the course of the next hour, they moved every stick of furniture in the cabin at least once. After the long day of work they'd had, they both should have been exhausted, but something about the process of finding just the right spot for the couch and the entertainment center and all the assorted tables and lamps and whatnots that made a house a home turned out to be more fun than either of them expected.

Laughing and talking as if they hadn't seen each other in a month of Sundays, they moved the couch twice before they realized they had it and all the furniture arranged exactly the way they both liked it. Chuckling, they sank down onto the sofa with just a cushion between them, stretched their feet out to the fire crackling in the fireplace, and kept right on talking.

"So how does it feel to be an aunt again?" he asked with a smile as he half turned to face her and propped his arm on the back of the couch behind her. "Is it different when your sister is the mother than your sister-in-law?"

A smile playing with the corners of her mouth, she nodded. "I didn't think it would be, but yeah, it is. Not that I'm not crazy about Emma and Cassie," she quickly assured him. "They're both adorable. But Merry's my sister. Watching her have the baby, I could almost imagine—"

When she hesitated, suddenly realizing what she was about to admit, he finished for her softly, "What it must be like to have one of your own? That's what you were thinking, wasn't it?"

Swallowing the sudden lump of emotion in her throat, she nodded. "You don't let yourself dream of something you can never have. It hurts too much."

"I felt that way when Victoria died," he said huskily, understanding perfectly. "We'd put off having children because we thought we had plenty of time. We didn't."

It was a night for confidences, for sharing, and with no conscious decision on his part, he told her about Victoria. "I know it sounds crazy, but I fell in love with her on our first date and never looked at another woman after that. She was all I ever wanted. Then she died, and I wanted to, too. Because I was the one who was driving that night.''

He'd never told anyone that but the police and his immediate family, and he wasn't sure how she'd take it. After all, there hadn't been a day that had gone by over the course of the past year that he hadn't thought about the accident and found a way to blame himself. He wouldn't blame her if she did, too.

He should have known, however, she would never be that coldhearted. Her eyes filling with tears, she reached across the cushion that separated them to take his hand. ''Oh, Reilly, it must have been awful for you. I'm so sorry.''

''A drunk hit us,'' he told her, tightening his fingers around hers. ''All the eyewitnesses said there was nothing I could have done differently, but that didn't make me feel any better. I kept thinking if we'd have left the party earlier or if I'd taken another route home, everything would have been different.''

He sounded so tortured that Janey couldn't help but ache for him. No wonder he'd been so miserable when he'd first moved to town. He'd carried all that guilt around and he hadn't told a soul.

''Don't,'' she murmured. ''I know how much you loved her, but you've worked in medicine long enough to know that even when you do everything right, it doesn't matter sometimes. The patient still dies. Because it's their time to go, and we have no control over that. Only God does. You could have gone miles out of your way, stopped at every intersection to make sure it was absolutely clear, and Victoria would have still died that night because it was her time to go. Nothing you could have done would have changed that.''

He wanted to believe her—she could see it in his eyes—and all she could think of was consoling him. Impulsively, she lifted her hand to his cheek and cradled his face in her palm. "Don't beat yourself up over this. You're a good man and you did the best you could. That's all anyone can do."

She hadn't meant to kiss him. She'd have sworn the thought was nowhere in her head. But he looked so sad that it just seemed the thing to do. His name a quiet murmur on her tongue, she leaned closer, eliminating the distance between them, and kissed him softly on the mouth.

It was just a featherlight kiss, a brush of her lips against his, a whisper of comfort that was over almost before it had begun. But with that simple, innocent kiss, the mood changed like shadows shifting in the night. One second they were talking about Victoria, and the next, something warmed and darkened in his eyes. Suddenly her heart was knocking against her ribs, and she couldn't look away.

"I didn't think I could love again," he said huskily. "Then I fell in love with you."

He said the words so simply, so easily, as if he himself was still amazed by his feelings for her, that she didn't know if she wanted to laugh or cry. In the end, she did both. "Oh, Reilly, I love you, too! So much it scares me sometimes. I wanted to tell you, but I just couldn't. I knew how you felt about Victoria—"

"She'll always have a special place in my heart," he admitted soberly, drawing her into his arms. "But she's gone and I can't live in the past anymore. Not when I have you."

He kissed her then because he'd been aching to all evening, because he couldn't resist the touch and taste and feel of her in his arms. She loved him! The wonder of that raced through him like a comet, destroying the last tiny dregs of darkness that clung to his soul, and with a murmur of need he wrapped her close and kissed her again as if he would never let her go.

"I love you," he rasped. "Let me show you."

She knew what he was asking and could no more have resisted him than she could have resisted the longing that welled in her heart like a spring that went soul deep. Without even knowing it, she'd been waiting for this moment from the second they'd first met. With a murmur of need, she kissed him back with all her heart.

Blindly reaching behind her for the lamp on the end table next to the couch, he found the switch and turned out the light. Darkness, warm and intimate and warmed by the fire that burned in the fireplace, engulfed them. Kissing her hungrily, Reilly groaned. "Do you have any idea how pretty you are? Tonight, when the baby was born and you looked up at me with tears in your eyes, I just wanted to grab you and kiss you."

She wanted to tell him he'd just been caught up in the emotions of delivering the baby, as had she, and firelight made everyone pretty. But she couldn't form the words. With just his touch alone, he made her feel as if she was the most beautiful woman in the world. He trailed a finger down the side of her neck, and she just seemed to go boneless. Gasping softly, she melted against him, only to moan as his mouth slowly followed the path his fingers had taken. "Reilly!"

"That's it, sweetheart," he murmured. "Just relax and let me lead the way. Just like I did when I taught you how to kiss."

Her senses swimming, she couldn't do anything else. How could she have known she was so sensitive? Everywhere he touched, he kissed, her nerve endings tingled. Then, just when she thought it couldn't get any better, he reached for the buttons of her blouse with fingers that weren't quite steady.

Her eyes wide, she looked up at him in amazement. "You're shaking!"

A half smile turning up one corner of his mouth, he didn't try to deny it. "I love you," he said gruffly. "I want this to be perfect for you."

He couldn't have said anything that would have made her love him more. Touched, tears spilling over her lashes, she covered his hand with hers and pressed it to her pounding heart. "With you, it can't be anything else. I love you so much. Love me, Reilly. Please."

Just that easily, she humbled him. How could he have been so blessed to fall in love with such an incredible woman? She was so special, and suddenly nothing was more important than showing her that. His nerves settling, he pushed her blouse from her shoulders with hands that were now steady and kissed his way down her throat to the curve of her breast.

When she gasped softly, he had to smile. "It gets better," he promised, and went about showing her how.

The fire burned low in the grate and the shadows grew longer, but neither of them noticed. Clothes melted away, and with soft whispers and even softer touches, they stroked and caressed and learned what made each other sigh. And then they made each other groan.

Janey was a nurse; it was her job to know the physiology of the human body. She knew the function of every organ, nerve, and muscle, but no amount of medical knowledge could have prepared her for the reaction of her own body to the lovemaking of the man she loved. Her breath hitched in her throat, her thoughts blurred, and all she could think of was how much he made her ache. And she didn't have a clue what to do about it.

"Reilly!"

A sob shuddering through her as he moved over her, she clutched at him, suddenly more unsure than she'd ever been in her life, but he was there for her, loving her, encouraging her every step of the way. "Easy, honey. Yes, that's right. Oh, Janey...sweetheart..."

At that moment she'd have walked over hot coals for him if he'd have asked. She moved with him, under him, in a dance as old as time, and couldn't have said when she learned the steps. Her blood hot and her body humming, all she knew was that she never wanted the loving to stop. Then he slowly, carefully, eased into her with a tenderness that brought tears to her eyes, and her life was irrevocably changed forever.

"I love you, I love you, I love you." She didn't remember saying the words, but they were like a song in her heart she couldn't stop singing. She should have felt pain from the loss of her virginity, but her every thought began and ended with him—in her, surrounding her, consuming her. She wanted to laugh with the glory of it—and cry from the beauty of it. She'd never felt more loved.

And when need curled tight in her belly and she found herself racing toward the stars in a dizzy rush, it was his name that she cried out in surprise. "Reilly!"

One step behind her, the pleasure more intense than anything he'd ever known before, he rasped, "That's it, sweetheart! Yes! Oh, Janey!"

A groan ripping from his throat, that was all he could manage. Then, before either of them could do anything more than gasp, the stars exploded around them. Spent, they collapsed in each other's arms, their hearts still pounding, sated with a pleasure that neither of them had ever dreamed existed.

Later Reilly couldn't have said how long they lay there,

content to never move again. The fire was nothing but embers that gave off a weak warmth, but still, he couldn't let her go. Not yet. Not ever.

"Marry me."

He hadn't meant to say the words just then, but they popped out before he even knew they were hovering on his tongue. And nothing, he realized, had ever sounded so right.

When she drew back in surprise so she could see his face, he smiled down at her with his heart in his eyes. "I know what you're thinking. People are going to say that it's too soon or that you need to date other men before you can make a decision like that so you'll know what you want. And maybe they're right. But I know how quickly life can change. You can lose the most precious thing in the world to you in the blink of an eye, and I don't want to lose you.

"I love you," he said huskily, cupping her face in his hands. "I want to marry you and have babies with you and grow old with you. If that's what you want, too, say yes, honey. Just yes."

Another woman might have needed more time. And if she'd have asked for it, she knew he would have given it to her. But she didn't need more time or to date other men to know in her heart what she wanted. Somehow, without even realizing it, she'd known in her heart that one day he would be there for her. She'd waited thirty-seven years. That was long enough.

Tears glistening in her eyes, happiness setting her aglow, she leaned forward to kiss him and answered the question she'd never expected to hear from any man and he'd never expected to ask. "Yes."

Just that easily, they gave each other their hearts.

Epilogue

The church looked like something out of a dream. Red and white poinsettias were everywhere, along with hundreds of white candles that set the air itself glistening with hope and expectation. And everywhere Reilly looked, he saw people smiling.

When he'd told Janey he didn't want to wait to start their life together, he'd been afraid she would want to take months to plan an elaborate wedding. If that's what she'd wanted, he would have seen that she got her heart's desire, but she'd been just as anxious as he to get married. So with her mother and sister's advice and help, she'd hastily arranged a wedding for New Year's Eve. Next week Sara and Dan were getting married themselves, but tonight was his and Janey's and one they would never forget.

It was a beautiful night for a wedding. Outside, fresh snow covered the ground and a full moon lit the star-studded sky. The church was packed to the rafters with her family and his, old friends and new, and patients from the nursing home whose eyes were already glistening with tears.

Standing at the altar, Reilly watched Janey walk down the aisle toward him on Joe's arm and felt his heart swell with love. Lord, she was pretty! And everything he wanted.

She reached him then and took his hand, and he couldn't stop smiling. He hadn't said anything to Janey, but deep down inside, he wondered about the ceremony itself and what he would feel when it began, but he needn't have worried. As Joe turned her over to him and the minister began to speak the well-known words that bound a man and woman in marriage, he felt nothing but peace. And that's when he knew Victoria was there. He couldn't see her, of course, but he felt her presence near him and a love that knew no boundaries. And just that easily, he knew she was beaming in approval. That was all he needed to make the night perfect.

* * * * *

CHECK IT OUT!

Silhouette®

INTIMATE MOMENTS™

PRESENTS THE LATEST BOOKS IN TWO COMPELLING MINISERIES

Into the HEARTLAND

BECAUSE SOMETIMES THERE'S NO PLACE LIKE HOME...

by Kathleen Creighton

LOOK FOR **THE AWAKENING OF DR. BROWN** (IM #1057)
On sale next month
and
THE SEDUCTION OF GOODY TWO-SHOES
On sale July 2001

❤❤❤❤❤❤❤❤❤❤❤❤❤❤❤❤❤❤❤❤❤❤❤❤❤❤❤❤❤❤❤❤❤❤❤❤❤❤❤

The Sullivan Sisters

LOVE IS AN UNEXPECTED GUEST
FOR THESE REMARKABLE SISTERS!

by Ruth Langan

LOOK FOR **LOVING LIZBETH** (IM #1060)
On sale next month
and **SEDUCING CELESTE**
On sale March 2001

*Available only from Silhouette Intimate Moments
at your favorite retail outlet.*

Silhouette®
Where love comes alive™

Visit Silhouette at www.eHarlequin.com   SIMCHECK

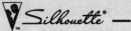

#1 *New York Times* bestselling author

NORA ROBERTS

brings you more of the loyal and loving,
tempestuous and tantalizing Stanislaski family.

Coming in February 2001

The Stanislaski Sisters

Natasha and Rachel

Though raised in the Old World traditions of their
family, fiery Natasha Stanislaski and cool, classy
Rachel Stanislaski are ready for a *new* world of love....

*And also available in February 2001 from
Silhouette Special Edition, the newest book in the
heartwarming Stanislaski saga*

CONSIDERING KATE

Natasha and Spencer Kimball's daughter Kate turns her
back on old dreams and returns to her hometown, where
she finds the *man* of her dreams.

Available at your favorite retail outlet.

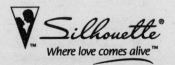

Where love comes alive™